UNKNOWN
HAND

Also by Gillian Linscott:

A Whiff of Sulphur
Murder Makes Tracks
A Healthy Body

UNKNOWN HAND

Gillian Linscott

St. Martin's Press
New York

Library of Congress Cataloging-in-Publication Data

Linscott, Gillian.
     Unknown hand / Gillian Linscott.
         p.   cm.
     ISBN 0-312-02996-9
     I. Title.
     PR6062.I54U55   1989
     823'.914—dc19   89-30090
                                           CIP

First published in Great Britain by Macmillan London Limited.

First U.S. Edition

10 9 8 7 6 5 4 3 2 1

Chapter One

The day it started, I'd watched my own hand as it scrawled 'Colin Counsel' in the space for reader's signature on the book order slip in the catalogue room of the Bodleian Library. I'd been working out, as I walked to the library that morning along Oxford streets overflowing with June sunshine and tourists, how many thousands of those little green slips made up the line that had swung me over the years from undergraduate to my present overcrowded height of junior research fellow. So, for the first time in seven years, I watched the hand in the act as if it had no connection with me, and wondered what it thought it was doing. Ironic, because it must have been on that order slip or one of the other three I filled in at the same time that I made the mistake that broke the line past repairing.

The red–headed woman was on duty at the desk when I handed the slips in. She had big breasts and a nervous smile as if apologising for them.

I said, 'I've just worked out, that's more than four thousand.'

'Four thousand what?'

She was checking I'd filled in the forms properly. She lectures me, now and then, about my nearly illegible block capitals.

'Order slips. At least four books a day, five days a week, say thirty weeks a year on average from eighteen to twenty-six.'

She looked up at me quickly, biting her lower lip, then away down the catalogue room.

'How many will it be by the time you're as old as he is? Forty thousand, more like.'

She was looking at a man so old and hunched that he didn't have to bend over to bring his thick lenses to focus on the catalogue page.

'Like him?'

I squared my shoulders and brushed the hair away from my forehead, trying to separate myself in her mind from the image of that aged grammarian. But she was looking at the slips again.

'This one, is it meant to be a two or a five?'

I said five at random, not knowing and not caring. I was too busy brooding about all those pieces of paper and the old man, and what Andrea had said when we'd had our row over holidays the night before: 'If you're not careful, Colin, you'll end up like the rest of them. Constipated brains and dehydrated balls.' (I should explain that Andrea is a biologist.) The crack sounded unfair to me at the time, particularly since we'd just had a grapple on the carpet that seemed to have demonstrated, to her satisfaction, that dehydration had by no means set in yet. But it had stayed with me, leading to my mental arithmetic on my way in and, by extension, to the mistake I made in writing the wrong shelf reference number on one of those slips now being sent to summon up books from the Bodley vaults.

The row had been about my need to spend the long vac on the work that was, with luck, to scrabble me up to the next academic ledge, as opposed to her holiday plans for us both. 'Aspects of Anglican Religious Poetry from the Oxford Movement to the "Four Quartets" ' versus three weeks' walking and other delights in Anatolia. We'd finished making love and I was trying to settle to some work while she ranged round the flat barefoot, tee-shirt skimming the top of her muscular brown thighs. I felt her foot caressing the nape of my neck in its high, sweaty arch (she also does yoga) and grabbed it so that it wriggled against my shoulder as we talked.

'We don't even have to carry the tents. Big hairy Anatolians put them up for you in the evening.'

I asked what else the big hairy Anatolians put up in the evening and she said I'd better come along or she might find out.

6

'Can't we go somewhere we can swim? Just for a few days.'
For weeks I'd had this hunger in my muscles for sea and waves, big unpredictable waves.

'There's always the swimming baths.'

'Look Andrea, I'm six months behind with this bloody thing already.'

She said she couldn't see that it would matter if it was a few weeks late, as only about four people would want to read it anyway. I'd admitted that often enough myself, but thought it was cheap to throw it back at me. I said something cutting about her research on the optical nerve endings of tadpoles, then she came back with the dehydrated balls line.

My usual end seat in the upper reading room had been taken by a Rhodes scholar wrenching his mental muscles on a Beowulf commentary. I sat beside him and opened a letter I'd collected from my pigeonhole at college on the way in. It was from my supervisor, Professor Lagen, a few black words on a large sheet of notepaper, clipped to photostats of a Texan literary journal. 'Dear Colin, I thought you should see this. L.L.' Ten pages villainously written but enviably annotated, announcing the discovery of a previously unpublished eight-line satirical squib by Clough that I'd turned up in my own researches. It was the only bit of the drudgery I'd enjoyed, and I'd been hoarding it to burst upon the world when my great work appeared. Now there it was, pulped by a transatlantic torpedo, and not a whisper of sympathy from Lagen. That, too, after he'd pushed the wretched Anglicans onto me in the first place.

I crunched up the Texan photostats, collected my overnight books from the reserve desk and tried to immerse myself in the work of a West Country clergyman who'd tried, with pitiful lack of success, to refute Darwin in a metrical scheme based on the Icelandic sagas. But it didn't grip and I was thinking about Andrea again. The fact was, work or no work, I didn't want to go on that holiday with her. I was coming to accept, regretfully, that the relationship that had lasted for two years was drawing to its close. So, I felt sure from many signs, was Andrea. The trouble was, I couldn't explain why, either to

7

myself or to her. We still liked each other. Sex was fine, no problem. But even as I said that to myself I suspected it was the problem, though not in any sense I could make Andrea understand.

I'd tried once to talk to her about my hunch that there should be more to it, that most of us were confusing with pleasure something that wasn't about pleasure at all. Something darker and more complicated than we could reach in even our most athletic episodes on divan, grass or carpet. Andrea, uncomprehending, accused me of having an outbreak of morality and said religious poets were getting into my nerve structure. So I stopped trying to explain and we went to bed. But that night I couldn't sleep and found myself counting, as with the Bodley slips. Sex on average three times a week, say, fifty-two weeks a year, from puberty to . . . to what? It shouldn't have depressed me, neither the sex nor the Bodley slips, but it did. I went over to the desk to see if the other books had arrived.

Three of the four were there. The missing one was something called *The Martyrdom of St Valentine*, a tedious work of sub-Hopkins metaphysical lyrics written anonymously by the prioress of a late-nineteenth-century religious order consisting of five nuns and a Birmingham gravel contractor who eventually went over to Rome. Published by a religious firm thirty years later, probably as a penance.

'Did you want it this morning?' the woman behind the counter asked.

The truth was that I didn't want it that or any other morning, but the decencies were preserved and she said she'd ring down for me.

'I'm sorry, they say it's taking a while to find. Try again in half an hour.'

That was the first indication I had that something strange was happening. I'd called up the book once before and it hadn't, as far as I could remember, been elusive then. Still, I didn't give it much thought, and when I came back to the desk after forty minutes or so the woman was beaming and benefactory.

8

'They've found it for you.'

When she gave it to me, it was on the tip of my tongue to say it was the wrong book. I remembered *The Martyrdom of St Valentine*. It was faded mauve, stiff board, dry and gilded. This one was quite different. A foreign-looking large paperback, bound in light primrose coloured paper with rough edges that flopped back, heavy and damp feeling, when I took it in my hands. Once I'd taken it, I thought that the woman had gone to some trouble to get it for me, wrong book or not, so I wouldn't disappoint her by handing it back at once. Better to take it to my desk, send it back with the others at the end of the day and re-order the right one next time. At the desk, I opened it at the title page and laughed.

'The Martyrdom of Valentine'. Type face gill sans bold, impressed deeply into thick receptive paper. Under it, lower case: 'A Novel'. My mistake, not the Bodley's. Reading the catalogue in an abstracted mood I'd mixed up the shelf references and put down the number not of my respectable prioress but of this, by the look and feel of it, anything but respectable foreigner. I laughed again, bringing annoyed looks from all round the table, and started reading.

It began, in a rather mannered style, with Valentine in his West End flat getting ready for a hard day's muck shovelling as a rising young MP and barrister. Quite rapidly we got the point that this Valentine was rich, good looking, pursued by most of the women in London but about to be married to a girl with a title. I flipped the pages, hoping the martyrdom was going to be sewing sacks in Wormwood Scrubs.

There were steps on the gravel and a shadow fell across him. Feet, long and white, stopped beside his face, turned sideways on the plants.

'Why are you lying on my camomile lawn?'

He was conscious, although he could neither see nor hear them, of other people watching and listening.

'Because of the smell.'

It was not what he had meant to say.

'Like this smell?'

9

She was kneeling over him, white thighs like the wings of a swan blotting out the sun, long calves against his cheeks.

'Like this?'

There was dark hair against his face, not harsh or springing but softer than feathers, drowning him in a universe of feathers, eyes, mouth and nostrils. Without any thought his mouth rose to the deep cleft in the softness, neck arching so that the back of his head pressed against the herbs and their bruised smell struck up to mingle with her smell, and the pain from his hurt skull mingled in the groan of his renewed, resented need.

The instant before his lips touched, when they were no more than the finest feather's breadth away, she flew up and out of his reach. He groaned again in pain and protest, grabbed for an ankle. She called out an order. He didn't hear what it was, but strong hands were dragging him to his feet, more hands turning his face away from her. He tried to fight them, bit one of the wrenching hands and heard curses in the rough accent of that part of the country, but there were three or four of them and he was hurt before the fight began. As they hustled him away from her he felt the gravel stinging his soles and realised for the first time that he was barefoot. He might even have asked them where his shoes were because he heard them laughing. They dragged him along the path under arches and swags of roses, threw him down the steps and slammed the door behind him. He found his shoes on the path outside, his socks neatly folded in the crown of his upturned hat.

'Excuse me.'

The blighted Beowulfian.

'Excuse me, do you have a pencil sharpener?'

I dealt with him and when I turned back to my book I found I'd closed it and hidden it under the clergyman. I felt disorientated, like someone who'd been woken up too early, and was suddenly very conscious of the people round me. I glanced around, but as far as I could see they were all absorbed in their own work. I opened it again at random, further on.

Warrinder's blood spread out across the sand, mixing with the gush of wine from the bottle they'd overturned. The sand was damp and sated with water from the incoming tide and absorbed both streams reluctantly, the blood more slowly than the wine. He sat there, his feet drawn away from the streams of red, his hand on Warrinder's bare shoulder as if consoling him, strengthening him, for the seeping away of life. That Warrinder might live if he did something to stop that flow seemed a possibility that belonged in another universe that had no connection, no common language with the place where he was sitting. The anger and drunkenness that had been on him when he'd found Warrinder had gone, leaving a clarity he'd never known before. He saw the sea moving up over the beach, surrounding the flat-topped rock where she'd stood with Warrinder, noticed two wasps probing a peach left over from their picnic. It never occurred to him to look for her or even wonder where she'd gone. The long semi-circles of the waves had come within a few yards of their picnic before she came back. His eyes were on the slow stain waiting for it to merge with the waves when he became aware of her. He did not look up, kept his hand on Warrinder's shoulder, now colder than the sea. She walked, in her white sandals, into the slow stream of red.

'I killed him.'

He said it quite coolly, like one reporting a small errand accomplished. Then he was on his feet, his hand transferred from Warrinder's shoulder to hers. Under the silk of her sundress, her flesh was still warm from the sun. He imagined wasps probing it as they'd probed the peach.

'I've killed him. As you ordered.'

11

He thought she said: 'I didn't order,' but he wasn't listening. He put his other arm round her waist, trying to drag her up the beach.

'No,' she said. 'Here.'

She stepped out of her sandals and lay down on the red sand beside Warrinder, the silk falling back from her thighs.

'Here.'

Later I sent the book back to the stack, sandwiched between the clergyman and a biography of Cardinal Newman. By then, the police had come for Valentine.

Chapter Two

From picture books behind the bike sheds, to Rabelais for 'A' level and the Earl of Rochester to cheer the undergraduate trudge through the seventeenth century, I was no virgin to literary erotica. Why *Valentine*, not especially remarkable of its kind, should have made such an impression on me that I emerged from the Bodley into the June sun like a sleepwalker was something I couldn't then begin to fathom. As I walked back to the flat, I got as far as the contrast between Andrea's sexuality, as healthy and accessible as a bowl of fruit, and the tortuous destructiveness of the woman in her locked garden. What I couldn't understand was why the picture of Valentine's woman standing there in her silk and white sandals should arouse in me such a complicated lust.

Andrea was there when I got home, mooching around in a tee-shirt, scientific journal in one hand, half-eaten apple in the other.

'Let's have some wine,' I said.

She raised her eyebrows because we're supposed to be trying to cut down, but didn't object when I prised the top off a carafe of Californian red. Massaging the back of her neck the way she likes it, I contrived to spill most of my glassful on the floor. Before she could start fussing about with Kleenex I had her tee-shirt off – with co-operation from her once she got over her surprise – and got her down on the carpet. I could see the wine spreading as we made love and, by deliberately blurring my hearing, made the traffic noise from the Woodstock Road a passable imitation of the tide coming in. When she sat up, pleased and breathless, I kissed the wine stain on her shoulder-blade.

'It looks like blood,' I said.

It didn't, being more mulberry coloured, but I was experimenting.

'Yeugh. It feels sticky.'

For one who spends her time doing terrible things to tadpoles, she's remarkably squeamish.

I said, 'I wonder what would happen if I wanted to make love to you and you wouldn't let me.'

She frowned, puzzled. 'When I don't feel like it, I say so. You know that.'

'Not that. Supposing you really wanted to make love, but you got more of a charge from exerting power, making me wait for it.'

She stood up from the floor to vertical in a split second, without using her hands, in the way she has.

'Colin dearest, if what you're looking for is a born-again virgin, you've come to the wrong counter.'

I gave up. I'd been half wondering whether to tell her about the book, but there was too much of a gulf. I sat on the carpet, drinking the remains of her wine, while she roved about getting dressed.

'You'd better get a move on if you're coming.'

'Coming where?'

An exasperated sigh. 'The demo. Against Lord Talisby. At the Union.'

'Oh, that.'

I'd forgotten, though a duplicated notice about it was Blu-tacked to the back of our door. Junior Home Office Minister Lord Talisby, widely rumoured to be polishing the next bit of gay-bashing legislation. After banning homosexual publicity at ratepayers' expense, the forces of repression were gearing up for a more serious putsch: an amendment to the 1967 Sexual Offences Act making it illegal to write, say or publish anything whatsoever implying that homosexuality was morally acceptable. Censorship, in other words. All people of good will, of whatever sexual orientation, to be outside the Union in St Michael's Street at six thirty to convince him of the error of his ways or, failing that, to put a few good dents in the bastard's ministerial Montego. I stayed where I was on the floor.

'No more demos. Remember the last one? Six half-witted Trots from five rival factions, sixty police and crowds of tourists filming under the impression it was an old university ceremony. Which it was.'

'This one's different.'

'Why?'

'Because if they get away with it against the homosexuals it'll only be a matter of time before they're stoning adulterers and we're back in the sexual dark ages.'

'Suppose sex is meant to be a dark age?'

She was so surprised she stopped what she was doing, standing on one leg, the other inserted half way into her denims.

'Colin, what's wrong with you? Has the Christian Union been getting at you or something?' She sounded genuinely concerned, as if I might have caught a nasty touch of the plague.

'Quite the reverse.'

'That bloody poetry then?'

'No. Prose.'

She clothed the other leg and turned away. 'You're just in one of your mollusc moods, aren't you? If you're not coming, I'll see you later.

I waited until about ten minutes after she'd gone, then let myself out. I felt restless after being cooped up in the Bodley all day and thought I might go for a walk in Parks. The book was still running round in my head and I wasn't sure whether I wanted to clear it or not. It occurred to me that there'd been no author's name on the title page and it was becoming important to me to know whether the author were man or woman. From internal clues, the careful way in which clothes were described, the sensitivity to the feel and textures of things, I'd have said woman. On the other hand, the passages dealing with Valentine's above-ground world showed a familiarity with Parliament and the law courts that would surely have been unusual for a woman in the 1950s. I

15

hadn't noticed a date, but I was reasonably sure of the period from the style and references to types of cars and so on. Then I began wondering if the author were still alive. If she, or he, was around thirty, say, when the book was written, that would put her or him in the mid sixties now. I imagined myself following the path to Provençal villa or doss house dormitory, up the university staircase, into suburban parlour or judge's robing room, confronting my quarry, asking my question. What question? The one that really mattered, of course. Did the woman, or somebody like her, really exist? And a follow-up: was there really a murder? The fact that they were such thoroughly unscholarly questions gives some indication of my state of mind.

Another indication is that, intending to go to Parks, I found myself at the point where St Giles joins Cornmarket, not far from the site of the demonstration against Lord Talisby. Like it or not, the responsible part of my mind seemed to have decided that I'd join Andrea and the forces of sexual rationality. I hoped Lagen wouldn't find out. Even at my comparatively lowly level, I was rather too senior for street hurly-burly.

I needn't have worried. By the time I reached the narrow entrance to St Michael's Street there was such a fight going on that my presence was irrelevant. As far as I managed to sort it out later, Lord Talisby had been driven up in his car and managed to make a run for it through the gate into the Union grounds, which had then been locked, leaving the demonstrators milling round furiously outside. Then the police had moved in to try to extricate the official car, hemming the demonstrators against the wall, and a predictable fight had broken out. For a while I stood there watching a seething mass of banners, limbs and helmets, then it struck me that Andrea was in there somewhere and I'd better do something about it. I looked for her among the mob, ready to plunge in.

'Excuse me.'

I couldn't see Andrea. I was trying to get closer to the police van at the far end of the street, in case she was already among those inside it, when I heard this voice behind me, clear and bell-like.

'Excuse me.'

It sounded like a voice that didn't usually need to say things twice. I turned round and saw a middle-aged woman, slim and cool looking, with grey appraising eyes, wearing a silk dress with blue swirls of flowers. She was leaning against the wall, supporting herself on one hand but looking more at ease than likely.

'I wonder if you could help me. I seem to have lost my shoe.'

One foot was in high-heeled blue leather, the other poised a couple of inches above the ground in nylon that glistened like ice. 'It's in there somewhere.'

She glanced towards the heaving mêlée, at the moment when a small Trot erupted out of it, pursued by two large policemen. The ranks closed behind them and the shouting got louder. Did she really expect me to plunge into that lot and emerge with her shoe in my mouth? It seemed she did, because she was looking at me as, I suppose, the shooting classes look at disappointing gun dogs.

'I'm afraid it may be somewhat difficult to recover,' I said, parodying her tone.

'In that case, I wonder whether you'd be kind enough to help me somewhere where I might sit down.'

My idea was to park her on a handy bench and go back for Andrea. But there was no bench available, so I found myself arming her across Cornmarket to a café in a side street. All the way, she leant on me with her full seven and a half stone. It occurred to me we'd have done a lot better if she'd taken the other shoe off as well and walked in her tights or stockings, but as she managed to give the impression that even one-footed nudity was an affliction to be borne with dignity, I could hardly suggest it. I'd intended to abandon her in the café and go back in search of Andrea, but more squiring was required. She sipped Earl Grey tea and delicately incised millimetres of frosted walnut cake with pearly little teeth while I made conversation, explaining about the demonstration and regretting, in courtly terms, that she'd been inconvenienced by it. As if it

—17

were my fault. I was thinking how scathing Andrea would be if she could hear me when, all of a sudden, Andrea was there along with another woman. She was panting and dishevelled and her jacket torn.

'Colin, I thought you weren't coming. For goodness sake order us some tea and look as if we've been here for a long time.'

She and friend plonked themselves down on the spare two seats at out table.

'The police are rounding up everybody. We broke out, but they may be coming after us.'

My companion raised her eyebrows fractionally, a demand for introductions. I formally presented Andrea and friend, with an effort to remember friend's name, and began explaining how I'd rescued my companion from the riot. I'd got far enough to make Andrea choke over her tea when there was another interruption. A man in uniform appeared in the doorway and friend's hand was closing over a slice of walnut cake, apparently ready to throw it, until we saw it was not a police officer but a chauffeur in peaked cap, black boots, the lot. He made a beeline for our table.

'Lady Talisby. I'm sorry you've had to wait.'

He presented an arm and she hooked herself onto it. The amusement had died out of Andrea's eyes and she looked at both of us as if we were exhibits at a zoo. Lady Talisby thanked me graciously, inclined her head to Andrea and friend and was gone, the eyes of everybody in the cafe following her and the chauffeur until the door closed behind them.

Andrea exploded. 'His wife. You've been sitting in here drinking tea with his bloody wife?'

I tried to explain but Andrea, possibly overwrought by her escape, had now got it firmly into her head that I'd joined the forces of repression and my rescue of the chief villain's wife had not been accidental. The row that followed, in the tea shop and back at the flat, may have had some influence on what I did next day. At any rate, I offer that in mitigation.

18

Chapter Three

Murder, rape and treason, given colourable excuse and style, are things which may be forgiven eventually to the senior members of this university. Stealing books from the Bodley is another matter. Before they even let you in there on your first day you have to swear an oath promising not to remove or to mark, deface or injure in any way any volume in the keeping of the library, or kindle any fire or flame therein. If I'd taken a blowtorch to the divinity section I could hardly have classed myself more thoroughly among the outlaws than by what I did. I date everything that happened afterwards from that first fall.

If there hadn't been the fight with Andrea, resulting in my spending the night in a sleeping bag on the kitchen floor, I might not have lain awake listening to the fridge juddering and thinking about the book. If I hadn't spent the night thinking about the book, and wondering about its author, I might not have looked it up in the catalogue. That was all I wanted to do at first, I'd convinced myself of it. Quick glance to settle a bet with myself about whether the author was male or female, then back to the paths of virtue and the high Victorians. I flipped through, trying to look casual. That in itself should have been a warning to me that things were getting out of hand. Why try to look casual when I'd got every right to be casual? But once it was in my mind, every movement became stiff and weighted, like bad amateur theatricals. Absorbed young academic runs eye down catalogue, reaches relaxed, careless arm out for a slip from the tray (drops half a dozen of them), scribbles down title and shelf number in sprawling hand, comes to space for author's name and stops. He thinks for a moment, consults catalogue again and pauses, raising quizzical eyebrows. Then, deliberately, he poises his Pentel over the slip of paper and, in capital letters, writes one short word: Anon.

The surprise was real enough. I'd assumed the lack of the author's name on the title page was a simple omission. A transparent pseudonym wouldn't have surprised me at all but 'Anon' was all wrong. Anon belonged with my poetical Prioress, not that other, more worldly creature. I hadn't intended to summon up the book again, but since I appeared to have filled in the slip, I thought I might as well hand it in with the rest. It was even in my mind, though goodness knows why, that the book itself might provide a clue. I reassured myself that the word 'Anon' wherever it occured was a challenge to any red-blooded scholar. In accepting this one I was merely allowing myself a little harmless diversion, like crossword puzzles. Except I would never have waited for a crossword puzzle with my heart beating as I waited for the arrival of the book.

It came in due course along with the others I'd ordered. To my relief it was handed over not by the red-haired girl but a lad who might as well have been selling fish for all the notice he took. I built myself a rampart with the other books, turned to the title page again, the copyright page, the opening, the end, and found no mention whatsoever of an author's name. The only fact to add to my knowledge was that it was published in Paris in 1959. This didn't surprise me. Although it's outside my field I knew there was a tradition among English authors from the thirties onwards of publishing in Paris to escape the British censorship laws. Several little publishing firms existed, mainly based on the Left Bank, to do just that; mushroom-like growths that appeared out of nowhere, published a book or two and vanished as suddenly as they'd appeared. The publishing firm's name, Chanterelle, seemed to accept that it was part of just such a process. Apart from that, it meant nothing to me.

I read the murder scene and some others, and hoped the effects weren't obvious to any of the other readers round the table. When a man I knew took the empty seat beside me I slid the book unobtrusively onto my lap, took a volume at random from my ramparts and immersed myself ostentatiously in what I was supposed to be doing. He grinned, would-be sympathetic, at my pile of ecclesiastical no-hopers.

'Lagen tells me a man in Texas has published something good on Clough.'

Lagen bloody would.

'Some serious flaws,' I said loftily, getting shut-up looks from round the table. Damn them all, and double damn Lagen. When I walked out at lunchtime, the book went with me.

It slid under my notepad like an accomplice, stayed quiet against my ribs as I carried it past the people at the issues desk, down the stairs and out into the quad. All the time I was expecting to be stopped and running through lightning scenarios as to why a piece of twentieth-century erotica which I'd so absent-mindedly walked off with was pertinent to my researches. Would they believe a footnote in T.S. Eliot? But I didn't have to try it. Although it seemed to me that I was moving as heavily and unnaturally as a man under water, nobody gave me a second glance. I took it back to the flat, relieved that Andrea was out for the afternoon, poured myself a generous tumbler of wine and settled down to read it.

By the time I'd closed it and swum back up into a hot afternoon with a bee buzzing in the window, I was as sure of one thing as I've ever been about a book – that the woman existed and that the murder, or something very like the murder, actually happened. I can't account for that certainty beyond saying that literary analysis is my trade, as far as I've got one, and that anybody in his own trade develops reactions that look like instincts but are really the sum of experience compressed into seconds. You see the same thing happening when a plumber cuts exactly the right length of pipe without having to measure. It wasn't that the book was so very good. Although rather high coloured in style, it was quite competently written, but the point was that there was nothing in the general style of it to account for the impact on me

21

of the scenes involving Valentine and the woman. Time and time again there were details, mostly observations of the way people looked and moved, that rang completely true to me. A good writer could have invented them, but it didn't seem to me that my writer was that good. Therefore, they weren't invented, they were observed. If so, that accounted for the anonymity – an anonymity that remained as complete now that I'd read the book all the way through as before.

There were, it's true, a few things I knew or could guess about the author. I still thought, for no reason I could explain, that the writer was more likely to be female than male. She, or he, had a good geographical knowledge of London, Paris and, as far as I could judge without going there, part of the coast of Brittany. She, or he, appeared to know something about the workings of Parliament and the law courts, of expensive hotels and motor cars and the chambers of successful barristers. She, or he, also knew a lot about gardens, or at any rate more than I did. It seemed to me too, although now we're back with the trained instinct, that the writer was not elderly. If I'd had to guess I'd have put him or her in late twenties or early thirties. That was as far as speculation could take me. For the next step, I'd need to find myself a bibliophile.

At that point I decided enough was enough and I'd better get on with my work. I opened my notebook and started sketching out the structure of my chapter on the Anti-Darwinians. Then it occurred to me that I'd missed breakfast because of keeping out of Andrea's way and lunch because of the book and that I should be hungry, but when I got out to the kitchen I decided I wasn't hungry after all and poured myself another tumbler of wine instead. Then I rang up a friend at Blackwell's who knows about twentieth-century books, and she gave me the name and telephone number of a man called Gus Prothering who lived in Observatory Street and was something to do with St John's. A phone call to him produced, without too much difficulty, an invitation to drop round at seven o'clock and have a glass of sherry.

His terraced cottage, plastered with window boxes and dripping with wisteria, looked as if it had been cut out of the backcloth for *White House Inn*. Gus himself, moving forward to meet me over thick beige carpet, was the shape of a Max Beerbohm caricature: large head, completely bald on top, chest and stomach one rotund curve over neat, tiny feet. Small eyes looked at me shrewdly under eyebrows shaped like the sharp end of an egg.

'I gather you're thinking of collecting?'

I'd made up the story while waiting for him to answer the phone. Small legacy from an aunt, friend who'd advised me to put it into books. I repeated it.

'There are, of course, pitfalls.'

Something about him made me nervous. I'd had a shock as soon as he invited me to sit down on an uncomfortable armchair, Regency striped. At eye level, in a revolving bookcase no more than four feet away from me, a block of primrose yellow. Six or seven books, all with the Chanterelle imprint across the base of their spines. Not my book, though. I had time to check while he was pouring the Fino.

I confessed to a nascent interest in English books published abroad, Paris particularly. It struck the right note and he was off beside the Seine in the 1920s: Hemingway and Ezra Pound, James Joyce and Gertrude Stein, Shakespeare and Company and the Three Mountains Press. He took sherry in quick little sips and gossiped about them as if he'd known them personally.

'But I should warn you, you may find that area a little over-subscribed for, er, a comparatively modest collector.' His pause invited me to state my means and I had to resist a temptation to say my aunt was called Getty.

'I suppose so,' I said humbly. 'I was wondering about the 1950s.'

'Yes. Yes indeed. A smaller field of course, though not without interest.'

He was off again; names from a quarter of a century ago, some familiar to me, some not. It struck me that he was about the right age to have been in Paris as a student in the 1950s. I asked him.

'Alas no. I missed my misspent youth.'

23

He went on talking and, as he talked, darting from shelf to shelf, bringing out book after book, showing me covers and title pages. At last, one of the Chanterelles.

'Not many of these, of course, owing to Cardell's little problems. They're becoming quite collectable.'

The word collectable and the slightly odd emphasis he gave it made me sure for a moment that he knew about my theft from the Bodley. I looked at his face. I could see nothing there but concern for the book I was holding, but felt I should be on my guard. I asked about Cardell. The eyebrows rose.

'He was Chanterelle. Owned it, ran the presses himself, everything.'

I asked if he was still alive.

'Alas, no. Alcoholism. He died about ten years ago when he was working on his autobiography in Provence. Unpublishable, unfortunately.'

I asked him, watching his face, if there'd been anything in it about a book called *The Martyrdom of Valentine*. He shook his head.

'I've heard of it, of course. It was the one that caused his first bankruptcy. Confiscated by Her Majesty's Customs when he tried to send a consignment to England in 1959. I suppose most of the copies were incinerated.'

His small fingers caressed the cover of the book he was holding, trying to reassure it. I asked if anybody knew who wrote *Valentine*.

'That was supposed to be the great secret, wasn't it?'

I pointed out that somebody must have known. It couldn't just have been dumped on Cardell's doorstep.

'As far as I remember from various letters, there was a running joke around the Rive Gauche that it was written by a consortium. They were supposed to have rented a house for the summer at Fontainebleau and taken it in turns to write the next chapter.'

I didn't believe in the consortium, but I said nothing.

'If you come across a copy you might certainly regard it as, um, a collector's piece. If your tastes happen to run

24

in that direction.' He looked at me, waiting for an answer to what shouldn't have been a question. I said if the output of the Chanterelle press had been small, it might be a good starting point for my 1950s collection. He agreed.

'But you will be careful, won't you. It's an area in which the, um, inexperienced, can make quite expensive mistakes.'

That made the third warning he'd given me. I asked if Cardell had any partners or assistants who were still alive.

'No. He was very much a one man band. Apart from Prudence, that is.'

He waited for me to ask. I did.

'You'll find her cropping up in letters. Prudence Belsire. A clergyman's daughter, um, kicking over the traces. Somebody said she had a face like a bull pup, but one has the impression most of them, um, shared her bed at some time. She was Cardell's secretary.'

Was she still alive?

'She was last year. I had a letter from her.'

He opened a drawer in an eighteenth-century writing desk, flipped through a small index file and took out three sheets of blue notepaper. The handwriting, clear scrawl in shiny black ink, was so large that there were no more than ten words to a page. 'Dear Mr Prothering, You ask about my collection of Chanterelle (page two) books. Please note that I sold them five years ago (page three) to a dealer in Shrewsbury to buy fertiliser. P. Belsire.'

He sighed. 'A complete collection of everything Chanterelle ever published, signed by the authors. Fertiliser.'

While he was replacing a book I memorised the address on the first page. Easy enough: Lapwing Cottage, near Clun, Shropshire. It was dinner time by then and I could tell he wanted me to go, but I spun out my sherry to ask if Cardell had wife or children.

'Oh no. Nothing like that.'

He was amused. As he was showing me downstairs he said casually: 'Lagen tells me you'll be publishing next year.'

That meant he'd been checking up on me. It also meant Lagen knew about my visit to Gus Prothering. That worried me, it seemed at the time, unreasonably. I walked around a bit, intending to find a quiet pizza bar and have something to eat, but they were all crowded with tourists so I went back to the flat, finding Andrea still absent, and drank the last of the wine. Then I got a map and started working out how to get to Clun.

Chapter Four

My departure from Oxford was as ambiguous as most of the other things I'd been doing over the past two days. On the one hand, I was still trying to convince myself that I was the dilettante with the literary crossword puzzle he could take or leave. On the other hand I got up when it was just light, rooted out the haversack and packed it with sleeping bag, anorak and two changes of shirt as if going on an expedition. The book came too, wrapped up in one of the shirts inside a plastic carrier bag. I was spared Andrea's comments because she hadn't come home, and I guessed she was spending the night with a friend. I walked to the station to catch an early train at a time when only the milkmen were up and about, and felt vulnerable in the empty streets, turning every so often to see if there was anybody behind me. Whether I was expecting secret police squads from the Bodley or Lagen dragging me back to my proper researches, I couldn't have said. I only know the interview with Prothering had increased the uneasiness I had felt since the book first arrived at my desk. And yet that uneasiness made me more, not less, set on finding what I wanted.

Ludlow, bustling on market day, came as something of a relief at first and I didn't mind having to wait two hours for the bus to Clun. By then a certain light-headedness made me conscious that I hadn't eaten for about thirty-six hours, and I toyed with an abrasive lentil rissole in a health food shop. Afterwards I was wandering round the market, the usual traditional rural assemblage of plastic plate racks and knitwear from Taiwan, when a new smell caught me by the scent buds. I traced it to a stall crowded with nondescript green plants.

When I first saw it there was nobody behind the stall, but while I sniffed at the plants a woman arrived. I think she may have been talking to the man on the basketwork stall next door. She was beautiful in a way that didn't go with the place at all. Quite tall. In her mid twenties, perhaps, but with the gravity of an older woman. Skin pale as milk of magnesia. Eyes big and shadowy, hair dark and hanging straight down, like a child's. Not at all like the other women I'd been noticing around the town who had a built-to-last look about them. She didn't say anything, just stood and looked at me. She was wearing a white shirt, open at the neck, with green smears on it from the plants. I asked if she had any camomile. I hadn't intended to ask that.

'Yes.'

Her voice was unremarkable, not with the accent of that part of the country. She looked down at the green things, expecting me to know which was which. When I made no move, a long pale hand drifted out, touched one of the plants, went back again. I took two of them. A price must have been named and paid, but I can't remember any other word being spoken. I carried them back to the bus stop and when I turned round on the edge of the market to look back at her, she'd gone again.

It hadn't been in my mind until then to take a present to Prudence Belsire. When I'd rung up, rather drunk, the evening before to introduce myself as a book collector and ask if I could come and discuss Chanterelle press, the welcome had been grudging. She'd even hinted, none too delicately, that time was money and if I expected any commercial help from her, I'd have to pay for it. Still, she hadn't actually forbidden me to come, so the plants could be thought of as a gift to my hostess. The appearance of the plants disappointed me, low and feathery things you tread underfoot at farm gates. I must have bruised them accidentally because their smell spread round me as I waited in the sun at the bus stop among the tractor drivers' mothers with their shopping bags; an odd, dusky sort of smell. I'd never thought of a smell being sinister before, but that was the way it struck me. The tractor drivers'

28

mothers smiled at me and my plants and went on discussing the price of meat.

The bus dropped me at Clun near a pub with a cat asleep in the sun outside. A plump woman who'd been on the bus with me gave me a funny look when she pointed out the way uphill to Lapwing Cottage, suggesting that Prudence Belsire was the subject of some local curiosity. The path was nothing more than two tractor ruts across fields with grazing ewes and lambs, through gates and over cattle grids. Quite steep. The sun was on its way down towards the Welsh hills by then but I was sweating, haversack on my back, camomile plants still balanced one in each hand. As I walked, I wondered if Prudence might turn out to be the end as well as the beginning of my search.

By Prothering's account she was in Paris at the relevant time, busy making up for a blameless English girlhood. I imagined her in a garret room with the Seine reflected in ripples on the ceiling, shutting door on latest literary lover, uncapping Swan fountain pen (parting gift from her old headmistress) and tearing across the paper in that sprawling handwriting her revenge on the men who'd shared her bed for half an hour and gone away to compare notes about her in pavement cafes. Or perhaps there'd been one man in particular and it was his story she was telling. Either way, where had it come from? That was what I wanted to ask Prudence, though the memory of the gruff voice on the phone warned me I shouldn't easily get an answer.

I heard the sound of an electric saw long before I got to her cottage. I walked on, the sawing getting louder, and saw a grey roof to the right of the path. Then, as I climbed higher, a stone cottage with a rowan tree beside it, the front door open onto a patch of rough grass. Prudence Belsire was holding the corpse of a small tree across a trestle, cutting it into logs as neatly as slicing bacon. Twenty-five years had done nothing to decaninise the bull pup face. She was wearing green corduroy trousers hazed with sawdust and a checked lumberjack shirt that was just wide enough for her broad shoulders, too long for her short body. I shouted an introduction over the noise of the saw. Two more logs hit the ground before she switched it off and took a long look at me, tilting her head back. I noticed, for a second, a glint in her eyes as if she liked what she saw. I think she'd had an idea of what an academic would look like and hadn't expected it to be young and tall. But the glint, if I'm right about it, was switched off before it could light up the rest of her face.

'You're the one who rang?'

I admitted it.

'Why do you want to know about Cardell?'

She hadn't put the saw down. I said I was thinking of writing a book about Paris publishers in the 1950s and, in propitiation, held out one of the plants.

'I brought you these. From the market.'

'Why? What's wrong with them?'

'Nothing's wrong with them. They're camomile.'

'Of course they are.'

She stared at me as if I were mad, one hand on the saw, the other on the butt end of the tree. I couldn't see the girl in the Paris garret, only the plain, competent daughter of the vicarage. And yet there was something about the grasp of those square, ringless hands.

'Do you think we could go in and talk?'

The direct appeal worked. She let the end of the tree drop and led the way inside, propping the saw in the porch. I left the plants balanced on the trestle.

That room of hers; I swear it had roots coming through the ceiling. Plants everywhere. Things with heart-shaped leaves writhing up the walls and along the ceiling joists, little spiky things on every protruding piece of stone chimney breast. It was still full evening light outside, but swags of greenery over the windows made it dusk in the room. There were a few pieces of heavy furniture. An open roll-top desk crowded with plant labels, insect killer, secateurs, some knives. A bookcase was stuffed with bundles of dried stalks and leaves. Not one book. Not so much as a pamphlet. She saw my eyes on the bookcase.

30

'I told him I sold them. Needed the money. Needed the space.'

But there was space enough in that low, rambling room.

'You mean mental space?'

She gave me a sideways look as if she knew what I was at and wasn't impressed.

'This book you're going to write – do I get any money out of it?'

And, for some time, I had to sit there and fence about terms. Since the book was, and would remain, hypothetical it was easy enough to promise her the twenty per cent she wanted and she agreed, reluctantly, that there was no need to sign anything yet. Then she settled herself back in her tub-like wooden chair.

'Well, what was it you wanted to know?'

I tried to lounge at ease on a chair with a sagging seat and unstable back. I said I wanted to know who wrote a particular book Cardell published.

'Which one?'

You had to be listening to her voice very carefully to notice the change, but I'm sure it was there. I made her wait, getting up to undo my pack, unwrapping my book, the Bodley's book, from its carrier bag and shirt. The she made me wait, fumbling among the plant labels for her glasses, before she'd take it from me.

'Oh, that one.' Her voice was dismissive. 'Nobody knows who wrote that one.'

She slipped off her glasses and stared at me. I could see it now, that look across a narrow bed in the room by the Seine. A look that said come and get it if you want it, but don't expect it to be cheap. From what Gus had said, I'd built up a picture of put-upon Prudence, the ugly girl they all took advantage of. I'd got it wrong, or Gus had. Prudence, I'm sure, always took more than she gave.

'Perhaps you wrote it.'

'I was too busy to write books.'

'You've read it?'

'Of course. I had to proof-read them all for him.'

31

'You must have wondered.'

'I didn't have time to wonder.' She thumped a clenched fist on her thigh. 'Why is everybody so interested in that book, after all this time?'

'Everybody?'

My voice was too eager. She tried to take back what she'd said.

'Well, you seem to think everybody's interested.'

Again that ultimatum of a stare. I sensed there was something besides the promise of money she wanted before she'd deliver, but I didn't know what it was.

I wrapped the book up and sat down again. The chair subsided another inch or two. With her on the higher seat, our eyes were just about level. Hers were brown and slightly protruding, like an elderly spaniel that would bite you as soon as look at you. I'm not sure whether we were going by human or vegetable time in that root-ridden place, but after a while I could see a change in the eyes. First there was a flare of hostility so clear that I expected her to order me out, then a kind of excitement as if she had ordered me out and I'd refused to go, making a fight of it. All this without either of us moving or saying a word.

Then she said, quite abruptly, 'Get it out.'

My left hand flew to guard my trouser zip and my mind was framing 'Madam, you are strangely mistaken', or words to that effect, before I saw it was the other hand that interested her. The one holding the book. I took it out of its bag and offered it to her.

'No. Read it to me.'

Very much I didn't want to do it, but as she stared at me I knew that Prudence yet again was naming her price. I gave her stare for stare, made her wait while I got myself as comfortable as possible in the precarious chair, then started at the beginning:

Two messages were delivered to him while he was still at breakfast. One, from his clerk, told him that he need not, after all, attend the High Court at ten o'clock

32

because the case he was concerned in had been deferred. The other, from Julia, asked him to collect her at seven from her grandfather's house in Piccadilly. He kept her note on the dressing table while he got ready, noticing that for the first time she signed herself with 'love'. 'Love Julia', in the neat round hand her first governess had taught her in the schoolroom at Tarnville. As he chose his tie he reflected that it was an imperative as well as a statement. Julia loved him: he was to love Julia. It seemed to him an eminently reasonable arrangement. When his car arrived he told the driver to go straight to the House, intending to dictate some constituency letters to his secretary. Rounding the corner of St James's Park he noticed that the first daffodils . . .

'Not there,' said Prudence.

I stopped.

'The middle of chapter eight, after he leaves Julia in the crypt.'

This only a few minutes after she'd pretended a total lack of interest in any books. But I was wondering about something more immediately disturbing. I was wondering by what witchcraft she'd pitched on the part of the book I least wanted to read aloud to anybody. Chapter eight is the one where he and his fiancée are at her grandfather's memorial service and he rapes hers, or imagines he rapes her, in the crypt of St Paul's. Then he goes rushing off in his memorial suit to meet the woman in the garden. Sometimes the garden's several days' journey away, but this is one of the occasions when it seems to be waiting just round the corner from Parliament or the law courts. Anyway, I found the place and read.

The door of the garden was closed. That day it was no more than a row of blank vertical planks, no latch, no doorknob, not so much as a hinge. He beat on it with his pigskin glove, then tore off the glove and beat till his knuckles were bleeding. After lifetimes, it opened quite

33

suddenly and he lurched forward, only just keeping his feet. When he turned round there was nobody who might suddenly have opened the door to him and closed it behind him, and yet it was closed. He moved along the path, noticing that there were more roses in bloom than last time, clotting the trellises with gouts of white and pink, sloughing the gravel with petals. After the trellis there was the camomile lawn as he remembered it, but no sign or scent of her. He thought she wouldn't come unless he were naked and he began to strip off his dark clothes . . .

I glanced up at Prudence. She'd been staring at the plant-covered window, but even this slight pause brought the spaniel eyes swivelling in my direction.

. . . jacket and waistcoat, black tie, shirt. As he dragged his shirt off, tearing away the buttons, his fingers scraped against his ribs and he thought how prominent they were, how thin he'd dwindled in the last four months. There was the scar too, still tender, slanting from his left collarbone. Shoes next, torn off with the laces still tied, socks. He couldn't see her but he knew she expected him to hurry. The scent of the herb, trampled first by his shoes with the dust of St Paul's still on them, then by his bare feet, rose round him stronger and stronger, increasing a panic that transferred itself from the hurry of undressing to a more aching urgency, so that when he took off his underpants his member was as rigid as a branch. Then he heard her laughing. It wasn't far away, but the smell of the herb and the swags of roses confused him. Then her voice.

'What did you do with Julia?'

He'd never told her his fiancée's name.

'Never mind her, I've come to you. Please . . .'

'Tell me.'

So he told her, from the time he'd taken Julia's hand and drawn her sobbing from the pew to the memory

34

of Julia on the stone floor of the crypt, torn black dress pulled up between her thighs, long ladders in her stockings. He was panting then, could hardly talk, but the cool voice from somewhere not far away milked him of the utmost detail. The ache in his crotch was thrusting out, trying to escape from itself, and his hand went down to help it, so that by the time he was describing Julia writhing against the stones, his seed was dripping on the lawn and he heard himself groaning. At each grown the voice would make him go on.

'Was she still crying?'

'Yes. Yes, I think so. Please . . .'

'What did you do then?'

'Left her. Left her and came to you.'

'Come here then.'

He walked towards where he thought the voice might be coming from and found himself at the edge of a pool he hadn't seen before. His feet . . .

I looked at Prudence again. She was still staring at the window, but I could hear the sound of her breathing, harsh and short.

Outside a lamb bleated and a tractor chugged home in the valley.

'Go on,' she said, not looking at me this time.

I closed the book.

'No. My turn.'

She glared, but she knew what I meant.

'Who wrote it?'

'Don't you know?'

'I thought you said nobody knows.'

'You're the expert, aren't you? Has anybody said anything to you?'

'Who?'

I didn't tell her that four days ago I hadn't known the book existed. I sensed a greed in her, a need to test the value of a commodity she'd cornered. I was more sure than ever that she could tell me what I wanted to know.

'Give me some clues, at least. How did it arrive? Who got paid for it.'

'I can't remember. It's a long time ago.'

'It got confiscated. It sent Cardell bankrupt. You can't have forgotten.'

'Quite a lot of our books got confiscated. We were always going bankrupt.'

'But this is the only anonymous one. You must remember something about it. Did it come by post?'

'It didn't come by post.'

A fact at last, albeit negative. I asked her how it did come.

'Cardell put it on my desk one morning in the autumn of 1958. He said we were going to publish it.'

'Manuscript or typescript?'

'Typescript. Quite clean.'

'Did he say who'd written it?'

'No.'

'Did you ask him?'

'I don't suppose so.'

'Didn't you think it was a bit odd, out of the blue like that?'

For the first time, she hesitated. The answers so far had been as glib as a talking toy, but this time she was thinking about it. She spoke slowly.

'Yes, in a way. I mean, I remember thinking that . . . that the timing was odd.'

'In what way?'

She sighed and shifted in the chair. Her eyes were on the book again and I knew it would soon be time to put more pennies in the slot.

'Cardell went over to England every so often, three or four times a year. He'd usually come back with three or four manuscripts to give me.'

'But this wasn't one of them?'

She shook her head. 'He hadn't been to England for about two months.'

'And it hadn't come by post. That means it was given to him in Paris.'

'I suppose so.'

36

'By somebody who was living in Paris at the time?'
'That's what I thought.'
'Did Cardell ever actually say it was somebody in Paris?'
'I can't remember.'
The meter was at zero. I opened the book again.
'I don't believe the next bit, do you?'
'I don't remember.'
'Of course you do. It turns out she's playing another trick
on him. It's a boy on the island, but he doesn't realise it until
he's . . . '
'Go on.'
So I soldiered on through the scene in the bamboo thicket
on the island, and I admit it stirred me more than I wanted in
the circumstances, hearing my own voice and her corrosive
breathing, with the few yards of dust-flecked air between us
as charged as a magnetic field. By the end of the scene the
light filtering into the room was turning gold and I knew it
must be late evening, but by then I was immersed in the
rules of this peculiar game and, even without my real need
to know, would have gone on playing it for its own sake. It
was at any rate more exciting than my conventional paths of
literary research.
'My turn again. We'd got as far as the book probably
coming from somebody in Paris in 1958, right?'
She nodded.
'So, the question is, who was in Cardell's set at the time?'
'Oh, everybody. They came and went.'
But I kept my temper and mined away and, by the time
the golden light had turned to copper, I'd got the beginnings
of a list. I'll summarise, as I jotted down in my notebook, the
fruits of that question and answer session, interspersed with
more readings from me. An odd thing about those readings
though. She put me through, unerring in her choice, the most
erotic passages in the book, with just one exception. That
was the scene on the beach in Brittany in which Valentine
murders his best friend then is allowed, at last, to make love
to the woman in the sand beside the corpse. She kept clear
of that and so did I, saving it for later. I kept it at the back

37

of my mind as I concentrated on what she told me about the little circle round Cardell and his publishing house in Paris twenty-nine years ago.

Cardell himself. Homosexual, in his late forties. A bit of family money soon swallowed up by his publishing enterprises, afterwards getting by on loans raised from anybody who stood still long enough. ('He could charm the fleas off a dog,' Prudence said.)

Among those occasional financial contributors was a rich young American woman called, or calling herself, Nicolle. The family made money from biscuits in Pittsburgh. Nicolle thought she was a poet and lived on the Left Bank. She was in her mid twenties at the time and had an income in her own right, so the family disapproval didn't matter. I asked if she was a good poet, but Prudence only replied that she didn't suppose so, in a tone that showed she'd never given any serious thought to the subject. Cardell had published a volume of her poetry, but considering she'd given him an unspecified but large amount of money, he probably had no choice.

'What did Nicolle look like?' I asked.

'Thin, tall. A lot of pale red hair.'

'Beautiful?'

'She had a long nose.'

The one they called Mimi, on the other hand, must have been beautiful because even Prudence had to admit it. At least, what Prudence said was they all seemed to think she was beautiful, which from the girl with the bulldog face seemed fair enough. It was obvious that Prudence had disliked this Mimi very much indeed and she hated talking about her. All I could discover was that Mimi came from London, had run away from her family and wanted to be an actress. She had no money at all, and Prudence threw out a few hints about how she'd managed to keep butter on her croissants.

I tried to find out their full names, but either Prudence had never known them or she was protecting some convention among the group of noms de guerre. This was especially so in the case of the young Englishman they nicknamed

38

'Milord'. He, like Nicolle and Mimi, was playing truant from his family and Prudence believed the family were aristocracy. Milord spoke beautiful French and was, when not slumming on the Left Bank, a student at Cambridge. Prudence said he was a great friend of Cardell's.

'Homosexual?'

'When he was allowed to be.'

'Meaning?'

'When the girl he was engaged to wasn't around. We did use to laugh at her.'

For the freewheeling little crowd on the Left Bank, one of the diversions of the spring of 1958 was watching Milord's betrothed playing sheepdog, trying to cut him out of the herd and return him to England, home and heterosexuality. Prudence, much more forthcoming when she started being malicious, described little scenes in pavement cafés, the betrothed one gloved, hatted and unshakeably demure, while the Bohemians rioted around her. There'd been a night, for instance, when the Mimi woman performed one of her stripteases on the table of a café in the Boul'Mich', Uncle Lazarus did a Turkish belly dance and they were all quite openly smoking cannabis. At the height of it the betrothed stands up, says politely what a lovely evening it's been but they must go now, and exits with Milord in tow. And yes, that was the surprising thing because soon after that Milord did indeed return to England and was seen on the Left Bank no more.

Uncle Lazarus? Here Prudence's brusque manner softened. She'd quite liked Uncle Lazarus. They'd all liked Uncle Lazarus. He was older than the rest of them, in his late forties or early fifties, and lived on a houseboat in the Seine. He was half French, half Vietnamese and a Buddhist, adopted by the group as honorary guru. He didn't, as far as she could tell, do anything like painting or writing and he lived frugally, probably on small handouts from the rest of them when anybody had a few francs to spare.

And was that all, I asked, counting them off on my fingers: Nicolle, Mimi, Milord, Uncle Lazarus and Prudence herself?

She bit her lip, then replied: 'There was Duncan.'

Her voice was quite different. When she stopped after those three words I knew it was from reticence this time, not stubbornness.

'You liked Duncan?'

She nodded.

'Was he a writer?'

'A painter.'

'Any good?'

She nodded again.

'What was he like?'

Even though I could feel the emotional current, the intensity of her reply surprised me.

'He was the most beautiful man I'd ever seen.'

Poor little dog-faced Prudence, head over heels in love with big, beautiful painter, having to watch that bitch Nicolle and that little slut Mimi setting their snares for him.

'He wasn't like the others. He was reserved. Quite shy. You wouldn't expect it in a man so strong and tall, but that's often the way, isn't it?'

I'd have preferred the old stubborn, grudging Prudence back again rather than hear this girlish devotion nursed over a quarter of a century, especially since it was in my mind that the Left Bank with Mimi stripping on every handy table was hardly the place for a tall bearded painter who was shy with women. I could think of reasons for that reserve, but if Prudence hadn't worked them out in all this time, I wasn't going to spoil it for her.

She'd turned away from me by then and though I expected to have to deliver another selection from the book, she said nothing.

'That's it then? All the little crowd.'

'That's it.'

She sounded tired. It was deep dusk by now but she made no move to turn on the lights.

'And one of them wrote the book?'

She burst out: 'Why do you keep on at me? Everybody keeps bothering me. They don't care what I want. Aren't I entitled to want something for myself?'

40

She wasn't playing or fighting any more, simply a tough middle-aged woman, angry and distressed. It was talking about Duncan that made the difference.

I said quietly: 'The woman in the book, did she exist?'

She turned her head away and didn't answer.

'I think she did,' I said. 'And the murder, I think that happened too.'

Even without seeing her expression, I could feel her tension.

'What murder?'

'In the book. Where he kills his friend for her. I think it really happened to someone.'

'That's nonsense. Why are you coming here talking nonsense?'

I expected her to fly at my throat. She had her fingers clenched on the arms of her chair, shoulders thrust forward.

'You're not writing a book at all, are you? What are you doing? What have you come here for?'

I don't know how it would have ended. I'd tucked the book under my arm getting ready, if she flew at me, to grab those capable hands of hers. But I was saved from having to do anything. Just at the moment when Prudence was ready to launch herself at me, the door opened and the woman from the herb stall walked in.

Chapter Five

She stood in the doorway, a slim silhouette against the last of the day outside, then clicked the light on. It dazzled me, so that it took me a second or two to recognise her.

'What are you doing here?' I said.

I had an irrational feeling she'd followed me from the market. I wasn't thinking clearly because when I saw her standing there I'd felt a shock of recognition that went further back than our meeting at the herb stall. It came from the cool way she was staring at me, as if I'd dropped from a previously unknown planet and she was trying to assess from me its level of intelligence. She looked tall in the low doorway. My age, perhaps, or a year or two older.

'She lives here,' Prudence said, settling herself back in the chair. If she'd intended to attack me, the arrival of the other woman had postponed it. 'She helps me with the herbs.'

So it was Prudence's own camomile I'd brought her.

The woman walked past us, bringing with her a scent of earth from the flowerpots and a current of cooler air from outside. She opened a door and went upstairs and I heard the sound of running water.

'Is she your daughter?'

'Mind your own business.'

Through the open door I could see the lights on in the valley farms.

'You'd better go,' she said. 'I'm not talking about this in front of her.'

I played for time, making a long business of putting the book back in my pack. The woman came downstairs before

I'd finished. She'd changed into a blue shirt, but there was still a smell of cool earth about her.

'Are you the man from Oxford?' she said.

Her voice sounded cool to the point of boredom, but I noticed she'd picked up a little pottery owl from the window sill and was twisting it round in her long fingers. Her feet were bare.

'He's just going,' Prudence said.

I picked up my pack and moved towards the open door, but I was still playing for time.

'Is there anywhere I can get bed and breakfast?'

'Clun,' said Prudence. 'Probably.'

And that was that. The glint of liking when she first saw me, the greed when I read to her, might never have existed. I found myself outside in the dark on the rutted track, with the door closed. I stood for a minute, waiting for I didn't know what, watching a square of light filtering onto the grass through the plant-latticed window, listening to the sounds of table laying inside. Then I turned downhill. I passed a parked van a few hundred yards down the track. The younger woman must have driven it up from the market.

I didn't fancy going all the way down to Clun for a doubtful bed. It was a dry night, not far off the summer solstice, with the afterglow still showing on the hills behind me. The temperature had dropped and I was glad I'd packed the sleeping bag. About half a mile down the track, just past one of the cattle grids, I found a grassy plateau between the roots of an old tree. There was a bank topped with a strand of wire behind it and, by following the sound of water, I found a little stream, raw and mossy tasting. I drank, ate a few mouthfuls of chocolate from the pack and climbed into the sleeping bag. I usually enjoy sleeping out but that night, although everything seemed peaceful enough, I felt wary, exposed. The sound of a sheep tearing grass on the other side of the stream had me twisting round in my bag like a nervy grub. I had a sense of something not benevolent close by me. It got so bad that I wriggled out of the sleeping bag and did a tour of my territory. Ten steps up

43

the track, ten steps down it, ten steps out into the dark field. Nothing, but I was still nervous when I rolled myself up again.

Later, half dozing, I thought I heard steps going up the track and, thinking it might be the farmer, kept quiet in case he turned me off his land. In spite of that, and in spite of hunger cramps in my stomach, I must have dozed off. It was near midnight when I heard the steps coming down that I knew weren't the farmer's.

Vibration first, rather than sound. My ear was against the ground and picked up the soft thumping of paws on earth, like an animal, but the wrong rhythm for any animal but one. It was coming down the track, down from the cottage, quiet but assured, knowing I was there as surely as if I'd been lit by searchlight. I thought they were Prudence's steps. I didn't believe for a moment that she'd repented of her inhospitality. There was something about that padding rhythm that conveyed trouble.

Then somebody called my name, quiet but very clear. 'Colin. Colin.' The way it was said made my own name seem foreign to me and again I had that feeling of having landed on an alien planet. I sat up, but I don't know if I made any noise or not.

In any case, she found me, walking unerringly out of the darkness, and stood over me. Her feet were bare and I noticed the toes were as pale and almost as long as her fingers.

'What were you asking Prudence?' she said.

It never occurred to me to lie to her.

'I wanted to know who wrote a particular book.'

'The one in your pack?'

Without asking for permission she crouched over my pack and opened it, hands moving so confidently I thought she must be able to see in the dark. She found it and peeled it, plastic bag then shirt, and held it closed, balanced on the flat of her hands. She seemed to identify it by the feel or smell, because it was too dark to see the title.

'My father wrote it,' she said.

A shiver went through me, starting at the nape of my neck and travelling down, because I thought she was mad but I tried not to let it get into my voice.

'Who is your father?'

'I don't know.'

She sounded both desolate and angry, as if she blamed me for it.

'But if you don't know who your father is, how do you know he wrote it?'

'Prudence told me. She didn't mean to.'

'Is Prudence your mother?'

'I think so.'

'Think so?'

'Have to think so. I've nearly torn myself apart from not knowing who my father is. Can't take not having a mother either.'

There was a forced jokiness about the last few words that made her seem more human than at any time since I'd seen her. I saw she was shivering.

'You're cold. You'd better get in the sleeping bag.'

I'd meant that I should get out and she should get in, but before I could do anything she'd slipped in beside me, bringing the cold with her. I could feel her breasts, firm and small, through the thin shirt, her bare feet striking cold through my socks. She gave a long, shuddering sigh.

'Will you help me find my father?'

There were, I suppose, any number of things I could have done. Not, though, the most obvious of them. Having a beautiful young woman appear out of the night and practically force herself into your sleeping bag may be the stuff of adolescent fantasies but the place, her coldness and, above all, that shock of recognition I'd felt when she walked in at Prudence's door made it more like some grim Nordic fairy tale – the kind where our hero ends up locked in the heart of a mountain or deep-frozen in a glacier. But I could at least have played the good responsible citizen, wrapped her up and returned her to Prudence, with instructions to take better care of her wandering daughter. Or, if my interests had been in

45

psychology rather than literature, I might have encouraged her to talk it out, patiently sort the fact from the fantasy in this father-seeking of hers. As it was, I did none of these things.

'What makes you so sure your father wrote the book?' I said.

I got the story, with my questions and her answers whispered as intimately as lover to lover, her face a few inches from mine in the sleeping bag. I don't know why we whispered, except that everything around us was as silent as mushrooms growing. She said her name was Kay. She was twenty-nine years old and had been born in France. But she could only remember growing up in England, and never anybody there but Prudence.

'She'd never tell me anything about my father. Sometimes she'd get angry when I asked, other times she'd just pretend not to hear. It wasn't until I was nineteen she started trying to explain.'

'Why then?'

'I'm not sure. It was just after she'd bought the herb farm. I'd dropped out of college. They tried to make me see a psychiatrist but I told them there was nothing wrong. I'd be all right if only I could find out about my father. She . . . I think she understood then what it was doing to me. She started trying to explain something about a book and my father. I knew it was the anonymous one, but when I tried to read it she took it away from me and wouldn't tell me any more. Then we had a real fight, a terrible fight, and I hitched to London.'

'Looking for your father?'

'I suppose so. I just wanted to get away from Prudence.'

'What did you do in London?'

'Worked round King's Cross.'

I said nothing, just let my arm tighten around her a little in what I hoped would feel like sympathy.

'I'd intended to get a flat and look for work as a typist, only I didn't realise how hard it is to find somewhere to live in London.'

There were days of rain and loneliness in her voice.

46

'It wasn't too bad, only sometimes with one of the older ones I'd wonder whether he might be my father, but my friend said I'd got to stop that, people went mad that way, so I did.'

'But you came back to Prudence?'

'I got ill and she looked after me.'

'Did you ask her any more about your father?'

'No. I knew it would be no good. I thought if I stayed and kept quiet she was bound to let something out.'

'And has she?'

Her chin moved against my shoulder. She was shaking her head.

'Then I thought, she'll have to put it in her Will. I'll find out when she dies. She wouldn't die and not tell me, would she?'

I thought Prudence looked the type to live forever.

'Has she made a Will?'

'Yes. Is there any way you can see a Will before somebody dies?'

'No.'

'It doesn't seem fair. Then last night, when she told me you were coming — '

'She told you?'

'After you'd phoned. She said a professor from Oxford was coming to talk to her about Cardell's books, and I'd better stay out for the evening. You were supposed to have gone by the time I got back. I'd have found you anyway.'

'Why did you want to'

'Because a professor can find out who wrote books.'

This over-confidence in the academic profession and my altitude within it took my breath away.

'So I decided I'd hire you to find my father.'

'Find your father!'

'Well, you'd be looking for whoever wrote the book, but it would come to the same thing, wouldn't it? How much do you charge?'

'It . . . um, doesn't quite work that way.'

But she'd somehow got her hand into her jeans pocket and was holding a folded-up wad of something in my face.

47

It's probably good commercial manners at King's Cross.

'It's a hundred pounds. Will that be enough?'

'Look,' I said, moving arm and notes aside as gently as possible. 'Look, I haven't said I'll do it yet.'

'Isn't it enough? I can get more.'

'That's not the point. Supposing it turns out whoever wrote the book isn't your father?' It was still in my mind that the author was a woman. 'After all, from what you've told me, Prudence never actually said it was your father who wrote the book. She only said your father was connected with it in some way, isn't that right?'

Even within the confines of the sleeping bag, I could feel her drawing away from me.

'But . . . but how else would he be connected with it?'

'Lots of ways. For instance, suppose Prudence wrote it and your father was one of the characters in it.'

Her back was straining at the seams of the bag by now.

'But how could I be the daughter of a character in a book? Besides, Prudence would never write a book.'

I might, from her tone, have accused Prudence of some obscure indecency. Kay wriggled out of the sleeping bag as smoothly as she'd got into it and stood up. I followed, less gracefully, and we were standing there with the moon coming up, I holding the sleeping bag, staring at each other.

'So you won't help me,' she said. Her white skin in the moonlight was near amethyst colour.

'I didn't say that. If I can find out who wrote the book I'll let you know, whether it's your father or not.'

'Thank you.'

Her arms were round me suddenly and she kissed me full on the lips. I felt a hand groping around my hips, but it was only to push the wodge of notes into my jeans pocket.

'I don't want that.'

'It's a fee. You've got to take it.'

She was triumphant now. She'd taken more than I was conscious of having given.

'Don't write to me here. Prudence will know. Meet me at the market stall when you've got anything to tell me.'

48

She'd turned to go when she thought of something.

'The book. You've read it?'

'Of course.'

'What's it about?'

I told her: 'It's about a man who becomes obsessed with a woman. She makes him destroy his own life and murder his best friend.'

Standing there, half turned away, she asked an unexpected question.

'What does she look like?'

And I gave the answer that had been in my mind ever since she walked through the door.

'She looks like you.'

Chapter Six

Later, lying awake, I heard the van go down. It was just before three o'clock and there was enough moonlight to recognise it as the one that had been parked below Prudence's cottage. I guessed that Kay was driving it and that her departure an hour before dawn meant there'd been another row with Prudence, probably over me. By the time I'd disentangled myself and run out to the track it was out of sight. I could hear it rattling over cattle grids down towards the valley. Even if I could have caught up with it, I don't know what I could have done. I went back to my bag and thought.

Kay's departure would mean that Prudence was on her own in the cottage, and there were more questions I wanted to ask her. If Kay's account had any fact in it at all, then there were things connected with the book that Prudence hadn't told me. I hoped the surprise of seeing me again in the early morning when she thought I was several miles away might jolt her into being more communicative. Also, I wanted to know what, if anything, Kay had told her about our meeting at midnight. Guessing that gardening people like Prudence probably rose early, I had a quick wash in the stream and was on my way up the track soon after six. It was a fine morning with the sun already burning the mist off the valley. My throat was dry and I hoped Prudence would at least rise to the elementary hospitality of a cup of coffee.

As I expected, the van had gone. There was no sound of sawing this time, only a skylark singing, and when I got within sight of the cottage the door was shut, exposing its flaking green paintwork. The dew on the long grass under the rowan tree was undisturbed, showing that if Prudence

was an early riser she hadn't walked out that way. I knocked
and called out her name, but got no answer. In case she was
already working out at the back I walked round the side of the
house. Sheltered between it and the hill, orderly rows of green
things, some tall and fern-like, some squat and leathery, were
already giving off a clamour of conflicting smells. But no sign
of Prudence. There was a back door beside a water-butt and I
knocked, then tried the latch. There was no lock or keyhole
so it must have been bolted on the inside. It didn't budge. I
put my ear to the door in case I could hear sounds of breakfast
preparation inside, but there was nothing. I decided I'd arrived
too early and went back round the cottage with the intention
of sitting under the rowan tree until there were signs of life
from inside. It was then I noticed that the living room lights
were still on.

The mesh of plants over the windows had prevented me
from seeing that before. Now, as soon as I saw it, I knew
something was wrong. Even after a blazing row with Kay,
Prudence didn't strike me as the type to go to bed without
switching the lights off. I wondered if she'd stayed awake all
night worrying about the girl, perhaps even drinking herself
into a stupor, although I could remember no signs of alcohol
in the room. At any rate, I should go in and see if she was all
right. I knocked on the door loudly with my knuckles, calling
her name again. No answer. I tried the latch, the door opened
and I was inside.

My first thought was that Prudence was drunk, dead drunk.
Even after I saw the blood I thought she'd somehow damaged
herself in falling and perhaps her nose had bled. She was face
down and I got my arms round her broad shoulders, hands
under the chest, to turn her over, muttering the meaningless,
consoling words one tries on drunks or injured children. It
was only when I turned her on her back and her head
lolled sideways, showing the great gaping cut under her
left ear, that I knew she was dead. Even then, my first
confused thought was suicide until I saw there were rents
in her blood-soaked lumberjack blouse and cuts deep into
her chest. Then I thought of the van being driven downhill

51

at three o'clock in the morning and Kay's voice: 'I'll find out when she dies.'

I couldn't see the knife, although I admit at that point I wasn't looking very closely. What had happened still wasn't real to me and I was watching myself as if through some transparent screen that would let through neither sound nor thought. I walked round the outside of the room, avoiding the blood, being careful not to touch anything. I had at least remembered that you shouldn't touch things. The secateurs and some gardening knives were on top of her old desk, just as they'd been the evening before. I thought one of the larger knives might be missing, but I wasn't sure of that. When I heard a car draw up on the track outside I thought it must be the police. I wondered who'd phoned them.

Not the police. Not even the most rural of police would travel in a seven-year-old Renault, its bonnet and doors pock-marked with dents. The man who unfolded himself from the driving seat was in his fifties, black hair and square-cut beard touched with grey. He was wearing corduroys and a dark fisherman's jersey, paint-flecked.

'She's dead,' I said. 'Prudence is dead.'

He looked at me and walked straight in, taking his time. I was behind him when he looked at the body, and couldn't see his face. He stood, shoulders bowed, and might have been praying.

'When did it happen?'

I started explaining about leaving her soon after dark, getting back at six, then trailed off in mid sentence as I understood what I'd got myself into. I leave Prudence after a row. I'm found alone with her body at an early hour of the morning. I had a wad of Prudence's money pressing like a tumour against my hip because it was surely the herb farm's money that Kay had taken for my fee.

'I didn't kill her,' I said.

He didn't reply. Still with his back to me he took a few steps into the room, avoiding the blood as I had done.

'Do the police know?'

'I haven't rung them.'

52

There was an old-fashioned black telephone standing on her desk next to the knives, but it hadn't occurred to me to use it.

'There was a daughter,' I said. 'She's gone away.'

He still gave no sign of hearing me but began slowly walking round the room, much as I had done, except I sensed he was noticing more. If I hadn't been so preoccupied with my own worries I'd have found his behaviour as odd as my own.

'Where's the knife?'

'I don't know. It wasn't in her.'

Saying that made me feel sick and I dashed outside, retching with my hand on the trunk of the rowan. I saw the camomile plants on the trestle where I'd left them the evening before and the pile of logs on the grass. As I went in he was bending down by her desk. I thought I heard one of the drawers shutting, and when he straightened up and turned round he was holding something out to me.

'Is this yours?'

'No.'

I took it from him. It was a crumpled theatre programme, Milton's *Comus* in performance at Ludlow Castle. I'd noticed posters for it while I was waiting for the bus.

'Where was it?'

'Down by her desk.'

'It wasn't there last night.'

I'd noticed the total lack of books or papers of any kind. Even a theatre programme on the floor would have struck me like water in the desert. Prudence did not seem to me a play-goer. Nor did Kay. I felt my brain toiling into some kind of life again.

'It's funny, the way it's creased.'

I knelt down beside him, noting that the bottoms of his trousers were covered with grime and oil, and looked at the shape of the handles of the desk drawers. Wooden rectangles. When I tried the programme against them, the marks fitted exactly.

'Somebody used it to open the drawers with, so as not to leave fingerprints.'

I didn't know whether to be relieved or not that the somebody was unlikely to have been Kay. Kay's fingerprints would, legitimately, be all over the cottage where she lived, so why should she worry? That suggested I hadn't, after all, shared my sleeping bag with a murderess. On the other hand, if it was somebody other than Kay, I had to face the fact that I was a prime suspect.

I said: 'Who are you?'

He'd been looking out of the back window. When he turned round he was actually smiling.

'I'm Duncan.'

He seemed to take it for granted that the name would mean something to me. A few hours ago, the woman on the floor had called him the most beautiful man she'd ever seen. Even twenty-nine years later it was possible to see why. The eyes mainly, I think. There was a gentleness about them that seemed at odds with the tall, powerful body. I'm nearly six foot and he could look down on me. He was doing it then, still smiling faintly, in what looked like sympathy.

'We'd better go,' he said.

When I got in beside him I naturally assumed we'd be making for the nearest police station. As he made a dozen or so attempts to get the engine to start, I was wondering how much I needed to tell them. While the car ground and clanged its way over the cattle grids, I wasn't liking the answers. The dialogue as I saw it went something like this:

'Mr Counsel, you tell us you first met the deceased a few hours before she was murdered. What made you get in touch with her?'

And I'd have to answer something about thinking that she might cast light on the authorship of a book I was interested in.

'What book would that be, Mr Counsel?'

'A 1950s sado-masochistic novel called *The Martyrdom of Valentine*.'

'Very interesting, Mr Counsel. I gather you're an academic at Oxford. Is that the kind of thing you're studying?'

'Well, er, not exactly, that is . . .'

Add to that the fact that even the most elementary of identity checks on me would bring my activities to the notice of Andrea and Lagen, and it's hardly surprising I was worried.

Then, as we drove at a rackety fifty along an empty main road, I thought of the next bit of the problem. Kay. When I found Prudence dead I hadn't the slightest doubt that Kay had done it. She'd been wrought up, a little mad. She had reason, as she saw it, for wanting Prudence dead. She'd talked about Prudence's death, walked back up the track, then, an hour later, driven down it.

But when I came to think it out, there were arguments against it. Kay, in paying me, thought she'd taken a decisive step towards finding her father. In the circumstances, wasn't a confrontation with Prudence on the issue less, rather than more, likely that night? Then there was the fact that somebody had used the theatre programme to avoid leaving fingerprints on the drawers. But neither of these was as conclusive as I'd have liked. It was possible that Prudence had discovered the theft of the money Kay gave me, confronted her about it and Kay had panicked. As for the programme, even if she didn't have to worry about ordinary fingerprints, it would be a different matter with blood-stained ones. I was still holding the programme. I looked at it but could see no traces of blood.

This, of course, like everything else, was a matter for the police. They'd test the programme for blood after I'd told them about Kay. I couldn't help telling the police about Kay whether I liked it or not. If I didn't I'd be concealing evidence, perhaps even be rated as an accomplice. Yet the prospect of sitting in a bleak interview room with somebody writing down Kay's pathetic meanderings about her father seemed to me nearly intolerable. It was at this point, when I gave my brain a rest and looked at the scenery, that I realised we were on a motorway and the signs said 'Birmingham'.

'Hey,' I said. 'Where are we going?'

I didn't know much about Shropshire, but I reckoned there were police stations nearer than Birmingham.

Duncan kept his eyes on the road, concentrating hard on passing a gravel lorry doing all of twenty-five.

'I thought,' he said, 'we'd go home and think about it.'

'Aren't we going to the police?'

'Do you really want to go to the police?'

We passed the gravel lorry and settled to a steady forty-five in the middle lane. The engine sounded as if it was feeling the strain. I could have pleaded the need to stop for a pee and made a run for it along the hard shoulder. I could even have insisted on turning off and making for the nearest police station and seen how he reacted. What I said was: 'All right. Where's home?'

I can see now that reaction had set in and I was in the grip of a practically insane over-confidence. I was pleased with my detective work about the drawer handles. I was even smug that in knowing about Kay, about the book, about Prudence's past, I knew more than the police were likely to know and was therefore better placed to find out who killed her. If it was Kay, didn't I at least owe it to her trust in me to find her before the police did, persuade her to give herself up and make it as easy for her as possible? And if it was not Kay, then there was even more reason for me to sort it out myself. Because if Kay was not the murderer, then I believed it happened because of the book. Not just the book but my researches into it. I'd stirred up something that had led to Prudence's death and, though I hadn't liked her much, I had a debt to pay for that.

I looked again at Duncan. I remembered the person I'd taken to be the farmer walking up the track, before Kay came to find me. Anybody could have parked a car down on the road and walked up the track in the dark, watched Kay go out and taken his chance. Kay might have returned from me to find Prudence already dead and driven off for help. Meanwhile the murderer could cut across the fields back to his car, ready to drive up in the morning and discover the body. Plus the bonus of a suspect there already.

'Did you often go to see Prudence?' I asked him.

He shook his head. 'Only once or twice in nearly thirty years.'

56

'So why come to see her at the crack of dawn this morning?'

'She said people were bothering her about the book.'

He knew he didn't have to explain what book we were talking about.

'People?'

'I suppose you're the one from Oxford. She rang me after you phoned her.'

And yet I'd only said I wanted to talk to her about Cardell's books.

'She wanted you to call me off?'

'Not really. She was trying to find out more about you, if I knew anything.'

'And you drove all the way out here because of that?'

We'd covered half a mile or so before he answered.

'I suppose you could call it a defensive alliance.'

'All of you, you mean? With Mimi and Milord and Nicolle and Uncle Lazarus?'

'Some of us.'

I filed that away for working on later.

'You say Prudence rang you yesterday. Why didn't you turn up until this morning?'

'I'd intended to be there when you arrived. There was some trouble at home so I was late starting. Then the car broke down and I spent most of the night in a lay-by.'

The condition of his trousers was a point in favour of that story. On the other hand, they'd have got pretty dirty on a walk in the dark across fields, and anybody can apply oil smears. I noted the reference to trouble at home and wondered where he was taking us. He didn't strike me as a domestic man.

'So,' I said, 'you come in and find me standing over the body.'

No reaction.

'It must be in your mind that I could have killed her.'

Still no reaction.

'So why aren't you taking me to the police?'

'I wouldn't take anybody to the police. Not anybody. Whatever they'd done.'

He said it with an intensity that was anything but reassuring. It meant he thought I'd done it.

'Why not?'

'Because if you happened to be a homosexual in the 1950s you don't take the same view of the police as other good citizens.'

After what Prudence had said, that didn't surprise me.

'You realise this could be just delaying things? If Kay goes to the police, she'll tell them about me anyway.'

He shrugged.

If Kay didn't kill her, I thought, she'll naturally go to the police and tell them about the man from Oxford. On the other hand, if Kay did kill her and is cunning enough to muddy the waters, she'll still tell them about me. I began looking out for police cars.

'Did you know Prudence had a daughter?'

'Guessed. I never saw her.'

'Is she your daughter?'

It was a fair enough question. He might have been bisexual. He pursed his lips and shook his head in a denial that looked convincing to me because it was so throw-away. No chance. Poor Prudence.

'So how did you guess?'

'That summer, Prudence went away to Brittany for months. Soon afterwards she went back home and stayed there.'

He'd said 'that summer' as if there could be no other.

'You mean, the summer before the book was published?'

'Yes.'

'The summer the book was written?'

He nodded.

'Did she write it?'

No answer.

I thought her death proved that she didn't. If Prudence had died because of the book it was because anon was determined to remain anon, because he or she suspected that Prudence was about to talk. I thought it over. Prudence, Mimi, Nicolle, Duncan, Milord and Uncle Lazarus. I'd met two of the six so far.

We turned off the motorway into the Birmingham suburbs. Duncan said, 'I should warn you, we've got a television team staying. They're doing a documentary on us for Channel Four.'

This surprised me. Prudence had said Duncan was a good painter, but she was prejudiced. If people were bothering to film him, he must be good. I wondered about the 'we' and decided it was probably one of those stable homosexual relationships, probably with another artist. The other aspect of it only struck me later, which shows I wasn't yet used to being a hunted man.

'Um, Duncan, if I'm supposed to be keeping out of sight of the police, won't a camera team make things a bit difficult?'

'Don't worry. They won't be interested in you.'

We drew up in front of a red-brick Victorian semi with rhododendrons in the garden and a couple of vans outside. I think it was probably in Edgbaston. Two lads were lounging about on the front steps, one pale with big dark eyes, the other looking like an amiable boxer with a multicoloured dragon tattooed up his arm and writhing under the shoulder of his singlet. Art students, I supposed, or possibly camera crew. Duncan asked them if everything was all right and they answered yeah. We went inside.

The first thing that hit me was the smell: stewed meat and cabbage. It was like being back at school. A Victorian stained-glass window on the landing spread light in the colours of cheap boiled sweets over a bleak hallway with a half-sized billiard table as its only furniture. Two lads looking younger than those on the steps were playing on it in an unenthusiastic way and hardly looked up when Duncan said hello to them. He led me straight upstairs past a mural depicting, I think, the martyrdom of St Eadmund in a modern shopping centre, to the second floor.

'We'll put you in Bartholomew for the moment while we decide what to do with you.'

That sounded ominous enough in itself, but what really unsettled me were the names on the doors we passed: Nicodemes, Damian, Cosmas, Crispian, that, owing to the specialised nature of my studies, I instantly recognised as those of early Christian martyrs. All men. No Catherines or the like. And, as far as I could see, no Valentine. The Bartholomew door opened into a small white-walled room. Its only furniture was a bed that looked like a hospital throw-out and a mattress, clean but biscuit thin.

'We'll find you some blankets,' Duncan said.

The assumption that I'd be staying the night or any number of nights threw me. I felt I was being taken over, and I didn't know by what.

'Hang on a minute, Duncan. What is this place?'

'I suppose,' he said, 'you might call it a kind of sanctuary.'

What it amounted to was that Duncan collected rent boys. They were homeless and jobless so they made money the only way they could. (I thought of Kay.) The police picked them up – trapped them was how Duncan put it – and sent them to approved schools. From which they emerged homeless, jobless so . . . et cetera et cetera. Except that somewhere in the middle of it, trying to break the vicious circle for as many as he could find houseroom for, was Duncan.

'But you're a painter,' I said.

He shook his head. 'I gave that up a long time ago. Except for the murals. The lads seem to like them.'

From the graffiti I'd noticed on St Eadmund I doubted even that.

'Duncan, can we talk about Prudence? About what I'm going to do?'

'Later. Are you hungry? I'll send Caleb up with some coffee.' He left, shutting the door behind him. He couldn't lock it because there was no lock, but the message was clear. It was probably a coincidence that the lad who brought the coffee and two Rich Teas carefully disposed on a plate was the tattooed young boxer. He too shut the door carefully when he went.

I was ravenous. As far as I could remember I hadn't eaten properly for days. The same applied to sleep. There hadn't been more than an hour or two of continuous rest since the helpful woman gave the book to me in the Bodley. Duncan must have picked up my pack when we left the cottage and I noted it as a sign that he'd been thinking more clearly than I had. It was on the floor by the bed. I opened it and checked that the book was still there, sat with it in my hands but had no impulse to read it. I looked at my watch. It was only just past eleven. Thirteen hours or so since I'd last had it in my hand, reading to Prudence. I stretched out on the thin mattress and slept.

Chapter Seven

I woke up thinking about Gus Prothering.

It was some time before I understood why, then I worked it through and realised it all hinged on who knew I was going to see Prudence. If she'd been killed to stop her talking to me about the book, then the killer must have known of my existence and my intention to visit her. That left a very narrow field. Kay knew. Prudence had told her about the man from Oxford. Duncan knew. He admitted himself that Prudence had telephoned him. That, as far as I could tell, was all. Except Gus Prothering. He knew I was interested. He knew I had Prudence's address because he'd shown me her letter. What he couldn't know was whether I'd follow it up, and when.

Timing was the problem. If Prudence's killer had wanted to stop her talking to me, the time to act would surely be before my visit, not afterwards. I remembered that I'd said on the phone to Prudence that I hoped to be with her about tea time. I'd been over-optimistic about public transport links with Clun, therefore it had been early evening by the time I'd arrived. Duncan had planned to get there earlier but he'd been let down by his car – or so he said. Gus, though, wouldn't know what I was going to do until I'd done it. If he'd checked on me, noticed that I wasn't in the Bodley as usual, he'd have been hours behind, even allowing for travelling by car instead of train or bus. The problem here was that, as far as I could tell, Gus Prothering had no connection whatsoever with the Cardell circle or the book.

And yet. And yet . . . He was steeped in the places and personalities of Left Bank Paris. He denied any personal acquaintance, claimed it was from books and letters. But then, he would, wouldn't he? Then there'd been those three warnings to me, ostensibly about the perils of book collecting but even at the time I'd sensed they were more than that. A circle like Cardell's, I thought, would have its casual hangers-on as well as the main characters. I needed to know more about all of them, much more. I was, at least, under the roof of a man who could tell me if he wanted to.

From the floor below I could hear the sound of a radio or television. I looked at my watch and found I'd slept seven hours and it was nearly six o'clock. Six o'clock news. I needed to hear it. Because of Duncan's clear intention that I should stay in my room, I felt ridiculously defensive as I walked out. But nobody tried to stop me as I walked down the stairs and through a half-open door into what was obviously a common room.

It had a ping-pong table scattered with cola cans, a few dog-eared books, a weights bench and one and a half pairs of dumb-bells. There were three people in the room: the boxer, the pale boy with the large eyes, and a red-haired lad I hadn't seen before who looked no more than twelve years old. They glanced round when I came in then turned back to the screen. The signature tune for the news was just starting. I hadn't expected it to be on the national news, and it wasn't. I wasn't really tense until the Midlands bulletin started. Woman found murdered in lonely cottage would surely rate a mention. I sat through jumbo jet near miss at Birmingham Airport, armed robbery in Wolverhampton and royal visit to Telford old people's centre. By the time we'd got down to Bertie the bantam who thinks he's a duck I knew it wasn't going to be on. I also knew that wherever Kay had driven after finding Prudence's body, it hadn't been straight to the police. The red-haired boy switched over to a pop programme.

'You another reporter?' he asked me.

I shook my head.

'Social worker?'

'No.'

'Don't you want to interview me? The TV people interviewed me.'

'No thanks. Where will I find Duncan?'

'He'll be in his room. Ground floor at the back.'

The boxer said, without turning his eyes from the screen: 'Won't it keep till you see him at supper? He likes some time on his own.'

It wouldn't keep. I went down another flight of stairs, noting that St Eadmund had acquired some more attributes, went along a narrow passageway and knocked on a white door. Duncan's voice, sounding weary, invited me to come in.

'It wasn't on the news,' I said.

It at least looked like a studio. The floorboards were bare and the large window curtainless, but after the rest of the house it felt light and clean. There were a few canvases turned towards the wall and one facing outwards, showing a figure among swathes of writhing foliage with a depraved looking pig at its feet.

'I thought you didn't paint now.'

'It's for a friend.'

He hadn't replied when I told him it wasn't on the news. There was no sign that he'd been doing anything when I walked in, no paper or palette.

'The question is, where Kay's got to. I think we should try and find her and talk to her.'

'Where were you thinking of looking?'

He had a point. Tracing Kay and the van would be a police operation; might be already.

'They're bound to have discovered the body by now, aren't they? Somebody must have missed her.'

But who, besides her daughter, would miss an unsociable woman in a lonely cottage? I thought of her still lying there and was angry with Duncan for not being more obviously concerned about it.

'She was supposed to be your friend, wasn't she?'

'She's dead. What can I do?'

'You can help me find out who killed her. We've got three main suspects so far. There's me. There's Kay. And there's you.'

He didn't protest, just sat down on a chair by the window as if this was going to be a longer interview than he'd expected. I took the other chair.

'Whatever you're thinking, it isn't me. And in spite of the way it looks, I don't think it was Kay either.'

'I didn't kill her,' he said. 'Why would I do that?'

I was glad that he hadn't asked why I thought Kay was innocent. I could have given him no reasons except a hunch, plus the flimsy evidence of the folded theatre programme. I had it in the pocket of my jeans.

'Right, that's three not guilty pleas: you, me and Kay in absentia. So who else have we got?'

He said: 'You really didn't do it?'

I kept my temper. He'd rescued me, as he saw it, believing I'd killed his friend. Either that or he'd killed her and was holding on to me as a handy fall-guy. Whichever it was, raging at him would do no good.

'I really didn't do it.'

'But what were you doing there?'

I made a quick decision and gave him an edited version of the whole story, not mentioning Gus Prothering by name and leaving out some of the conversation with Kay, like her questions about the Will. Afterwards he sat quietly for a while.

'There's one thing I don't understand.'

'Yes.'

'Why did you want to know about the book? It's nothing to do with you.'

'I wanted to know who the woman was. Why she wanted to destroy him.'

'She was an evil woman, that's all.'

'He knew that. He chose her. That's the point. He wanted to be destroyed by her more than he wanted anything else in the world.'

Silence.

'Did she really exist?'

'Yes,' he said. 'Yes, she existed.'

'And the murder. Was there really a murder?'

Silence.

'That was the last thing I asked Prudence. She was so scared and angry I thought she was going to attack me. I think there really was a murder.'

I saw that he was nodding his head, very slowly. When he lifted it the eyes were closed, lips pressed together.

'There was a murder?'

His 'yes' was so quiet it was almost lost in the clattering of feet down the stairs.

'Supper time,' he said. From the look in his eyes he might as well have said 'dying time'. I've never seen a man look so hopeless.

'You've got to tell me about it,' I said. 'If somebody killed Prudence to keep her quiet, they might be after the rest of you.'

'Afterwards,' he said. 'Afterwards.'

Supper was macaroni cheese, thick and slimy. I'd thought I was famished but I couldn't eat. There were a dozen of us round the table: seven rescued rent boys and three from the TV crew. They'd been out filming in the Bull Ring when I arrived. All of them looked at me curiously, but fortunately the place didn't seem to go in for introductions. Afterwards we took our coffees and went back to his room.

'So who wrote it?' I asked.

'I don't know.'

'You were there. You must know. You must have some idea.'

'All I know is it should never have been written.'

'You say the woman was real and the murder was real but you don't know who wrote the book.'

'I've told you, I don't know.'

I didn't believe him. I thought it was part of a self-protective network they'd built round themselves for twenty-nine years. But it hadn't protected Prudence.

'You accept that Prudence might have been killed because of something to do with that book?'

66

'It's an evil book.'

'Either because somebody doesn't want it known who wrote it, or they don't want any questions asked about the murder. So why has it happened thirty years later?'

'Because you stirred it up. You stirred up the evil.'

He didn't even sound angry about it. He was just stating it as a fact.

'If you're saying Prudence was killed because she talked to me, we come back to this: who knew I was seeing Prudence yesterday? You say she told you. Did you tell anybody else? Anybody from the old crowd?'

'Yes. Angela. Angela Arless.'

I stared at him.

'The Angela Arless?'

'If you mean the actress, yes.'

The name in these surroundings came as a shock. I knew Angela Arless the way most people did, through the television screen. Ten years ago, when I was young and impressionable, she'd done her bit for my literary education by showing me why Oedipus married his mother. By which I mean she was an admitted thirty-eight when I first saw her on the screen and she lifted the popcorn right off my lap. Ten years on, she's still doing the same thing for fifteen-year-olds at an admitted forty-six, but that's show business. I'd been watching her with Andrea in a late night movie just a few weeks before and she'd had a mock strip scene that . . .

'Ye gods,' I said. 'She's Mimi. Angela was Mimi.'

I had a mental picture of Mimi stripping on the café table, the time Milord's little fiancée said thank you for a nice party, and it just slid into place. I knew I was right when I saw Duncan's face.

'She's the friend you're painting the picture for, isn't she? The pig, Circe, Ludlow . . . oh my god.'

It came to me in a flash as these things do, so I'd better backtrack.

Who in literature lurks in forests and changes people into pigs? The enchantress Circe. And where, outside Homer, do we find the enchantress Circe? Please sir, in Milton's *Comus*,

67

sir? And where do we find Milton's *Comus* being performed? At Ludlow Castle, that's where. An easy drive from Clun. I took the programme out of my pocket and turned to the cast list. Sure enough, there it was, 'Circe: Angela Arless.' Slumming it at Equity minimum plus mosquito bites in the cause of art. Or something.

'Prudence didn't like Mimi,' I said. 'I suppose it was mutual.'

'Angela's a very generous woman. A very kind woman.'

'And you just happened to ring her up yesterday and mention to her that I was going to see Prudence.'

'She rang me up about the next sitting. She's coming tomorrow morning.'

'Coming here?'

I couldn't associate what I knew of Angela Arless with thin mattresses and macaroni cheese.

'Why not? She owns the place, after all.'

'Owns it?'

'It costs a lot of money to run. We could never have managed without Angela.'

'She's into rescuing rent boys, is she?'

Duncan should have resented my tone, but didn't. He even smiled. 'I believe some women in Angela's position go in for cats. We're lucky.'

Yes, I thought, and you're not going to do anything to threaten that luck, are you? There was a biography of Angela Arless at the back of the programme. No dates, just a glancing reference to studying acting in Paris and London. I reckoned she was probably about five years older than her age in the papers, which put it about right. Interesting that she should choose to be painted as an archetypal cruel woman, or had that been Duncan's idea?

I'd guessed Mimi, by a piece of good luck. That left three I didn't know about.

'Prudence wouldn't tell me their real names. What about Uncle Lazarus?'

I started with him because, by Prudence's account, he was the easy one, the man they all liked.

'I've never known him as anything other than Uncle Lazarus.'

68

'Is he still alive?'

'Living in his houseboat on the Seine, just as he's always done.'

He'd be in his seventies or eighties by now. He might have flown across the Channel and knifed Prudence, but I could rule him out for the while.

'And Nicolle?'

'She really was Nicolle. Nicolle Banderberg.'

'Are you still in touch with her?'

'Not for years.'

'Where does she live?'

'Paris too. I'm surprised you haven't heard of her. She writes poetry, but mostly in French now. She's taken French citizenship.'

'How do you know about her?'

'Angela sees her sometimes when she's filming in Paris.'

The bitch and the slut, as Prudence had called them. I wondered what they talked about.

There was one more to go, but that extra name I'd woken up with was still on my mind.

'I suppose there'd have been a lot of hangers-on as well as the main crowd. People who drifted in and out.'

'Of course.'

'Can you remember a plump Englishman in his twenties, probably an undergraduate, interested in collecting books?'

'Rich?'

'Probably some money to spare.' Houses in Observatory Street didn't come cheap.

He frowned. 'It sounds like one of Milord's crowd. Can't say I remember him; there were quite a lot of them.'

His voice, which had been warm when he talked about Angela and Uncle Lazarus, neutral for Nicolle, dropped to freezing when I mentioned Milord.

'You didn't like him. I thought he was . . . '

He glared. 'Colin, do you like people just because they happen to be heterosexual?'

'Of course not.'

'Well then . . . '

I tried to apologise but he was well launched, striding round the room, setting the floorboards creaking.

'The old myth, isn't it: freemasonry of homosexuals. If it exists at all it's between people like me and those lads up there, and that's not because of what we are but because of what people have done to us. If you think we've got anything in common with the only here for the day thank-you-kindly-my-man tourists like him and his friends, you're not as intelligent as I took you for.'

I said I'd gathered from Prudence that Milord had taken the coach trip back across the sexual divide unwillingly, in the grip of the betrothed.

'It was there all the time,' he said. 'Underneath all the posing it was there all the time. I wasn't a bit surprised by what happened.'

'This Milord, who was he?'

He was still standing, looking down at me.

'Oh, you haven't guessed that one yet?'

I told him I'd got no idea.

'Come with me,' he said. 'Come with me.'

He led the way downstairs into the basement. The staircase curved down to a concrete floor stacked with cleaning equipment and cartons of baked beans, presumably provided by the voluptuous Angela Arless. He stopped at a heavy oak door, knocked on it and, when he got no reply, walked in. I think at one time he must have tried to set it up as a disco. There was a semicircular platform, coloured lights, speakers. But the mural that dominated the place, spread over the long wall facing the door, wasn't the sort you usually expect in discos. St Sebastian in the middle, tied to his tree but smiling, untouched by arrows. On either side of him, a regular rogues' gallery. The Marquis of Queensberry, I noticed, sundry judges and moral campaigners, a Puritan cleric in white bands, an eminent Victorian in a top hat. The texture of their chests and faces looked odd until I saw that they'd been painted on roundels of cork and the residents had been encouraged to use them as dart-boards. And there, standing at the left hand of St Sebastian with a face considerably dart-pocked

70

but quite recognisable, junior Home Office Minister Lord Talisby. Duncan had even painted in his elegant little wife alongside. Looking down, I noted that she was wearing both her shoes.

'That's your Milord,' Duncan said.

He picked up a dart from the table and flung it. It missed Lord Talisby but hit his wife.

'That's your Milord. And wouldn't he be in a nice position to frame either of us?'

Chapter Eight

Later that evening I slipped out to phone a friend who
works as a parliamentary reporter. I chose a time when
Duncan was in the common room and nobody tried to stop
me, but Caleb the boxer just happened to be sitting on the
steps and watched me go. I turned and backtracked around
the streets for a while in case he was following me, but saw
no sign of him. For a wonder, I found a phone box that took
pound coins in working order, and got through to my friend
without much trouble. She said I was lucky to get her as she
was just going home to bed.

'So early?'

'So early, forsooth. I was up till four o'clock last night,
in the bloody Lords of all places. Committee stage of the
rape bill.'

'Agriculture or Home Office?'

'Home Office, half-wit.'

'Does that mean Lord Talisby?'

'Yes, God rot him, explaining every bloody new clause
at dictation speed down to the last comma. Government fili-
buster. Trying to bore the Opposition off to bed so that . . . '

A lot of parliamentary detail followed. I cut through it.

'What time did all this start?'

'Four o'clock in the afternoon.'

'So he was in the Lords all night.'

'Every bloody minute, except when he went out to pee. I
suppose you've got to give it to the sod for stamina. How's
Andrea?'

I said vaguely that she was all right, wondering how far
I could go without her wanting to know why.

'Do you know much about Talisby?'

'Such as?'

'Where he was educated, for instance?'

'Eton and Cambridge, I think. Or Harrow and Oxford.'

'Do you happen to know if he spent much time in France?'

The pips started and I fed in another pound.

'I do know he speaks very good French because he was a junior minister at the Foreign Office before this. Scared his civil servants stiff because he'd rattle away to the French Ministers and they didn't know what he was saying. Got him replaced with a man who can't sound his Rs so everybody's happy again.'

She'd heard about the anti-Talisby demo at Oxford and guessed, correctly, that Andrea was in there somewhere.

'She'll manage to get herself arrested one day.'

I wondered what she'd say if she knew I was the one closer to arrest.

'Not that I don't sympathise,' she said. 'You can tell Andrea from me that Talisby means it. The government thinks the voters have had enough of "glad to be gay". Got to go. Somebody on the other phone.'

I said thanks, put down the receiver and walked out into the June suburban evening. There were sounds of tennis being played in a park, strains of Dave Brubeck from an open window. Normality. I didn't have to go back to Duncan. I could stroll to the main road, bus to the station, home before midnight, apologise to Andrea and everything back the way it had been. For a while, strolling past the roses and syringa, I genuinely thought it would be like that. If I walked away from it, Prudence and Kay and Duncan would slide back to that other universe where they'd existed before I picked up the book.

It was the thought of Kay that showed me I was wrong, making the bridge between one universe and the other. Kay's long, cold feet and desolate voice. Kay's face when I'd told her she was like the woman in the book. Kay, who had, or had not, gone straight up the track and plunged a gardening knife into Prudence. I had to know and, in the absence of Kay

73

herself, my only contact with the world where she existed was Duncan. I walked back slowly, noting a newspaper shop on the way. At seven o'clock the next morning, before anybody in the house was stirring, I was its first customer, buying every morning paper they had in stock.

The *Birmingham Post* had the fullest account. I sat on the steps and read it. Prudence's body hadn't been discovered until around six o'clock the previous evening, by a farmer who'd called to discuss parsley. The victim had been dead for some time, probably since the night before or the early hours of the morning. There was no sign of forcible entry, leading police to believe she knew her attacker. It was not known if any money or valuables were missing. Local people described the deceased as a woman who worked hard and kept herself to herself.

Then three paragraphs that came like successive punches to the stomach:

> Police are looking for Miss Belsire's companion, a young woman called Kay, thought to be a relative. The van used by the herb farm was found abandoned last night on the hard shoulder of the M4 about twenty miles west of London. Police have not ruled out the possibility that Kay was abducted by the murderer. They are anxious to interview her. She is described as in her mid to late twenties, tall and slim, with long dark hair.
>
> Police also want to talk to a young man who asked directions to Prudence Belsire's cottage on the day the murder is thought to have taken place. He travelled on the afternoon bus from Ludlow to Clun and was last seen walking up the track to the cottage.
>
> He is described as in his mid twenties, above average height, slim but broad-shouldered, with thick collar-length brown hair and brown eyes. He was carrying a rucksack and spoke with a cultivated voice.

Worse than I'd expected, much worse. Reading between the lines I'd murdered Prudence, taken her money, stolen her van and abducted – possibly murdered – her companion to keep her from talking. (Companion. Why hadn't they said daughter?) And, give or take the voice which sounds to me just like anybody else's, the plump woman from the bus had given them a description of me that was accurate enough as far as it went. It was repeated word for word in the national papers and I wondered if it would mean anything to Gus Prothering, or even Andrea if she'd come home and discovered my absence. The only bright spot was that, judging from where the van had been abandoned, they'd be looking for me in London. Even that wasn't very bright. It meant Kay was probably in London and my chances of finding her were zero.

The consolation I'd had till then, that it was still possible to go to the police, had gone as soon as I'd read that report. I was hunted. If I went to them now I wouldn't be citizen reporting discovery of body. I'd be murderer giving himself up – and with a story I wouldn't believe either. I was sitting on the step, head in my hands, when I felt a touch on my shoulder and there was Duncan.

'It's in all of them.'

He read, but said nothing.

'It's nonsense about Talisby, you know. He was in the House of Lords all night.'

'He doesn't have to dirty his own hands,' Duncan said.

I didn't argue. I recognise an obsession when I see one, and perhaps Duncan had cause to be obsessed.

'The police are looking for me.'

'Then you're in the right place here.'

The worst of it was, he was right. His neighbours must, long ago, have given up being curious about the comings and goings next door.

'Don't the police come here?'

'From time to time, but we won't be seeing them while the film crew's around. No public harassment.'

What it amounted to, as long as I stayed in Duncan's sanctuary posing as a superannuated rent boy, I was as safe as I was likely to be. Or, put another way, he'd got me just

75

where he wanted me. I didn't need any heavies on the steps
to keep me from wandering.
'The crew's getting curious about you,' he said. 'I think
you'd better give them an interview.'
'An interview!'
I thought he meant about Prudence.
'About your life on the streets. At your age, I think we'd
better say you lost your job as a teacher after you decided to
come out. They'll like that.'
So would Lagen.
'I can't do that.'
'Don't worry, it won't be going out for a long time. And
it's Channel Four so nobody will see it.'
By which time I'd probably have started a life sentence.
'Do I have to?'
'It will all help the protective colouration.'
And all help to trap me. I considered it.
'I'll do it on one condition. You let me talk to Angela Arless.'
The bargain was struck. I wondered why he hadn't been
more reluctant.
The film crew closed in later that morning. 'Stand there,
would you, by the tree. Left an inch or two. That's lovely.'
I stood, feeling a prat, while they lined the camera up.
A few of my fellow inmates watched and giggled.
'Do you want his hair combed, Les? No, you're right.
Better a bit dishevelled. What about another shirt button
undone?'
I hadn't slept much and still wasn't eating, except biscuits
and coffee. I'd had to tighten my belt two holes and the most
martyred ex-teacher could hardly have looked more haggard
than I did. They were thrilled with me.
Duncan had warned them that I didn't want to go into
too much detail about the sacking, 'because of his family',
so that went smoothly enough, apart from a retake because
the interviewer dropped his clipboard and couldn't remember his next question. When it got to the mean streets bit
I'd been carefully coached in the details by Caleb and had
quite a convincing little saga of nights in the Bull Ring all

76

ready for them. Only, when the interviewer wiggled his face about sympathetically and said, in reverent tones: 'And when did you first turn to prostitution?' something else took over.

'I'd gone to London,' I said. 'I'd intended to get a flat and look for work as a typist, only I didn't realise how hard it is to find somewhere to live in London.'

I hadn't needed to write the script. It was what Kay had whispered to me in the sleeping bag, word for word. Behind the cameraman I could see Duncan, looking puzzled. The interviewer asked me what the worst thing about it had been.

'Sometimes with one of the older ones I'd wonder whether he might be my father, but my friend said I'd got to stop that, people went mad that way, so I did.'

That properly put the interviewer off his stroke.

'Thank you,' he gulped. 'A very interesting angle. Thank you.'

'Have you got enough?' Duncan asked him. He looked ill at ease. They said they had. As they switched the lights off me, somebody started clapping.

'Very nice, darling.'

She must have parked her car in the road and walked in while I was being interviewed. I'd thought the camera crew looked fidgety and when I turned round and saw her I didn't blame them.

She was much smaller than she looks on screen; a head shorter than any of us there and several stone lighter. But there was something about her that made me think of a bird of prey in an aviary of budgerigars. Her hair gleamed like a newly shelled chestnut and, if it was dyed, I couldn't spot the join even in full sunlight. She was wearing pale suede trousers and a blue silk blouse. When she stood on tiptoe and slipped an arm round my ribs I smelt perfume that reminded me of mulled wine, only not so innocent.

'I think you're very brave,' she said.

She was looking up at me and I could see the little lines round her eyes, the pucker marks round her lips. She seemed to make no attempt to hide them. It was almost a challenge: 'Yes I know, but look at the rest of me.' It struck me that she was taking a lot of trouble for a visit to a house full of homosexuals down on their luck, but who was I to cavil at somebody's charity. Besides, she was there to be painted. That's what she said to the film crew, her arm still round my ribs, when they diffidently suggested an interview.

'Darlings, I've committed most of my sins in public. You must let me do some of my good things in private.'

They were impressed. They went off with Caleb and the large-eyed lad to do some more filming in the Bull Ring, leaving her and me and Duncan standing in the sun.

'Everything all right, Duncan?'

She looked tiny beside him, but he was the nervous one.

'I think so. We've got seven now. Plus Colin.'

'Plus Colin, of course.' She still had her arm round me and I could feel her little fingers digging in.

'He's so thin, Duncan. I can feel all his ribs. We must feed him up, mustn't we?'

For what, I wondered, thinking of the pig.

'Yes,' said Duncan. 'Yes, we must feed him up.' He didn't sound happy about it.

She let me go and hooked herself round Duncan. 'Are we ready then? Let's get on with it. If I'm not back by four I'll miss my nap and all the little rivets will start popping.'

We went to Duncan's studio, with him carrying her bag. When we got there she decided she couldn't start posing before she'd had a coffee.

'Do go and get us one, Duncan, there's a darling. Colin will help me change and I'll be all ready for you when you get back.'

As he went out of the door she called after him, 'You'll do it nicely won't you, darling? With ground coffee beans? That instant muck's murder for the skin.'

Duncan said he'd see if he could find some. As soon as the door closed behind him she had her arm round me again.

'Don't worry, darling, Duncan's told me all about you.'

I hoped she meant the sacked schoolteacher story, not the other one.

I said, experimentally: 'It wasn't an easy decision, coming out, I mean.'

'I'm sure it wasn't. You must tell me all about it. Darling, would you ever look in the case and find my sandals?'

Surely if it had been the other story he'd told her, she wouldn't be treating it so casually. It seemed to me, too, that she didn't know about the report of Prudence's murder. Although, from what Prudence had said, there was no love lost between them, a little polite regret would seem appropriate. It was quite likely that she didn't read the morning papers. On the other hand, why hadn't Duncan told her? Perhaps he was leaving it to me.

I opened the case. It contained a mass of white jersey material and a pair of silver sandals, vaguely classical in design with four-inch heels.

'Size three,' she said, seeing me looking at them. 'I've got ridiculously tiny feet.'

She was perched on a chair and I was kneeling by the case, more or less at her feet. There was something avid about her expression, like a gourmet before plunging the fork in. It was me she was feasting on. I realised it when I saw she was looking at the shoes in my hand. Her feet, small and pink as sugar mice, were bare. She rested them on the bar of the chair and wriggled silver-varnished toenails. She saw my eyes going to them and a great smile of satisfaction spread over her face, practically orgasmic.

'There. Put them down for now and help me off with these.'

'You bitch,' I thought, and felt a welling up of anger that had nothing to do with the trouble I was in. Some women in her position, Duncan had said, went in for stray cats. She went in for young homosexuals. The stray cat line is more honest. If you torture cats when you're pretending to have their best interests at heart, people know what to think of you. Torment confused young men who've got no other alley way to go to, and it's their own fault for being like that. I should have thrown the shoes at her and walked out, but I couldn't afford that luxury. She eased the suede pants down over hips, little pink point of tongue between her teeth, looking at me all the time. She was wearing nothing underneath them. I watched closely every inch of the way as she rolled them down to her ankles.

'This is the difficult bit. Will you help me please?'

Two kicks with her size three feet would have got her past the difficulty unaided. I stayed kneeling, took a handful of suede and eased it over a heel as round as a ping-pong ball.

'That didn't hurt, did it? Now the other one.'

She undid the blouse herself, slowly. The strapless bra under it was blackberry coloured and lacey over skin white as vanilla sorbets.

'Undo it for me please.'

No darlings now. She was serious, almost severe. I walked round her slowly, unhitched the hook, possibly with more expertise than she expected. When I came back to face her she was smiling at me over the globes of her breasts like the gourmet at the sweet course. She probably mistook my anger for frustration. She wasn't far wrong.

'Get my dress out.'

The swathes of jersey felt heavy in my arms. She stood, her arms in the air, armpits smooth as cream, waiting for me to drape it over her.

'There,' she said. 'Circe. Would you like me to turn you into a pig?'

Duncan had been gone a long time, even for proper coffee. I wondered if this was the way he paid his dues.

'Put my shoes on.'

I knelt again and she put one hand on my shoulder while I slipped on the sandal and did up the ankle strap. Her hairless calf was inches away from my face. I ran my finger along it very slowly.

'That's a nasty scratch,' I said.

That wasn't in the game. The leg went tense.

'How did you get that?'

There was a moment's hesitation.

'Mosquito bites. You know how you scratch them.'

'It doesn't look like that to me,' I said. 'It looks as if you've been scrambling through hedges in the dark.'

'Do I look like the sort of woman who scrambles through hedges?' The high heel clicked abruptly to the floor.

'Do the other one.'

I held the leg out horizontally, running my fingers along it.

'Stop it. What are you doing?' She was scared and angry.

'Just checking.' I took my time. 'No, that one seems to be all right.'

'Put my shoe on then.'

She was fighting for control and thought she was winning. Only a stronger tang to her perfume showed the effort she was making.

'Put it on yourself,' I said, and gave it to her. Her hands were small but strong looking. The silver nails might have been made of titanium. She bent to wiggle it on her foot, looking missiles.

I went behind her chair while she was doing up the ankle strap. I clamped one hand on her left upper thigh, the other on her right breast, tilted the chair back and, as she opened her mouth to protest, enclosed it in a long, thorough kiss, working my tongue inside. Her teeth are her own, and sharp. I know, because she bit me on the lip.

'Duncan,' she yelled, when I'd let her go. 'Duncan.'

'Naughty Mimi,' I said, dabbing blood.

I sat on the other chair and watched her. Twenty seconds or so later Duncan came rushing in, carrying the tray, asking what was the matter.

'Duncan, where did you find him? What have you been telling him?'

'Not much,' I said. 'Not enough.'

Duncan put the tray on his desk, looking down at both of us sorrowfully.

'Has he told you? Prudence is dead.'

I could see nothing in her eyes but surprise, but then she is an actress.

None of this was the way I'd planned it. I'd counted on some casual talk with Angela before we got to the hard questions, working gently if we could to the old days in Paris. She'd made me angry. Perhaps it was first round to her after all.

81

'He means she's been murdered,' I said.

The gasp, the hand to the throat, might have been the same, acting or not.

'When? When did it happen?'

I found that odd. Wouldn't a more natural first question have been how or by whom?

'She was stabbed in her cottage,' Duncan told her. 'The night before last.'

'Didn't you see it in the papers?' I asked her.

She gave me a furious look, then tears started washing down her cheeks and she buried her face in her hands. Duncan knelt down beside her and put his arm round her. At the same time he gave me a glance that appealed to me to go gently.

'I don't know why you're so upset,' I said. 'From what she said, she didn't like you and I don't suppose you liked her much.'

She wailed through her hands: 'Duncan, who is he?'

I could see that Duncan had a problem. He wanted to keep me in his care. It might be because he saw it as his mission to look after me. Or possibly he wanted to keep me away from the police until I'd entangled myself even more thoroughly as a suspect than I was at the moment. On the other hand, he couldn't afford to fall out with Angela. It was odd that he'd found time to tell her about my cover story, but not to pass on the news of Prudence's death.

Duncan said: 'He found the body. He was talking to her just before she was killed.'

'Just before . . . at night in her cottage?'

She looked at me. Her eyes go larger when she cries, whereas most people's go smaller. It must be a great professional advantage to her. Duncan was persuading her to drink some coffee. She took the mug from him, still keeping her eyes on me. This question of time mattered a lot to her.

'I was there in the evening. Then she turned me out at about ten and I slept beside the track about half a mile away. In the morning I went back to ask her something else and she was dead.'

If she had been the person whose footsteps I'd taken for the farmer's, that should worry her. She was frowning.

'Had she been robbed?'

'There was no sign of it.'

The bundle of notes was now stowed away in my pack.

'But why?'

'Nobody knows,' said Duncan, a little too hastily.

'Have you any ideas?' I asked her.

'Why? Why should I? I hardly knew her.'

'And yet you seemed very upset when you heard.'

'So would you be upset if somebody tried to rape you, then just after that you hear a person you know has been murdered.'

She was recovering fast. Duncan took his arm away and stood behind her, still protective.

'You must have known her quite well once, in Paris.'

'Darling, that's twenty years ago and anyway, I was never really part of that circle. Prudence was a lot older than me.'

I caught Duncan's eye but he looked away. Nearly thirty years it was, and Prudence could be no more than five years older at the most. Still, that needn't signify anything more than professional self-preservation. More serious was the direct conflict of evidence, Prudence and Duncan on the one hand, Angela on the other, about how deeply in she'd been.

'Did you see much of Prudence once you got back from Paris?'

She sipped coffee and carefully rearranged her legs, letting the dress fall back from the flat muscles of her thighs. 'Nothing. Different worlds. I didn't even know she was still alive until you told me she was dead.'

'And yet Duncan rang you up the day before yesterday and told you a man from Oxford was going to see her.'

That rocked both of them. Duncan scowled at me, but she recovered first.

'He tells me all sorts of things, don't you, darling? I probably thought he was talking about one of the boys here.'

Whatever delicate balancing act Duncan was performing, he decided to throw in some weight on Angela's side.

83

'I don't see why you have to cross-examine her about this. You can surely understand that somebody in the public eye like Angela wouldn't necessarily want every last detail of her past raked up.'

'You mean studying acting in Paris is OK; associating with Cardell's lot isn't?'

'Something like that.'

'Bad for the image, is it, books about women inciting men to murder?' I licked the blood on my lip.

'What's that got to do with it?' She was alarmed, no doubt about it.

Duncan explained. 'Cardell published a book called *The Martyrdom of Valentine*. Colin went to ask Prudence who wrote it.'

'Is that the one with the woman in the garden?' She tipped the chair back and stretched out her legs, sipped coffee with stagey precision. 'I thought everybody knew who wrote that.'

I probably looked as surprised as Duncan. His mouth opened, his eyebrows rose and he stared as if sparks were erupting out of the top of her head.

'Nicolle wrote it. They're going to make a film of it.'

'Do you believe her?' I asked Duncan.

He shook his head slowly, but whether that indicated disbelief or puzzlement I didn't know.

'Nicolle Banderberg, the American?'

'That's right. Only she's French now.'

'And she admits writing it?'

'She does now.'

'And somebody's going to film it?'

'That's right. I'm going to play the woman. The woman in the garden. Nicolle says she was based on me.'

'Never,' I said.

Two chops at the jugular with a double-headed axe. If the authorship of *Valentine* was now an open secret, there'd be no possible motive for somebody to murder Prudence to hush it up. Take away that motive and you were left with Kay, asking me about Wills and going straight up the track to stab her mother to death. But there was a worse loss if I believed her. I could not and would not lose the woman in the book, the woman who could drain a man dry of profession, affection, life itself, and replace her with a videotape seductress like Angela Arless.

Unreasonably, you might say, since I've admitted that in my impressionable years this woman, now sipping coffee at me in a pointed fashion, was one of my erotic reference points. Even more unreasonable, since I'd just been exposed to a seduction technique of studied cruelty. I only know that I didn't want her to be the woman in the book. Even if I thought of her thirty years younger and tried to put her there, what I saw wasn't Angela. The place was already occupied, more palpably and disturbingly than when I'd first read the book in the Bodley. It was occupied by Kay. Put in the cardboard cut-out of Angela and what you got was pantomime.

'It's not your part, duckie,' I said.

She pouted. 'Nicolle thinks so.'

'What about the murder in the book, where he kills his friend? Did that happen?'

'No, of course not.'

Again I looked at Duncan, but this time there was no response. Stalemate. I changed tack.

'What time does the play finish?'

'Ten fifteen. They have fireworks at the end, just as it's getting dark.'

'And you're there for the curtain call.'

'Of course.'

'What do you do after that?'

'Go back to my hotel and go to sleep.'

'Straight to sleep?'

She flared up. 'Duncan, for goodness sake, why does he keep cross-questioning me? I want to go.'

I answered for him. 'I'm trying to establish whether you could have seen Prudence on the night she was murdered.' I made it less than a half hour's drive from Ludlow to Clun.

'Is he saying I murdered her? Is he saying I murdered Prudence?' She was on her feet, eyes flashing, hair flying. 'Get out! Make him get out.'

I went. I didn't wait to see whether she'd need Duncan's help in changing back to her street clothes.

In the road outside two of Duncan's boys were looking at a new red MG. I had an idea they'd been fiddling with the locks until I appeared.

'Is that hers?'

They said yes, they were looking after it for her. I looked inside. Very tidy, white leather upholstery. On the passenger seat was a map, folded back. Since she'd been for at least one previous sitting, it struck me as odd that she needed a map to get from Ludlow to Birmingham. I peered in, pretending deep interest in the dashboard. It was a large scale map of Shropshire, the type walkers use, folded back to show the road from Ludlow to Clun. Outside Clun, the black square of a cottage was circled in red biro. I made sure I wasn't there by the time she came out.

Chapter Nine

After Duncan had seen her off he came to find me in my room. Furious.

'She says you attacked her.'

'She asked for it.'

'And all those questions.'

'Yes, I got it wrong there.'

He calmed down a bit. 'I'm glad you admit it. I know you feel you're under pressure but— '

'All those questions,' I said, 'and I didn't ask the one that mattered. I didn't ask her why she's got a map in her car with Prudence's cottage marked.'

That rocked him. 'How did you know?'

'I looked. I'm supposed to believe she hasn't seen Prudence since Paris, and there it is, on the passenger seat. And you think I was hard on her.'

'It's a plant.'

'Oh, come on. How— '

'It's a plant. Anybody can open a car door. It's part of the basic course.'

'Whose basic course?'

'It's not even an intelligent plant. If she had something to hide, would she drive around with a marked map in her car? It's typical of them.'

'Hang on a minute, Duncan. Who are these people?'

'The same people who'll be framing you or me for killing Prudence.'

I felt cold. He was so certain about it. Either he was right or I was in the care of somebody who was probably murderous and certainly paranoid.

'We're back with Lord Talisby, are we?'

'As far as I'm concerned, we never left Lord Talisby. I told you last night, but you still had to bully Angela.'

'Me bully Angela! She'd make Messalina blush. You admitted yourself she wouldn't want her public to know about the Paris goings-on.'

'It would only embarrass her. It would wreck him.'

'Him being Talisby?'

He nodded.

I said: 'I've only got your word for it that Lord Talisby was Milord. Prudence didn't say so.'

'Ask the others.'

'The others being Angela, who's gone off in a huff, and Nicolle and Uncle Lazarus, who just happen to be in Paris. Very convenient.'

He said nothing.

'Of course, if you've got any proof . . . ' I let the words trail off, watching him. He had a trick of keeping very still, not even blinking, as if he'd put himself into a trance.

'Come on,' he said.

The red-haired boy and a couple of others watched us from the top landing as we went downstairs to his room. They were beginning to get on my nerves. I guessed they were curious about me. The tension seemed to be affecting Duncan as well because he went to the window and made sure there was nobody watching from the overgrown garden before taking a key from his pocket and unlocking an old metal filing cabinet. In a place where it seemed to be an article of faith to have no locks on doors, it was the first time I'd seen anybody use a key. I noticed he opened the drawer only halfway and screened it from me with his back while he rooted about. When he turned round he was holding two photos, one large and one small, in transparent plastic covers.

'There.'

I took them from him. The large one showed a group of people round a café table. My first thought was they all looked so respectable. Most of the men were wearing jackets. Of the two women in the picture, the one who was obviously

Prudence was wearing a flowered top that wouldn't have been out of place at one of her father's vicarage teas. The other one, with a long nose and a serious expression, was in black jersey, pointing a cigarette in a white holder straight at the camera. Nicolle, probably. Duncan was immediately identifiable, casual arm round Prudence (poor Prudence), bearded head flung back, laughing. There were three more men in the picture: a small man with a hooked nose and a bald head, a plump, younger man – and Talisby.

I'd only seen him once in the flesh, but Andrea collected cuttings. More than any single feature, it was the arrogant tilt to the head that did it – a tilt that said I'm superior to the rest of you and isn't it a joke because you can't do a bloody thing about it. Duncan brought a newspaper over for comparison. A gossip column had run a few hundred words about Talisby, linked to the House of Lords marathon session, and there was a recent photograph of him with eldest son in Cotswold seat. The son was the image of the young man in the photograph.

'All right,' I said. 'It's Talisby. But it doesn't prove he asked somebody from MI5 to please nip up and kill Prudence for him and frame you or me or Angela on the way back.'

Duncan said nothing. I looked at the other photo. Just two men this time, Duncan and Talisby, arms round each other's shoulders, slightly out of focus against a background of trees. I gave the photos back to him and he returned them to the filing cabinet, although I noticed he forgot to lock it.

'One thing I don't understand. You know Talisby was part of a happy little homosexual set in Paris. You've got photos to prove it. Now he's doing his damnedest to drive homosexuals back into the closet, you hate his guts, but you don't seem to be doing anything about it.'

'Such as?'

'In your place, I'd have had those pictures straight round to the *News of the World*.'

He looked at me, and the look was genuinely pitying.

89

'You just don't know, do you? You just don't know where you're living. What do you think happens when you do something like that? Friendly call from editor to Talisby's office. "Some nausea here, old boy. Greasy old pervert trying a bit of muck spreading. Right, old boy. Discuss it over a drink at the club, what?" Then they think of some reason to get pervert put inside for a year or two to remind him not to make life difficult for his sexual betters.'

'I don't believe— '

'You don't, don't you? Doesn't happen in your world. Well, it happened to me twenty years ago. Remember the great swinging, sexually liberated sixties? He'd just taken over the title then. I hinted at it, just hinted, in a little magazine I was helping with. The editor got two months inside for publishing a blasphemous poem that happened to be in the same issue, magazine went bust, killed himself when he came out. No mention of Talisby. But these things don't happen, do they?'

'I wasn't saying— '

'They could be up in that cottage now, carefully applying your fingerprints or mine or Angela's to a knife that the police will just happen to discover— '

'The police haven't got my fingerprints,' I said.

He laughed, throwing his head back. 'How do you know who's got your fingerprints? Do you wipe every glass you drink from?'

That got to me. I thought of the occasions when I'd been invited to sherry parties given by dons rumoured to have links with Five or Six. Was there somebody in the pantry busy with labels and dusting powder?

'Who killed Marilyn Monroe?' he said. 'Who killed Stephen Ward?'

'Who killed Kennedy? All right, I get the picture.'

I did, too. If he wanted to make me even more nervous than I was, he was succeeding. I made an effort to get back the initiative.

'What Angela said – did Nicolle write the book?'

'I don't know.'

'You don't think she did, do you? But why would Angela lie about it?'

He said nothing. I could see from his eyes that he was still back there down paranoia gulch, and I knew its shadow was now on me too.

'She said the murder in the book didn't happen. You say it did.'

'It happened.' He stated it like a tenet of faith.

'By Talisby?'

Silence.

'You think it was Talisby, don't you?'

'I didn't say so.'

I sensed a deliberate drawing back. The man was scared, even of me, who had more reason for fear.

'I've got to go out,' he said.

It was a meeting down in the town about welfare benefits with somebody from the DHSS. I told him to be sure not to leave any fingerprints on the tea cup.

'They've got mine already,' he said, and went lurching off in the old car.

I felt oddly unprotected when he'd gone, in a house occupied only by red-head and friends. I heard them shuffling and whispering in the corridor outside when I went up to my room. Caleb and the camera crew hadn't come back yet, so we had the house to ourselves. I lay down on the bed and tried to get things into some order. Milord was Talisby. Duncan wanted to get Talisby. The question was, did he want to get him so much that he'd use me for it? Was I being manipulated by Duncan into making the accusations that wouldn't be believed if they came from him? They wouldn't be believed from me either, but that was beside the point. Duncan might be past rationality.

But how did Angela fit into all this? One of my problems in trying to get my mind round that was that I didn't want to believe what she'd said. I didn't want my book to be the property of some Francophile American poetess with red hair and a long nose. Above all, I did not want to see it filmed with Angela Arless vamping away as the woman. It would

91

be like giving a pint of blood then seeing somebody use it to make bad drawings of cartoon animals. My book couldn't be filmed. My woman wasn't Angela. If I had to choose, I was on Duncan's side about that – the dark side that said the book was wicked, that sex was a bed partner with death, not a diversion for a wet afternoon. I took the book out and read the passage leading up to the murder, when Valentine makes love to Warrinder then kills him.

He ran a hand over the soft skin at the back of his neck, pressed his lips to it and tasted salt. Warrinder lay like one already dead.

'Is it true?' he said, softly still. 'Is it true she came to you?'

Warrinder's 'Yes' breathed softly into the sand, sounded as casual as the question. He didn't resist when Valentine slid an arm under him and turned him on his back. His eyes were open and accepting. Only when the other man picked up a knife from the cloth and plunged it clumsily just under the left collarbone, pain and the will to live came to him in spite of himself. His hand closed on Valentine's neck, forcing his head back.

'Not like that,' he said. 'Not like that.'

Lying on Duncan's thin mattress, still blanketless, I read through the scene, half murder, half ritual sacrifice, and thought of Talisby and that look of pitying arrogance. I make the rules, you live by them. How do you know when you're paranoid and when they're really out to get you? I suppose the answer is: Too late.

I slept. I think I was beginning to run a temperature, from nerves and lack of food, because I sweated rivers and had an odd dream. I saw Kay, standing by her van on a motorway lay-by, but there were branches growing all round it like the ones in Duncan's Circe picture. I saw she was doing something to the side of the van and I asked what. 'Putting on your fingerprints,' she said. She was holding a sherry glass.

92

I tried to stop her and found I couldn't do anything because I was tied to the back of the van. Then it started to move off and, when I shouted a protest, Lord Talisby looked out of the window, smiled at me and said: 'Who killed Marilyn Monroe?' I heard my own screams as I was dragged down the motorway, and Kay laughing.

When I woke up there really was laughter, or sniggering rather. It was coming from the next room, which I believed was inhabited by the red-haired lad. The walls were thin and I could hear two or three voices. One of them sounded as if it were reading something. I got up quietly and put my ear to the wall.

Valentine picked up a knife, a knife they'd used for cutting the peaches in half. He held it at Warrinder's throat, and at first Warrinder didn't move. Valentine said to the woman: 'Will you be sorry if I kill him? If you don't love him, you won't be sorry when I kill him?' He didn't see that, behind her back, she was passing another knife into Warrinder's hand. Warrinder took it and kept it behind him . . .

My first thought was that the red-haired lad had stolen my book while I slept and was amusing himself reading it to his friends. I was about to rush next door and grab it away from them when something struck me: it wasn't the book at all. My book was still on the floor beside my bed, where I'd put it. More than that, this was an entirely different account of the fight between the two men, a cruder version without the weird sacrificial quality of the one I'd been reading. I rushed next door

'What's that you've got there?'

They looked guilty, but not very. There was red-head, sitting on his bed and reading, with two others down on the floor listening to him. They giggled a bit when they saw me, but red-head handed over the pages he was holding without resistance. There were three of them, thin paper filled with small, tidy script in blue-black ink.

'Where did you get that?'

'He wrote it,' said one of the friends. 'He's writing a tele series.'

'Of course he didn't. Where did you get it?'

They didn't consider their transgression a serious one, so it took very little questioning to find out. As I guessed, it had come from Duncan's room.

'From the filing cabinet, the one he usually locks?'

Red-head nodded.

They'd got a pile of other stuff on the floor: sixties magazines, piles of photos.

'That all from the same place?'

It was. As I bent to pick it up I noticed something incongruous on top of the pile: a seed catalogue. From the look of the garden, Duncan didn't have much to do with those. I looked closer. 'Lapwing Cottage Herb Farm, near Clun. All types of plants and seeds supplied.'

'It was inside that,' red-head volunteered. 'The stuff about the fight was inside that.'

I remembered that Duncan had been on his own in Prudence's cottage when I'd gone out to be sick, also that he'd been standing near the drawers of the writing desk when I'd got back. There was the theatre programme too, folded carefully so as not to leave fingerprints on the handles.

'I'll put these back,' I said. 'I won't tell him this time, but don't do it again.'

They didn't seem too bothered. I took the things back downstairs. One the way I compared the handwriting on the three sheets with a notice about claiming benefit money that Duncan had written and put on the common room notice-board the day before. No resemblance. Duncan's was a fine, flowing italic hand. The other was rounded and almost schoolroom neat. There was no resemblance either to Prudence's bold scrawl. I replaced the other things in Duncan's cabinet, but kept the pages and the seed catalogue. I had no doubt that I was holding part of a manuscript draft for the first version of the book, later elaborated. I had little more doubt that it had been brought by Duncan from Prudence's cottage

94

after the murder. But if it wasn't his writing and wasn't hers, then whose?

I was nervous as I waited for Duncan to get back, hoping he wouldn't check his filing cabinet. As it happened, I was lucky. The camera crew provided a diversion. They got back with Caleb before Duncan did, nursing three black eyes, various sprains and a sense of professional triumph. They'd actually been attacked by a group of skinhead neo-fascists, kept filming and got some tremendous, but tremendous, footage. Their lighting man had come off worst and had his arm in a sling. Duncan got back soon afterwards and was so excited, in a gloomy way, by this latest evidence of persecution that he had no time to worry about files. So everything was all right until after supper.

I was sitting in the common room, scanning the late edition of the *Birmingham Mail* in case there was anything new about the Prudence murder. Red-head was looking out of the window over the front drive and he gave the alarm.

'Here, it's the fuzz.'

Caleb told him not to worry, they'd probably come to take evidence about the attack on the camera crew, but there was a feeling of hostility and tension when he left the room and everybody went quiet. We could hear doors opening downstairs and a murmur of voices as they went through to Duncan's room. I walked over to the other window, trying to look unconcerned, and started weighing up escape routes. Foothold of two inches or so on brick course projecting from back wall, long step across to reasonably solid-looking drainpipe, slide down to outhouse then an assault course of suburban walls and fences. Caleb came back in time to save me, for the while at least, from finding out if I meant it.

'It wasn't about that. They're doing a vehicle check.'

I couldn't concentrate. The print blurred in front of my eyes. I listened as the front door opened again, heard an official voice thanking Duncan for his co-operation, a vehicle driving off. I already knew the worst before Duncan put his head round the door and asked if he could have a word with me. Red-head's avid eyes followed me as I went out. Whatever I'd done, they were on to me.

'They're asking about the car,' Duncan said. He looked as pale as I felt.

'How do they know?'

'Somebody in Clun must have spotted it the morning we found her. They gave quite a good description of it but didn't get all of the number. The police say it's just a routine check.'

'You don't believe them?'

'Do you?'

He watched me. At least he didn't say I told you so.

'I'd better get out,' I said.

The police already had my description. If they added that to Duncan's car, they were there.

'Another thing. Angela. She'll have read the papers by now. She'll recognise the description of me.'

'Angela wouldn't do anything,' he said.

But I remembered the look she'd given me and wasn't so sure.

'Duncan, I've got to get out.'

He walked to the window and stood looking out over the garden.

'I think,' he said, 'we'd better send you to Uncle Lazarus.'

Chapter Ten

In a couple of hours they'd got everything arranged between
them, Duncan and Caleb. He had to bring Caleb into it
because he owned the passport. I said I'd chance going back
to Oxford for my own – hoping I wouldn't meet Andrea –
but Duncan said it wasn't worth the risk. Why Caleb had a
spare passport, in a name that wasn't his own with a photo
that didn't look much like him or me, was a detail I decided
not to go into. Duncan seemed to think Caleb was doing
something very magnanimous in letting me have it. When I
thanked him he said not to worry about it. I needed it more
than he did. That worried me more.

Then there was the question of my clothes. The wretched
woman from the bus had given the police a fair description
of them: grey corduroys, blue open-necked shirt with the
sleeves rolled up. Duncan produced from the house store
stone-bleached denims, a bit short in the leg, Motorhead
tee-shirt, a beige bomber jacket. Then he started on my hair,
reducing it to a kind of modified crew cut, like Caleb's.

'Then if they query your passport picture, you can tell
them you've just had your hair cut.'

When I asked him, sarcastically, if I shouldn't grow a beard
as well he said there wasn't time, and went on cutting round
the back of my neck. His fingers were cold and deft. They sent
a current through my nerve-endings every time they touched
me, and it was all I could do to keep still. When I looked in
the mirror in his room I hardly recognised the face that stared
back. The short hair made me look even more gaunt, the eyes
shadowed, with a wariness about them even in front of their
own reflection. I was looking at a scared man, a guilty man.

If anybody had walked in then and offered to get me back to my seat in the Bodley, all cleaned up and no questions asked, I'd have leapt at it, even if it meant an eternity of catalogue slips.

Duncan was watching me. Caleb had gone out of the room by then.

'Colin, at Prudence's cottage – did you take anything?'

I watched my eyes in the mirror get even more wary and turned round. The three pages and the seed catalogue were in my pack upstairs.

'No, nothing. What were you thinking of?'

'A diary, an address book. Something like that.'

'No. Was there one?'

'I just wondered.'

He turned away. I thought, if he had discovered the theft from his files he couldn't ask me about it openly, because then he'd have to admit taking the things himself.

'I've got it sorted out with Caleb,' he said. 'After breakfast tomorrow he'll back the van up to the steps as if we're loading something. You get in the back. He'll drive you a good way down the motorway and let you out when he's sure you're not being followed. You can hitch from there to the Channel ports. I'd recommend Dover, but it's up to you.'

I thanked him. There was no point in doing anything else.

'Have you got some money?'

'Yes.' About thirty pounds of my own, plus Prudence's hundred pounds that Kay had pressed on me. I reckoned I was justified in using it.

'I'll write you a letter to Uncle Lazarus. You can stay with him until it blows over.'

'You mean, until they've arrested somebody else for killing Prudence?'

'Yes. I'll keep in touch.'

I foresaw myself going old, grey and mad with an ancient guru in a rotting houseboat. If I got that far.

'You'd better go and get some sleep. I'll give you the letter in the morning.'

On my way up to the second floor I stopped and looked out of the common room window. It still wasn't quite dark but the street lamps were on. A figure was standing by the pillar box on the corner, a tall straight figure, very patient. Waiting for a girl, perhaps, or trained to stand on corners looking as if he were waiting for a girl. There was a commercial travellers' hotel opposite Duncan's house. Rooms from £15 a night, the sign said. Not much in tax-payers' money if you were keeping a murder suspect under surveillance.

I thought about Prudence's cottage, wondered if its lights were on and the experts on hands and knees inside. 'Conclusive, sir. This kind of dust is only found in the Bodley Library. We're looking for an eleven-stone Oxford academic who hasn't been seen around his normal haunts for three days.' Lagen would say he was sure there was some explanation, licking his lips, thinking one less for the lectureship. Andrea would probably throw things at them from the landing window. 'No need to take it like that, miss.' The figure on the corner still hadn't moved. A light had been switched off in the commercial travellers' hotel. I thought: 'I could walk out and see what happens.' But Duncan's precautions had made it a sea full of sharks and to take those few strokes away from the steps was more than I could manage. 'He's got me hypnotised.' And I was supposed to walk down those steps tomorrow and get into the van like a sacrificial lamb.

I believed his scenario as far as it went, up to the point where Caleb dropped me by the motorway, but what happened after that? Quick call from Caleb to Duncan: OK, go ahead. Slower call from Duncan to the police. Sorry to bother you, Officer. No, not the usual. The fact is, we've had this man staying with us for a couple of nights we're worried about. You remember that report of the murder of the woman in Shropshire? Yes, quite a bit. Only he changed his appearance while he was with us. Cropped hair, jeans, bomber jacket. Hitching south, we think. He was asking about Channel ferries . . . . When they picked me up it would be my word against Duncan's. I told myself that I was getting hysterical, that Duncan was what he seemed. Then I thought of those three pages he'd stolen and decided nothing would induce me to get in the back of that van. The question was, what I intended to do about it.

While I was standing at the window I saw the television crew drive up and come into the house. Wisely, they'd decided to eat out at a curry house, possibly to celebrate their epic battle with the forces of reaction. They came into the common room and turned on the light, apologising when they saw me standing there. After that they ignored my presence and got down to a crisis meeting.

I soon gathered that the problem was their injured lights man. The hurt arm had been diagnosed as a nasty sprain, must be rested for at least a week, and since the lights man had to cart heavy weights around, that ruled him out of action. What made it worse was that they had some important filming to do the next day that they were nervous about already and couldn't get another lights person in time.

'Would he do it the day after? We could get somebody up from London for— '

'No chance. I had to spend three weeks on my knees to the Home Office press office before they'd give us this slot. Anyway, he's off to Brussels the day after tomorrow, so it's that or nothing.'

'Can't we just call it off? We've got enough from here.'

'No we bloody can't call it off. We need conflict, don't we? Without the Talisby interview, we haven't got conflict.'

I'd been looking out at the street until then, half listening, but the name caught me. They went on bickering, putting up various suggestions and knocking them down again. I waited for a lull and moved in.

'Are you going to interview Lord Talisby?'

They looked surprised. I'd forgotten I'd changed my appearance since they last saw me. When they recognised me they relaxed.

'That's right. We're going to put some really intensive questions to him about these government proposals for changing the law on homosexuality. In the light of the kind of thing that's happened to you.'

100

I remembered that, as far as they were concerned, I was still a martyred gay teacher.

'I'm glad somebody's doing it,' I said.

'Yes. The problem is, Pete got his arm done by those fascists today so we've got nobody to carry the lights. And we've got to leave at the crack of dawn tomorrow so we can't get anybody else in, even if we could afford it.'

'Perhaps I could help.'

They stared.

'I used to help with the lighting at school plays,' I said, lying wildly. 'If Pete told me what to do I'd probably manage all right.'

The producer said, on a sigh: 'Union?'

They sank into deep silence. Then the man who'd interviewed me said: 'If he doesn't want paying and Pete's there anyway getting paid, I don't see the objection as a one-off.'

'Particularly if they don't know about it,' the producer said.

'I shouldn't want paying,' I said eagerly. 'Glad to be useful.'

They talked it over some more, then accepted. It would be an early start because they were interviewing Lord Talisby at his home deep in the Cotswolds. I was instructed to be down in the hall at six ready to load up.

I slept no more than the previous night and was down before any of them. On the letter board was an envelope addressed to me in Duncan's handwriting, inside it the promised letter to Uncle Lazarus, sealed and addressed with only the boat's name: *Rêveuse*, near Pont de l'Alma, Paris. I put it in my pack, along with the book, the three pages in unknown hand, the *Comus* programme and the seed catalogue. The crew came down some time later, bleary-eyed and already arguing. Hoping neither Duncan nor Caleb would come down to see us off, I got loaded up in a time that would have sent the Union into convulsions, handling lights, tripod and sound gear under the anxious supervision of Pete. When the producer saw me putting my pack on board he said wasn't I coming back with them? I murmured something about walking round the Cotswolds for a few days, which seemed to satisfy him. He and Adrian, the interviewer, spent the entire journey crouched

101

in the back of the van having a ferocious argument about tactics in the interview with Talisby, while the cameraman, driving with Pete as navigator, got us comprehensively lost in Cotswold by-ways. I ignored them as far as I could and concentrated on my own problem: namely, whether to go into the attack on Lord Talisby.

That Milord and Talisby were one and the same I was, in the face of the photographic evidence, ready to accept. That the Talisby of thirty years ago had been, however fleetingly, involved in homosexual affairs that would embarrass him seriously if they surfaced now seemed at least possible. Any ideas the government might be cherishing for the harassment of homosexuals would be laughed out of court, for the while at least. All this was fair enough, as far as it went, but Duncan had implied much more than that. Duncan thought, or wanted me to think, that Talisby had arranged the murder of Prudence and was framing him, me or both of us. If there was anything in that at all, if it was more than Duncan's paranoia, then the Talisby of thirty years ago must have been involved in something worse than the undergraduate buggery that seems more or less routine for the public school classes. Something like murder, or writing a pornographic novel or possibly both. Given this chance to meet Talisby, could I go rushing off on other courses without at least trying?

Well, yes I could. I'd already achieved escape from Duncan's little nest of martyrs without, as far as I knew, attracting the attention of anybody who might be watching it. By the time Duncan found out from the film crew that I'd gone off with them, I'd be well clear of him and Caleb. So, I was already ahead of the game if I got out there and then. It could be done, too. Help unload the gear on the steps of Talisby's stately home then melt into the shrubbery and away while the crew were still getting themselves sorted out. It would leave them without a lights lugger, but judging by the way Adrian and the producer were going at each other, that would be the least of their worries. There was just one little drawback. Once I'd accomplished my smooth getaway and found myself on the open road with my pack and my little collection of documents that didn't add up to evidence, what the hell did I do next?

I was still a man the police wanted to interview, with shorn head and borrowed clothing, in possession of a passport not my own. I still had no hope of ceasing to be a wanted man until somebody found out who really killed Prudence. If I was to be that somebody, I still had no idea of how to set about it.

I had four leads, if you could dignify them with that name. One, I needed to talk to Kay. But I had no idea where Kay was. Two, I needed another session with Angela Arless, now that I'd seen the map in her car. But if I went anywhere near Angela she'd probably call the police. Three, and connected with two, I needed to talk to Nicolle Banderberg who, if Angela was telling the truth, claimed to have written the book. But the only way of getting to Nicolle was via Paris and Uncle Lazarus and my introduction to him might be part of a Duncan plot to incriminate me. Four, I needed a nice cosy chat with Lord Talisby to ask him if he'd done any murders or written any erotic books. But Lord Talisby, in his capacity as Minister at the Home Office, helped control a police machine that was even now combing the country looking for a man of my description. It was a mixture of desperation and passivity that made me decide to follow through the Talisby option. Once I'd decided that, I too had to think about tactics.

I shouldn't have been surprised to find the Talisby mansions so thoroughly well guarded. I'd imagined honey-coloured gateposts and long sweep of gravel drive with walnut trees. What faced us when the van ground to a halt and the crew in the back were let out to breathe was a new brick wall and a ten-foot gateway of new wood, very solid. There was a cabin outside the gate with two uniformed men inside it and a television camera on top of the gatepost trained on anybody who arrived outside. I grabbed a battery pack and made a big business of checking the fastenings, hoping the camera hadn't already caught me gawping. There was some fuss because I wasn't on the security man's list of expected names, but the producer talked me through. By this time the two security men had their hands full because a minibus had

103

drawn up behind us. I heard one of them say to the other that it was Lady Talisby's gardening women, and they were to go round to the greenhouses.

The gates opened for both lots of us and, while the gardening women went off somewhere to the right, we continued to a sweep of gravel in front of low stone steps, frothed over with creeping plants in purple and white. It was an eighteenth-century house, perfectly proportioned, larger than it looked at first glance.

'Over-privileged shit,' said Adrian loudly. He sounded nervous and I didn't blame him.

The producer told him to shut up and stop ego-tripping and a flunkey in a tracksuit appeared and told us we could follow him and start setting up inside. As I carried a light and two tripods up the steps and into a long corridor lined with what I swear were Turner sketches, the book stuck close to my ribs, clamped by my elbow. It was getting used to that by now and I felt comforted to feel it there. I needed comforting because my heart was banging like a disco in a dustbin and I knew I was crazy. If there was a place above all I shouldn't be, it was the house of a minister at the Home Office. If I'd got myself there, then the only sane thing to do was get out as soon as possible without drawing attention to myself. What I intended to do was insane, and yet I seemed to have opted for insanity. In a daze of fear I tried to attend to Pete as he told me to put that here and plug that in there. We got it together. The producer told the flunkey we were ready and, a few minutes later, in came Lord Talisby.

Pin-stripes and pale blue shirt, silvergrey tie, blue handkerchief protruding an inch and a half from top pocket. Black casuals of such fine leather that cows probably had to put their names down at birth to get made into them. Behind him, a young man with a pink, worried face who I gathered was the Home Office press officer. He and the producer immediately got together in a corner and started whispering ferociously at each other while Talisby did the gracious bit. Would we like coffee? Coffee was ushered in by a woman in white overalls. Had we had far to travel? So nice of us to come and interview

104

him at home. So much to do before his Brussels trip. He did it well. Since he was obviously no fool he knew their television programme wouldn't be on his side, but you'd have thought they were there to do a party political. I could see Adrian gritting his teeth and holding on to his prejudices. In the corner the producer and the press officer hissed their way to some sort of truce.

'I've told them no tendentious editing,' said the press man to Talisby. 'And no questions about the Bill – I mean no questions that assume it's already been decided.'

Talisby gave a remote nod, as if this haggling had nothing to do with him. For a second, his head was exactly at the angle of the young man in Duncan's photo. I caught my breath, wondering how much pinker the press officer would go if he knew why I was there, and Pete gave me an anxious look as one of my lights trembled on its tripod. Adrian was looking anxious too. I knew from the conversation in the van that all his questions assumed that the Bill, making it an offence to speak in favour of homosexuality, was cut and dried. He scribbled miserably on his clipboard while Talisby was manoeuvred politely into position. I was holding a light reflector only a few yards away from him but he didn't give me a second glance.

I knew enough by now of what the crew were after to see that the encounter went game, set and match to Talisby. Adrian led off with a question about consequences if laws ensuring an individual's sexual liberty were reversed. Talisby countered with Milton's line about liberty and licence that Adrian should have seen coming a mile off, but it wasn't on his clipboard so he didn't. Adrian said what about people who lost their jobs, blackmail and so on? Talisby said nobody was proposing to outlaw homosexuality. Anyway, was Adrian saying that an individual's sexual behaviour was not a legitimate concern of society as a whole? Adrian, ill at ease, said it wasn't, was it? and Talisby asked him if, in that case, he was in favour of child prostitution. Adrian said, of course he wasn't, but wasn't the point . . . ? By this stage the producer had his head in his hands and the press officer had toned down from peony pink to milky piglet. They worried at it for some time more, until Adrian ran out of questions but didn't get near jolting him out of his tolerant superiority.

All the time, standing so close that I could smell Talisby's aftershave, I had the book inside my bomber jacket. As the interview ground on and Talisby's confidence radiated brighter than the light that was scorching my ear, I had to fight down suicidal impulses to produce it there and then, to ask if he'd written it, to ask if Duncan had been a good fuck back in 1958. It was like the urge you have to throw yourself under a tube train, even when you're feeling quite happy, to know what it feels like. The difference was, unless my nerve failed me completely, I would be jumping under this particular tube train and in a few minutes or so I'd know exactly what it felt like.

Funny, this nerve business. There can be any number of things you don't want to do and don't see the point of doing, like jumping into cold water or out of a plane with a parachute. You could spend your life quite happily doing neither. And yet once you ask yourself whether you've got the nerve for it, jumping into the water or out of the plane becomes the only thing that exists in the universe. By this time, beyond all rational calculation, what I'd planned to do had narrowed itself down to just one question: had I got the nerve for it? There was nothing beyond that.

They'd finished. Pete was signalling to me to put down my reflector and switch off the lights. The press officer was making the producer even more miserable by telling him it was a good interview. Talisby was shaking hands with Adrian and, as far as I could gather, wishing him well for the future. Adrian looked as if he'd just gone off the idea of the future altogether. Talisby was leaving the room, followed by the press officer. Now or never. I abandoned my lights, ignoring questions from the crew, and went after him.

Deep in conversation, he and the press officer didn't notice me as I followed them along a stone-flagged side corridor, walking softly in my training shoes. Inferior pictures along here, ancestral watercolours, probably. The passage led to a courtyard at the side of the house where the press officer had his car parked.

The right-hand side of the courtyard was closed off by the ends of two long greenhouses. In one of them, through gaps in whitewash daubed over the panes, I could see people moving about, probably the women's gardening party under the care of Lady Talisby. Lord Talisby and the press officer stood, elbows on the car roof, deep in discussion. I was waiting for the press officer to move off, and wished he'd hurry up. My position by the back door would be hard to explain if a servant or the tracksuited flunkey came out that way. While Talisby and the press officer were comparing diaries, I made a cat-footed dash across an angle of the courtyard and through a door into the unoccupied greenhouse. From there I could keep watch and be less in the way.

When I got inside I thought I'd been gassed. It was hot as a sauna and the air so saturated with moisture that it settled like a sticky blight on the skin of my face and neck. I tore off my jacket and the fabric of the tee-shirt clung to me for company. There was a smell of rotting straw and indecent greenness, as if every chlorophyll-bearing plant that ever crept had been distilled and poured into one small, steaming space. What it was all about was cucumbers. I could see them hanging like green lacquered truncheons among leaves that flopped with their own weight. One thing, I thought, when I'd got my breathing started again: she won't bring the gardening ladies in here. Couldn't stand all that sodden Crimplene. I stood near the door, peering out through leaves. The press officer still showed no sign of going.

I'd been there perhaps two or three minutes when I heard a movement at the far end of the greenhouse. A door opened and closed. Footsteps came in a little way, echoing on the concrete path, and then stopped. The greenhouse was a long one, divided into three, with what looked like tomatoes in the middle section, then vines of gourds, and I was fairly sure that whoever had just come in wouldn't see me cowering among the cucumbers. With luck it would be a gardening lad who'd do his work and go. But when the footsteps started up again it didn't sound like a gardening lad, or anybody else who had a right to be there. They were tentative, stopped and started again. I risked a look out, and there was a woman standing halfway down the path in the middle of the tomatoes. She wore white trousers, a blue tunic and a headscarf, and had a hunched look about her as if she didn't want to be noticed.

I cursed. One of the idiot women must have wandered away from Lady Talisby's party and got herself lost. If she didn't turn back before she got to the cucumbers I'd have to pass myself off as one of the gardeners and hope she'd be more nervous than I was. In three days I'd been biographer, sacked teacher and lights man. Gardener should be a pushover. She was coming on, slow and unseeing, with her head bent, but there was no avoiding her. I waited till she'd come level with the first gourds, then I stepped out.

'I shouldn't come in here, m'm,' I said, in what I hoped was a Gloucestershire accent. 'We be fumigating the cucumbers.'

She gasped and jumped back, like Eve meeting the snake. Her eyes were wide, her lips that were only a shade darker than her pale skin drawn back from sharp little teeth, blue white. The last time I'd seen her had been by moonlight. Here in the filtered, green-stained light there was still this cold, glowing quality about her, like radiation.

'Hello Kay,' I said. 'What are you doing here?'

Chapter Eleven

Her hand went up. She tore a gourd off its stem and stood there holding it like a grenade. If it had been a grenade I think she would have thrown it. She whispered something I didn't hear. I asked her to say it again, and she kept on saying it.

'Why are you following me? Why are you following me?'

'Where have you been? What happened to you?'

Her lips shaped three words so quietly that they seemed to come to me only by vibration, up and down the gorged green stalks.

'It doesn't matter.'

I don't know why that should have had such an effect on me. I only know that when the words got to me at last I felt the tides of green heat rushing in as they had when I first came through the door, only worse. It seemed to me that she was saying the murder of Prudence didn't matter and that the instant she said it I'd accepted it, become an accomplice with her. She was telling me she'd killed Prudence and it didn't matter, or she thought I had and it didn't matter. I was Valentine and this was the woman in the book, telling me to kill. The bit of my brain that resisted tried to fight its way up through the smothering green waves.

'I didn't kill her.'

She was still holding the gourd. Her eyes were huge and dark as moleskin. The scarf had dropped back and her dark hair spread out over her shoulders. I didn't know if she was hearing me.

I said: 'I hadn't got time to kill her, you know that. You went straight up to her after you'd left me, didn't you?'

She nodded, but I still didn't know if she understood.

109

'How would I have time to get up there in front of you, kill her and get away again?'

Her eyes hadn't changed. I don't think I was making any sense to her. I heard the sound of a car starting. The press officer was going at last, but that would have to wait till later.

I took three steps towards her and put my arm round her. There was the rough fabric of her tunic between my bare arm and her shoulder, but I'd never felt more conscious of contact between my own and another body. It felt literally magnetic, as if my arm couldn't have gone anywhere else if it had tried.

I said: 'I want you to tell me exactly what you did after you left me. You remember, after telling me about looking for your father.' I didn't say, after talking about Wills and Prudence's death. Her shoulder jerked, but stayed where it was under my arm.

'Don't be scared, Kay. I'll help you, whatever it is.'

I stroked her hair with my free hand, feeling it moist and sticky from the humidity, and noticed I was trembling. My voice was the only calm thing about me, but it got through to her.

She said, not looking at me: 'I found her.'

'Dead?' I made the word as gentle as I could.

'She'd . . . her throat had been cut. There . . . there was a lot of blood . . . all round her.'

She was looking at me now, huge eyes staring into my face. 'Was there anybody else there?'

She shook her head. 'Not there. Not in the room. Upstairs.'

I tried to keep my voice calm. 'You came home and found Prudence dead and you heard somebody moving about upstairs. What did you do then?'

Silence. I couldn't tell anything from her eyes, although they were inches away from mine.

'Did you shout out?'

She shook her head.

'Did you run away?'

There'd been at least an hour, I was sure, before her van had come down the track. Another headshake.

110

'What did you do then?'

She moved away from me, half turned, her hand with the gourd in it resting on the cucumber bench.

'You must have done something.'

'I . . . I waited.'

'Then what happened? Did you see the person upstairs?'

'No.'

'Did you know who it was?'

'No.'

'So you came away in the end, and the person was still up there?'

'No '

'Something must have happened, Kay.'

She said quietly, into the cucumbers: 'He . . . he came down.'

'So you did see him?'

'No. He came down the stairs and out of the back door.'

I tried unsuccessfully to remember the geography of Prudence's cottage, whether a person could come downstairs and out, unseen from the living room.

'If you didn't see him, how do you know it was a man?'

'I . . . I don't. I just . . . '

I was certain there was something she wasn't telling me, but decided to approach it sideways on.

'When you came out to meet me, did Prudence seem quite normal then?'

'What do you mean?'

'Was she working? In bed asleep?'

'Downstairs. Doing labels.'

'Was she angry when you said you were going out?'

'No. She told me to go.'

'She told you? But it was dark by then. She sent you out in the dark?'

'I often went out for walks in the dark. I don't sleep much. Anyway, it gave me a chance to find you.'

'But why did she send you out?'

A long sigh. 'She told me somebody was coming to see her and she wanted the house to herself.'

'Somebody coming to see her at getting on for midnight?'

'She said so.'

'Who was this other person? Man or woman?'

'I don't know.'

'How were they getting there?'

'I don't know. I didn't see a car.'

She was still turned away from me, but talking more normally now. Our voices were no more than murmurs inaudible, I hoped, to anyone outside. Two things were in my mind. I remembered the person I'd taken for a farmer, walking up the track before Kay came down it. Had she, or he, been waiting outside the cottage till Kay went walkabout? The other thing, if you believed Kay's account, was that Prudence had been waiting for her murderer, so it was someone she knew, like Duncan or Angela Arless. I glanced out at the courtyard. The car had gone and there was no sign of Talisby. No sign either of the gardening women in the greenhouse next door.

'The person upstairs, did it sound as if he, or she, was looking for something?'

'I don't know. Yes. Perhaps.'

'Had anything been disturbed downstairs? Drawers open and so on?'

'No. No I don't think so.'

The impression of something being concealed was even stronger. It was almost as if she wanted me to be aware of it and do something about it.

'So you're telling me that you stood there until whoever it was went away, then you just got into your van and drove off? You didn't go to the police?'

She shook her head.

'So what did you do?'

'I . . . stayed at a hotel in London. In Earl's Court.'

'And now you just happen to turn up here. Why is that? Sudden interest in horticulture?'

I was forgetting for the while that my own presence in Lord Talisby's grounds would need some explaining. She didn't answer.

'You know who this house belongs to?'

112

'Lord Talisby.' She pronounced it wrongly, with a long 'a'.

'Yes, Lord Talisby. So what are you doing here?'

I thought she was ignoring the question again, until I saw she was groping in the pocket of the tunic. Her hand came out with something cradled in the palm and she held it out for me to look at. A signet ring, small enough to be worn on a man's little finger. Rubbed, old-looking gold with a blurred coat of arms.

'I looked it up. In a library. It's his family crest, Lord Talisby's.'

She let me take it from her.

'Where did you find it?'

'On Prudence's finger.'

I nearly dropped it.

'When . . . after she was dead, you mean?'

'Yes.'

She must have seen my shudder. It was like the time in the sleeping bag when she'd told me about working at King's Cross in that flat, almost childish voice, only more so. This woman, who seemed almost too insubstantial to open a door, had knelt by a corpse, by her mother's corpse for heaven's sake, and taken a ring off its finger. There was something wrong too, something worse than that. She saw it in my face.

'What's up?'

'Nothing. That is . . . nothing.'

I remembered my first sight of Prudence: one square, ringless hand on the log, the other on the saw. True, some women take their rings off when they're working, but I've noticed they slip them on again as soon as the job's finished. There'd been no rings on Prudence's hands when she sat listening to me reading. She didn't look like a woman who wore rings.

'Kay, when you were in London, did you speak to anybody about all this?'

She shook her head.

'You weren't in touch with Duncan at all?'

'Who's Duncan?'

113

She seemed to mean it.

I tried to go on talking to her as I had been before, but it was difficult. I thought she'd hear the suspicion in my voice or sense it from my body, but for all that I couldn't stop myself putting my arm round her again or smelling the musky scent of her hair. I noticed it needed washing, that there were bits of grass clinging to it. My hand twitched, wanting to brush them off.

'So when you'd found out whose coat of arms it was, what did you do?'

'I looked up where he lived in *Who's Who*. It took me a long time to hitch here.'

'Where did you sleep last night?'

'In a field.'

'Alone?'

'Of course.'

'And how did you get in here? It's guarded like the Tower of London.'

'There were some women in a minibus. I got in with them while the men on the gate were talking to a film crew or something. The women thought I was someone from the house, and the men on the gate thought I was with them.'

I was past being surprised now at the lengths she'd go to.

'What are you going to do now you're in?'

'Find Lord Talisby.'

I felt her hand on mine, prising my fingers apart, then realised she was only taking back the ring. I hadn't realised I was still holding it.

'And then?'

'I want to see what he looks like.'

I should have seen where we were heading, but I hadn't. 'You're thinking he might be your father?'

'Why else would she be wearing his ring?'

'You can't do that,' I said.

She drew away from me, disappointed, but if father-hunting were the only thing in her mind, it wasn't in mine. I'd risked a lot for a chance of a conversation with Talisby and the last thing I wanted was to have it sabotaged. Disaster, likely anyway, would be assured if I turned up with Kay in tow, waving a ring and claiming him as her long lost father.

'Why not?'

'They'll never let you near him. He's surrounded by body-guards.'

She took that in and her shoulders slumped a little.

'I'll tell you what.I've got an appointment with him in half an hour. You lend me the ring and I'll let you know how he reacts to it.'

'Appointment?'

'I'm with that film crew you saw.'

She wrinkled her forehead, drew a hand through her hair.

'I . . . I thought . . . '

She thought I was an Oxford professor.

'One of my other jobs. Literary consultant. His ancestor was a famous poet.'

She looked down at the ring in her palm, up at me.

'Can I trust you?'

'If you can trust anybody, you can trust me.'

I don't know which of us moved first. The heavy air swirled, I felt her hand putting the ring into mine, then our bodies were pressed hard against each other. I kissed her, forcing the thin lips back, felt her teeth against mine, then her tongue inside my mouth, moving over it like a slow methodical search. Perhaps she thought I had her father hidden in there. She pushed me away from her, looked at my face and smiled, apparently satisfied with what she saw there, though I don't think it had anything to do with trustworthiness. It was a smile from the pale lips only, tongue put away.

'Where shall I meet you afterwards?'

'You can't stay here. You'd better go with those women and get off at the first loo stop.'

She nodded, decisive again. 'There's a café just before exit nine of the M5. I'll meet you there after ten o'clock tonight.'

I wanted to ask what she'd be doing until then, how she'd got her familiarity with the motorways, but it wasn't the time for it. I agreed to meet her there.

115

'I should go and wait by their bus. I'll stay here until it's time to meet him.'

I watched her walk back up the greenhouse, adjusting her scarf, adopting her hunched-forward walk. As soon as the door had closed on her at the other end I walked across the empty courtyard and in at the back door. Contact with her had given me a shot of recklessness, of her odd, boneless confidence. I found my way back to the corridor with the Turner sketches, walked along to the far end as if I had a right to be there, knocked on a white door that was standing ajar. As I walked in, the man at his desk turned to face me.

'Can I have a word with you, Milord?' I said.

Chapter Twelve

At first, I don't think he recognised me as one of the film crew. He didn't react at all to what I'd called him, but perhaps he was used to being my-lorded by the peasantry. Even without the television lights there was a confident gloss to him. Dark hair greying at the sides, statesmanlike. Face bred to look intelligent with high, square forehead. Eyes no warier than most politicians I've seen, fixed on me, trying to place me.

'Aren't you with the television people?'

'Yes, but it's not about that.'

Her ring had given me my start. I took two steps towards him, holding it in the palm of my hand like a sugar lump to a horse. Like a horse, his first reaction was to draw his head back, squinting down his nose at it. The book meanwhile was in my left hand, with the bomber jacket thrown over it.

'What is it?'

I stayed where I was. He stood up, waiting. I waited too, and he had to take the next few steps towards me.

'It's got your coat of arms on it.'

I hoped she'd got that right, at least.

He picked it off my palm, stared at it, walked over to look at it by the window, though the light had been perfectly good where we were.

'Where did you get it?'

'A friend bought it in London.' I'd decided on that while I was walking along the corridors. 'Is it yours?'

'It was lost a long time ago.'

'In Paris?'

117

He'd forgotten about me, absorbed in the ring. That brought him back and he gave me the look a bull gives the picador: impertinent chap this, but could be trouble.

'It might have been.'

'You were a student there, weren't you?'

'Paris, London, Cambridge. It could have been anywhere.'

But you'd know, I thought, when and where you lost a family heirloom. I didn't say it because I didn't want to get him angry too soon.

'How did you say your friend came by it?'

'She bought it off an antique stall in Camden Lock. She got interested in the coat of arms and looked it up.'

He walked across the room and gave the ring back to me, reluctantly I thought. It was warm from his hand and being in the sun but I still felt like shivering when I touched it, thinking of Prudence's dead finger or Kay's lie. He must have invited me to sit down, because I was in an armchair and he was back sitting at his desk. The book was in my lap now. I crossed my legs and tried to look comfortable.

'Would your friend be willing to sell it back to me?'

I'd expected that.

'I'm not sure. She seems to have got quite attached to it.'

'Of course, if it could be proved to be our property . . . '

He let it trail off, hardly more than the shadow of a threat. I'd expected that too.

'The law would be complicated though, wouldn't it? I mean, if somebody had found it and kept it, not knowing its value, then sold it honestly after nearly thirty years . . . '

Neither of us had mentioned how many years ago the ring had been lost, but he didn't pick me up on it.

'Quite. Oh quite. I'd make her a reasonable offer. Say twice what she paid for it.'

'I'll ask her,' I said.

'I'd be very grateful. Perhaps if she'd write to me here . . . '

I made my voice sound as deferential as I could. 'I'll tell you what. It might be a good idea if you scribbled her a couple of lines. How glad you are it's turned up, how

118

much you'd like it back and so on. I could take it to her. I mean, she could hardly refuse then, could she?'

I'd got the flattery right. He smiled.

'You think so? If you won't mind waiting a moment . . . '

He took a piece of crested notepaper from the Victorian stationery rack on his desk, picked up his pen and asked my friend's name. I made one up. He wrote for a minute or so, then brought it over to show to me.

Dear Ms Green, Your friend will have told you about our conversation. I can only add that if you feel you can help in this, I shall be very grateful to you. Yours sincerely.

Neat. Not a mention of the ring. Handwriting distinctive, with angular loops, words evenly spaced. Not remotely like the unknown hand on my three pages. I gave it back to him and he put it in an envelope. The crest on the flap was identical to the one on the ring. He remained standing, right hand a little advanced, waiting for me to get up, shake hands and go. I stayed.

'Funny Paris should come up,' I said. 'I think you used to know a friend of mine there.'

'Oh. Who?'

The hand went back. The voice made it clear I was outstaying my welcome.

'Duncan. Duncan McMahon, a painter. Big, bearded man.'

He shook his head. 'I can't remember. I was there to learn French. I didn't see much of the bearded community, so to speak.'

I thought of Duncan's photograph. He'd been on close terms with at least one beard.

'I should have thought it would have been a small world,' I said.

I was still scared, more scared if anything, but I felt my heart beat and my lungs expand when he said that, the way I imagine an athlete feels when he's out in front. If he'd casually admitted acquaintance with Duncan, hinted –

119

however passingly – at student wildnesses, my case would have crumbled. Now, three times already, I'd got him lying: about not knowing where he lost the ring, about Duncan, about keeping clear of the bohemian crowd. The question was, now I'd got my three lies, what was I going to do about them?'

'Not really. Won't your friends be going?'

Short of ordering me out, he couldn't have put it more clearly. I reminded myself that even if his ancestor had been a bastard son of Charles II, the same might be true of any of us. I recrossed my legs and settled more deeply into the chair cushions. Glazed chintz they were, but very comfortable, a design of red and blue parrots on berries. I could have stayed there for days.

'There was another one,' I said. 'Prudence. Cardell's secretary. You must remember her.'

I'd stepped over the line now. No going back. I wondered how much it would cost to get a chair like this one for my room, then thought I wouldn't have a room any more.

'Prudence . . . '

Hesitation in his voice, nothing like the confident way he'd denied knowing Duncan. But there could be more than one reason for that. Home Office ministers surely read reports of murder investigations.

'Prudence Belsire,' I said. 'The one who was murdered.'

I watched dust motes moving up and down in the sunlight through the window. I watched his face and couldn't read the expression on it at all.

He asked: 'Was she a friend of yours?'

'I went to see her once, last year. I wanted to know who wrote this.'

I stood up and handed it to him. He stared at it for a while, opened it at the title page, then at random, page 37. It's the one where she makes him stand there and runs a knife down his ribs while her maid is . . . That one. I looked over his shoulder while he scanned halfway down the page. Then he tried to slam the book shut but, being a paper cover, it wouldn't slam satisfactorily, and turned round on me. He was

120

actually blushing. His elegant eyebrows had come together and his eyes were hard and furious.

'Why are you showing me this muck?'

I picked up my book as calmly as I could. 'Is it the first time you've seen it, then?'

'Of course it is. Do you think I read books like that?'

The odd thing was that, at the time, I believed him. There was a raw quality about his surprise and anger quite different from his reaction to the ring. The air round him quivered with it. If he'd written the book, however long ago and in however different a life, I couldn't believe he'd handle it with such hatred. We stood there staring at each other, and I don't think either of us knew what to do next. I sensed though that the question of what to do about me had now become a more serious one than how to get me off the premises. I was more than a nuisance, I was something deeply offensive to his scheme of things and to let me walk unrebuked and unchecked was almost unthinkable to him. And yet, what could he do about me? I'd come into his house, as far as he knew, legitimately. I had, like a good citizen, offered him a means of getting back some long-lost property. If I'd then bored him with impertinent questions about my acquaintances, that was a social offence, not a legal one. As for the book, there was nothing in the law as I knew it to prevent you showing an erotic book to a government minister.

The one thing, as far as I could see, that he could legally have held me on was to help inquiries into the death of Prudence Belsire. But I'd told him I'd visited her last year, and there was no reason why he should connect a crop-headed film crew member with the man the police were looking for. No reason yet, that is. If he did find some pretext to hang on to me, awkward connections might be made. I thought of the flunkey in the tracksuit and the two security men at the gate, and the confidence that had got me there sank very low.

'Darling, did you ring up the airport?'

A voice from the corridor, through the half-open door. I recognised it. The first time I'd heard it, it had been ordering me to collect its lost shoe.

'Not yet, darling. I've been busy.'

Lady Talisby came into the room in slacks and violet silk blouse, feet in grey casuals suitable for showing gardening women round the estate. She stopped when she saw me and looked me up and down. His eyes went to the book in my hand and, to help him calm down, I slid the bomber jacket back over it.

'This young man's here with the film crew,' he told her.

So hostilities were not to resume in front of her. It was some relief, but not much, because her blue eyes were still on me and they were looking thoughtful.

'Don't I know you? Yes . . . yes.'

I stood there and she actually walked round me, as if I were a statue that might do for the garden.

'You've had your hair cut. You're the young man who rescued me in that dreadful affair at Oxford.'

Until I'd heard her voice, I'd entirely forgotten the episode. It belonged to another world, the world of Oxford and Andrea, that I'd left so far behind it didn't seem to count any more. It had never even occurred to me that I might meet her, as I had imagined her to be busy with the coachload of women.

'I'm glad to see you again. I was afraid I hadn't thanked you properly at the time.'

'I suppose you were filming the so-called demonstration,' Lord Talisby said. 'There's nothing like a film crew for encouraging rent-a-mob, is there?'

Another black mark for the poor wretched producer, but I didn't correct him. If it stopped him connecting me with Colin Counsel, the little-known Oxford academic, that was all to the good. I'd seen Lady Talisby's sudden entrance as a threat. Now I was beginning to see her in the light of the lion coming to the rescue of Androcles.

'Darling, he was really very kind to me. After you'd scuttled off inside and left me.'

Pow. The lion had a nice line in domestic fighting. He blinked and shuffled.

'I explained, darling. I had no choice. The security people insisted— '

122

She cut him short. 'Anyway, I really am most grateful to you. Most grateful. And now here you are again. I hope he gave you a nice interview.'

Yes, very nice, I said, while Lord Talisby scowled. Any plans he might have for giving me in charge would clearly not be popular home policy. The best thing he could do now was get rid of me as soon as possible.

'I expect your people are packed up by now. They're probably out the front waiting for you.'

She put her hand to her mouth in mock horror. 'Oh dear, I'm afraid they've gone already. I've just remembered I saw their van driving off after my flower club ladies.'

This was no surprise to me as I'd told them not to wait, but it didn't please Lord Talisby.

'I'll get somebody to give you a lift back to the main road. You'll have to hitch from there.'

That suited me fine. He picked up a phone on his desk and gave orders, while Lady Talisby asked me if I'd like some coffee. If my nerve had been stronger I'd have said yes please, just to annoy him, but I reckoned I'd done enough in that direction for one morning. A minute later tracksuit arrived to escort me off the premises and Lady Talisby thanked me yet again as I went out. Lord Talisby said nothing, but I noticed him looking at the shape of the book under my jacket.

I made sure that we went back via the room where we'd done the interview to pick up my pack and check everything was inside it. Then I was escorted to the gate where a car and driver were waiting, and that should have been that. Only it wasn't. The driver insisted on getting out to put my pack in the boot. While I was watching him, one of the security men in the hut called out: 'Everything OK, sir?' I turned, surprised, to tell him that it was and I'm certain that the man beside him was holding a camera. It was done so quickly that there'd have been no chance to protest, even if I'd been in a stronger position. Looked at reasonably, you couldn't even blame them or Talisby. I was a suspect character that they didn't want in again. Looked at less reasonably, the way Duncan looked at it, the way I seemed to have caught from him, it was a very

123

bad sign indeed. It meant that Talisby, if he wanted it, now had something for comparison.

If he checked with the film crew – and the press officer would have their address – he'd trace me back to Duncan's refuge and a false identity. Two false identities if you counted the school teacher and the name on the passport. If he looked closely, now that he knew about the Prudence connection, he might see resemblances to the police description. If he needed fingerprints, there'd be plenty on the coffee cup I'd handled so casually while the crew were setting up for the interview. What it added up to was that if he wanted me, he'd got me. When we came to the main road the driver asked casually if I'd be hitching north or south. North, I said. I waited until he was well out of sight, then crossed over for south.

Chapter Thirteen

It was still only midday, more than ten hours to go to my meeting with Kay. The café she'd chosen was about forty miles away but I used some of the time to cover my tracks, shuttling to and fro on the main roads and the motorway itself, only hitching lifts from commercial drivers, watching for anything that might be a car from the Talisby stable. Once on a feint northwards, a truck driver said hadn't he seen me hitching the other way an hour or two ago? No, I said, must be my twin brother, and spun a long and unnecessary story about having to get to Liverpool for a wedding. I was becoming an addict of identities. Twice police cars passed me as I waited at service stations, but they were only motorway patrols, not interested in tatty hitchers.

Towards the end of the afternoon I thought I'd shuttled enough and found myself a field not far from the motorway. The grass had been razored off for silage, but there was still a long fringe of it by a river bank under pollarded willows where I could lie out of sight of anything except a few birds that came, looked and went away again. A truck driver had given me a piece of chocolate bar. I ate it slowly, trying not to feel thirsty, then thought what the hell and took a few gulps from the river in the palm of my hand. Why not liver fluke, on top of everything else?

That photograph at Talisby's gates had got to me badly. I was full of the need to escape, but didn't know where. Everywhere seemed barred to me. Not back to Oxford – the trail might have led them there already, not back to Duncan until I knew what he was trying to do with me. London was dangerous. The van had been abandoned near there and the

125

police thought that had something to do with me. Paris had its attractions, but my way of getting there with the false passport led me straight back into the Duncan net. In spite of that, I was tempted, if only by the thought of twenty-one miles of clean sea between me and all the rest of it. It had too the attraction of one of my remaining missing links: Nicolle.

Which brought me straight back to the main problem. Getting clear away from it all, to Cardiff, say, or Edinburgh, wherever you like, looked the most sensible thing to do in the short term. Find myself a room somewhere, lie low, wait for it all to blow over. That was all very well if I thought it would blow over, that Prudence's murderer would be caught without my interference and I could crawl out with some more or less convincing story of what I'd been doing in the meantime. But the more I thought of it, the more I was convinced that, without my interference, Prudence's murderer would never be found and I'd be there in my lodging house in Cardiff or Edinburgh until old age or madness supervened and I took to the streets with my carrier bags, muttering to the smelly air about plots in high places. I'd seen them coming often enough, these people, and crossed over. Now it came to me, supposing they're not mad, supposing they all of them started where I am now? A black panic came over me that made me want to go back to Duncan and Talisby and Angela and beg or batter out of them some key that would save me from such disintegration.

Or Kay. That was the root of it, what kept me here tethered to a few dozen miles of motorway like a tortoise on a string. I couldn't go anywhere or think of doing anything until I'd seen her again. I wanted to touch her. I wanted to put my arm on her shoulder again and get that same desperately clear feeling that had sent me straight into Talisby's room with the ring. I wanted to see her tongue come out between her lips, like a snake's head between stones. I wanted to brush the grass out of her hair. Mixed up with all this, but quite different, I wanted to ask her where she'd really got that ring.

It seemed to me that the solution to the murder now depended on that. I knew now, what I didn't know when

126

she first showed it to me, that it was what she claimed it to be: Talisby's. He hadn't even denied, though he'd tried weakly to backtrack, that the ring was lost in Paris at the time when the book was written. The question was, what had it been doing ever since? If I accepted Kay's version, the answer seemed to be that it was in Prudence's possession all the time. If so, how come she didn't wear it when she was alive but had it on her hand when she died? Two possible answers to that: either she'd put it on, for some purpose of her own, between the time when I left and the arrival of the murderer, or it had been put on her finger after death, to be found by whoever discovered the body. If the first option, in the light of Kay's claim that Prudence was expecting a late-night visitor, then she might have worn it as a threat, as part of a blackmail attempt. In which case, who would Talisby's ring threaten but Talisby? If, on the other hand, it was put on after her death, then the inference was somebody else trying to incriminate Talisby.

My hipbone had dug a pit into the grass and was pressing on the ground. I turned over to face the hedge and the declining sun, heard the traffic noise from the motorway. The trouble was, all this hinged on the idea that Kay was telling the truth about taking it off Prudence's hand. If she was lying, two questions. Why? And how had she got hold of the ring in the first place? The why had to wait. The easy explanation of the second question was that she'd found it somewhere among Prudence's belongings and the dead finger was just a piece of drama. The second was that somebody had given it to her, which brought us back yet again to somebody trying to incriminate Talisby. Which brought us back to Duncan, whose name apparently meant nothing to her.

After ten, she'd said, so there was no point in getting to the café early. I made myself wait till the sun was below the hedge and the shadow had reached the grass where I was lying before I picked up my pack and started trudging back to the motorway. I got a lift from a van on the approach road almost at once and was at the café by about quarter past nine. I looked carefully at the vehicles in the car park – a couple of Belgian

127

heavy transports, three British, a broiler factory truck, a dozen unremarkable cars. It was fairly quiet inside with half a dozen drivers fuelling up in the commercial section, a sprinkling of commercial traveller types eating alone, a family party with a kid that howled intermittently. I'd intended to eat if I got there early, not because I wanted to but because I calculated I'd gone about four days now without a real meal and I didn't know how long it would be before I started feeling weak. But when it came to it, the smell of sausages and the glutinous film round the beans churned my stomach, so it was coffee and biscuits again, the shortbread sort with currants in them. Ten o'clock came and went, then half past, but there was no sign of her.

Over another cup of coffee I started wondering whether she'd meant inside or outside the café. When I walked outside the car park looked dark after the neon, though the sky was still pale, with a few rags of clouds where the sun had gone down. Heat and diesel fumes were rising off the tarmac, but there was a cool breeze coming in with the darkness that got to me under the bomber jacket and made me shiver. Very few vehicles left in the car park now: two cars, one green, one dark coloured, the Belgian transports, the broiler truck. I stood in the middle of the empty space, so that she could see me if she was waiting. I strolled over to the parked cars, but there was nobody inside. Then I walked out and round the trucks, intending to make a circuit of the car park before going back to wait inside.

'Colin.'

A woman's voice, no more than a whisper, so low I couldn't make out where it had come from. I looked round at the parked cars, at the truck cabs.

'Colin, here.'

It seemed to be coming from the far side of the broiler truck. I can't remember whether I called out anything in reply. I ran because there'd been urgency in the whisper, round the front of the transports, along the side of the broiler truck, smelling chicken shit, hearing my feet pounding the tarmac. As I was rounding the back of the truck, a figure stepped out.

128

'Where do you think you're going, mate?'

The rough accents of that part of the country. A figure a few inches shorter than I am, but broader. I mumbled an apology and tried to dodge past him, thinking he'd just happened to come out of the back of his vehicle at the wrong time. But he wouldn't have it, stood in front of me, blocking me, his shoulder against the side of the truck. When I tried to swerve past him to the left another man appeared and blocked me there. Alarmed by now, I swore at him and kicked out at his shins but he caught me by the arm, turning me back to face the man by the truck. I didn't hit out at first because I still thought that these were just a pair of drunks who could be talked out of it. I only got seriously worried when I saw that there was a third man, standing a little way back from them and watching.

'What's this?' I said. 'What's going on?'

The man by the truck drew back his arm and swung a punch to my jaw. I got my free arm up in time to divert it but not block it entirely and it made contact with my cheek hard enough to send me lurching back against the man holding me. I had enough sense left to stamp hard on his instep and pull free, throwing a punch as I came forward in the general direction of the face of the one who'd hit me. It must have connected because it crunched my knuckles and he started swearing, but by then the one behind me was back in action, pulling at my shoulders with all his weight, and the third man, bigger than the others, was closing in. I landed another few kicks and punches and heard one of them grunt like a toad, but with the three of them against me, I couldn't delay it long. The first two got me up against the truck and pinioned my elbows so that the third man could pound into my face as it suited him, left and right.

I'd forgotten, because it was a long time since it had happened to me, the sheer griminess of pain, the sickness running through you from throat to bowels, the gulping that's wrenched out of your body uncontrollably, that you hear from a long way off as if it had nothing to do with you. The third man kept landing punches, two, three – a pause as if selecting a part of my face less pounded than the rest, then starting again. At first I tried to dodge them in the only way left to me, moving my head to the side, but then one of the others got an arm locked round the back of my head and stopped even that. While I could talk I pleaded with them to stop but they took no notice. After that first remark, none of them said anything.

Later the two who were holding me let me slide down to the tarmac and I thought that was an end of it, but they started kicking at my ribs and legs and shoulders as comprehensively as they'd battered my face, regular and methodical as if they were counting. I couldn't talk by then, there was nothing but retching and groaning. When they stopped, I couldn't understand what was happening. The universe had become pain and there was nothing in it but waiting for the next kick. The man who'd first spoken, the only one whose voice I'd heard, was saying something. It sounded like grating gravel. I tried to listen, tried to let him know I couldn't hear.

' . . . out of it. You keep out of it.'

Then they went away. From a very long way off, I heard a car start. I lay there, eyes closed, feeling blood running from my nose down the back of my throat.

'Are you there?' I said. 'Are you still there?'

I wasn't talking to the three men. They'd gone in the car, I knew that. I was talking to the woman, the one who'd called out to me. The one who'd been watching. How I was so sure she'd been there all the time, I don't know, only that I was, throughout, as certain of her presence as of the fists and feet pounding into me. She'd ordered them to do it, and now I needed her to make sense of it to me.

'Please, are you there?'

I tried to open my eyes, in case she was standing over me, looking down, but the lids were too swollen. Still asking if she was there, I passed out.

The two Belgian transport drivers found me much later, when the daylight had gone completely and the tarmac was cold as marble. As a trade, they are not inclined to fuss. They treated me efficiently from well-stocked first aid boxes, seemed to accept my story of a jealous husband and not wanting to involve the police for the wife's sake. One of them gave me a lift as far as the turn-off to the next town, advising me to see a doctor about my ribs. I'd asked them to look for my pack before we started. It had gone, of course. All I had left were the ring, the fake passport and a hundred and thirty pounds in cash, in the zipped pockets of my bomber jacket, and I wondered why they hadn't searched those. I watched the transport drive off down the motorway, walked along the slip road and found a grassy ditch, where I passed out again until morning.

There are events so concrete that everything else becomes ghost-like by comparison. That's what happened to me. When I managed to get my eyelids far enough apart to see sky and grass blades, I could remember everything that had led up to the café car park but I didn't know what to do with it. It had all happened in another world, inaccessible to the creature that was performing the long, painful process of getting to its feet and heaving itself up out of the ditch to the edge of the road. And yet the creature seemed to know what it was doing, after a fashion. It walked away from the motorway noise, in the direction of the town the transport driver had indicated the night before. After a yard or two it worked out that, since both legs hurt equally, there was no point in limping. It could count, too. Twenty steps and stop, thirty steps and stop. The eyelids crept open, millimetre by millimetre. Breathing was a problem. The ribs would only take short breaths but the nose, propped up by Belgian lint and plaster, couldn't cope with that. The mouth could manage, but there were broken teeth that every intake of air rasped. Still, the components came to some sort of arrangement. Thirty steps and stop, forty steps and stop. After a long time of this, I asked the creature where it thought it was going. Paris, it said. Where else? Where else.

Duncan had wanted to send me to Paris and Uncle Lazarus. I'd resisted, and this had happened. At that stage, I still wasn't up to sorting out cause and effect. Whether I'd been beaten up for not doing what Duncan wanted wasn't clear. What

131

was clear, though, was that if Duncan had been involved in the attack the night before, only Kay could have told him where to find me. The same applied to Talisby, unless the cucumbers had been bugged. But need Kay have told either of them? She'd have needed protectors in her King's Cross life and could, presumably, whistle three of them up the motorway at need. But why would she need? I didn't know, and that was why I was in no condition to resist my automaton's determination that I was making for Paris and Uncle Lazarus.

It was only eight o'clock by the time I got to the town, but there was a transport café open by the bus station. The girl at the counter, talking to a couple of drivers, hardly gave me a glance as she handed over the mug of coffee. My attempts to drink it, though, attracted the attention of all three of them.

'You OK, mate?'

Yes, I said. Got in a bit of a fight. Own fault. Too much to drink. At least my voice, filtered through gauze and blood and broken teeth, could hardly now be described as cultivated. They were passingly sympathetic and the girl said the dentist on the corner opened at nine and might fit me in. The nearest hospital casualty department was twenty miles away, which relieved me of the decision on whether to get the ribs and nose seen to. The dentist must have graduated in Dodge City. He made no comment on my condition beyond calling me a bloody fool, did some temporary shoring up of the teeth with the subtlety of a motorway contractor and relieved me of two of my ten-pound notes.

'Don't eat on that side, but I don't suppose you'll want to anyway.'

This small act of reconstruction helped me to feel more in control of things. I bought antiseptic cream and glucose tablets and caught the bus for Cheltenham.

Once I'd accepted that I was going to Paris, I checked all the time to see if I was being followed. There was quite a crowd waiting for the London train at Cheltenham station and I was a conspicuous object, but as far as I could see nobody gave me a second glance. Paddington seemed full of police,

132

uniformed and strolling in pairs. I froze at the ticket barrier, then told myself they wouldn't have sent so many for me, and creaked unimpeded into the underground. In London, at least, I didn't even feel peculiar. It was bad on the platform, though. There were three men standing by the tunnel entrance in workmen's overalls, and when I first saw them they looked in build like the men in the car park. I'd shrunk, crouching against the wall, before I got a hold on myself and realised it wouldn't need all three of them to follow me. Anyway, even if they had been the same three, I was doing what they said, wasn't I? Leaving the country would surely count as keeping out of it.

All the time, too, I was looking for Kay. I felt she must be somewhere near, that she could hardly do what she'd done to me and stay away. But perhaps she'd gone ahead of me to Paris. There was a girl with her back to me on the Dover train, slim and with long dark hair, but when turned round she had full, rosy cheeks and lips and she smiled at me sympathetically. All the journey I missed the book badly and wished they hadn't taken it from me. I didn't want to read it, just to feel it under my hand or lightly against my hurt ribs. I'd deliberately spun out the journey for a night crossing, so that it was dusk before we got to Dover and I looked out of the window, seeing and not recognising my own reflection. I half slept, seeing the woman in the book with Kay's face, and dreamed that I was travelling to meet her.

In the café on Dover harbour front, with the games machines pinging and hamburger wrappings blowing in the sea breeze, I suddenly thought I should let Andrea know I was going. Not directly, though. I couldn't face questions. I found a phone and dialled her friend's number. At first she didn't recognise my voice.

'Colin, you sound odd. Andrea's been worried sick about you. Where are you?'

'Sorry. Will you tell her I'm all right. I'm going to Paris.'

'Paris. Why Paris? She'll be— '

'Some research I've got to do. Tell her not to worry. I'll be in touch.'

133

That last sentence was meaningless. I put the phone down, visualising her friend's flat, its Indian rug with the cat asleep and collages of postcards. A day ago I'd have felt tugged by the normality of it. Now it meant nothing to me at all. The side of the ferry came suddenly out of the dark and I lined up behind the motorcyclists with the other raggle of foot passengers. As far as I could tell, there was nobody to see me off.

Chapter Fourteen

It hardly got dark at sea that night, which added to my wariness. I felt as exposed as a fly on a plate. Quiet too. Although I stood on deck for most of the crossing, I've no memory of engine noise, only of moving across a flat sea like being drawn by a magnet over a bowl of mercury. It felt like an experiment, an irreversible one for me as I was taken, yard by yard, away from identity. I hadn't chosen the clothes I was wearing; they'd been imposed on me like the name on the passport. I had no luggage, not so much as a razor or comb. Even the last of the paper tissues I'd bought to dab at my damaged mouth disappeared bloodstained into the wake when we were halfway across. If I'd followed it and been taken out eventually, there'd be no telling who I was. On the other side, the official at the passport desk gave me one routine glance and let me through. It hadn't occurred to me to worry about him. By then my false identity seemed neither more nor less likely than any other.

The exposed feeling was still there though, as we waited at dawn on an open platform for the Paris train. There were five besides me and we stood far apart. I looked at them as carefully as I could, but didn't see any resemblance to anybody I'd met before. We all got into different carriages and I had an uninterrupted journey, free to concentrate on what the vibrations of the SNCF rolling stock were doing to my teeth and ribs and find out what this assemblage of sensations that seemed to have taken my place intended to do next.

Uncle Lazarus. That seemed to be the beginning and end of it for the moment. Uncle Lazarus because Duncan had told me to go to him and whether he'd intended me good or harm by doing it, I might find out when I got there. Uncle Lazarus because all of them, when the book was written, liked him and talked to him. Uncle Lazarus because he might tell me what sort of woman stood and watched while a man's teeth and ribs were kicked and broken, and whether she'd ordered it and why. Because I was bone tired and bewildered and couldn't think of anywhere else to go.

The letter of introduction from Duncan had disappeared along with my pack, but I could remember the name *Rêveuse* and knew from four days I'd spent in Paris with Andrea where most of the boats were moored. I changed money at the station, got the métro to the Trocadero and drank coffee at a pavement café among groups of American tourists comparing guide books. I got some alarmed glances and the tables on either side of me were left carefully vacant. From the way I'd looked in the mirror at the station lavatory I wasn't surprised. The bruises were beginning to come out and dabbing with cold water hadn't shifted the blood from my tee-shirt. In spite of the suppressed alarm all round me, I almost went to sleep there in the sun and the traffic noise until a waiter loomed and managed to convey, without saying anything, that I'd better settle up and go.

I was so tired by then I couldn't even get out of the way of the Paris traffic and let it hoot and pile up around me. A gendarme shouted and I exaggerated my shuffle across the pavement, hoping he'd think I was just another drunk. I kept it up over the shiny flagstones of Trocadero square, zigzagging in and out among kids on roller-skates, Arabs selling pseudo ethnic carvings, other salesmen launching whirring paper pigeons at head height so that I flinched and ducked away. The gendarme didn't follow, but why should he? Just another drunk, just another identity. Down the steps by the fountains, across another road with more hooting and there was the Seine. It was a relief to see something that seemed to know where it was going. I walked against the current along the embankment until I came to the line of houseboats and, within a few hundred yards, found *Rêveuse*.

It was on its own mooring, not double-parked and linked by gangplanks like most of the others, and when I got a proper look at it I could see why. Its neighbours were bourgeois affairs with bay trees in pots on the deck, wine bottles on tables under parasols, while *Rêveuse* looked as if the tides of several decades had washed over it, leaving it barnacled with a detritus of lost causes, good causes or causes the world had abandoned and outgrown. The windows of the deckhouse were plastered with fading posters, facing outwards, demanding that LBJ should end the Vietnam war now, announcing that Che Guevara lived. A row of cannabis plants, grey with exhaust fumes, stood in pots on a hatch cover, so obviously plastic that they wouldn't rate a second glance from even the most excitable *agent de police*. A peace symbol on what looked like a tattered tea towel hung from a pole at the stern and a couple of fat white pigeons sat on the deck-house roof and cooed at me.

'I'm coming aboard,' I told them.

The gangplank was little more than a rotting stick but the mat on the other side said 'Welcome' in at least four languages. There was no sign of life apart from the pigeons.

'Hello. Anyone on board?'

I tried it in English and French and at first nothing seemed to be happening, then I noticed a foot coming round the edge of the deck-house door, sliding it open, an old brown foot, wrinkled but sinuous.

'Come in and sit down,' said a voice, speaking in English but with a strong French accent. 'You'll be all right now. Come in and sit down.'

It sounded amused. The door was wide open by then and the foot had gone. I walked in and found a small man sitting against the wall in what I assumed to be a yoga position, soles of feet together, thighs flat against the deck boards, a batik-printed sarong covering his genitals. I looked down on a head as shiny as a pecan nut, and a pair of brown eyes looked up at me with, as far as I could see, nothing but kindly interest.

'Sit down,' he said. And again: 'You're all right now.'

The deck-house was completely bare. I realised I was meant to sit on the floor and hoped I wasn't supposed to

137

copy the yoga posture. I couldn't help wincing, from the pain in my ribs, as I folded myself up with my back against the wall, and could see that he noticed.

'Duncan sent me,' I said. 'There was a letter but it got stolen.'

'Yes, yes. You're breathing wrong.'

It struck me as remarkable, all in all, that I was breathing at all. I said so, but he didn't seem curious.

'From the stomach more, from the diaphragm, then it won't hurt you so much.'

I tried to explain about Duncan and the letter but he wouldn't let me.

'Don't talk. Breathe, like so.'

He spread his palms outwards, on either side of a brown stomach that went rhythmically from flat to concave. Seeing that we'd get nothing discussed until my breathing satisfied him, I did my best to imitate it, but didn't get it right and he came to crouch beside me, fingers pressing against my stomach, eyes looking dispassionately into mine, like a doctor's. This went on for some time until I got into the trick of it and he put himself back into his soles-together posture and watched me.

'That's better. Now, close your eyes.'

'If I close my eyes, I'll sleep.'

'Sleep then. Let the violence and the pain go away from you.'

'They don't though.'

'They don't last forever. Even Franco won't live forever.'

'Franco?' I had almost been dropping off, but this brought me wide awake again. 'What's Franco got to do with it?'

'If you move quickly like that, you'll hurt yourself. Everything slowly. Weren't you one of them who went to fight Franco?'

I was wide awake now, realising I'd got myself shut in with a nutter and hoping he wasn't going to turn violent. He looked over eighty and about six stone, but the way I was feeling I couldn't have coped with one of his pigeons if it had got fractious.

I said, as tactfully as possible: 'I was born about fifty years too late to fight Franco, though of course I have the deepest respect for the International Brigade.'

He nodded. 'So you refused to fight in Vietnam. And now the CIA are even coming to find you in Paris. You'll be safe here, and when you're well we'll get you to Stockholm.'

I tried his breathing techniques to fight down a tide of panic. By this time he'd gone into his concave stomach, palms-outward routine again. I spoke as calmly as possible.

'I'm not a draft dodger either. I wasn't old enough. Duncan sent me because Prudence is dead and the police probably think I killed her.'

I don't know why I tried it, since I was convinced he was sunk in senility, but if he were mad it couldn't matter either way. Anyway, it got results. When his eyes opened again there was an alert, hard look about them.

'Why should the police think you killed Prudence?'

'Because I'd been with her the evening before, and I discovered the body. Except I don't think it was me. I think somebody else got there first.'

'Why do you think that?'

I didn't tell him about the draft pages from the book I'd found at Duncan's house. He was, as far as I knew, Duncan's ally.

'Something I found there.'

He crossed his ankles and stood up in one movement, without using his hands. The sarong flopped down over calves skinny as a bird's.

'Shall we go inside?'

Inside turned out to be down a flight of steps to the boat's belly. As I followed him I thought that he'd shown no surprise at all when I told him about Prudence's death and expressed no regret, but perhaps that went with the yoga.

'Sit down.'

At least there was somewhere to sit apart from the floor. Two deckchairs, the old-fashioned kind with wooden frames and faded green canvas, stood in a clearing of what looked like a distillation of the world's jumble sales. Watery light

139

from the bottle glass portholes, rocking and wavering as the *bateaux-mouche* went past with their cargoes of tourists, glanced off stacks of paintings framed and unframed, piles of books, heaps of clothes and curtains. The smell, though, was of citrus fruit and spices as fresh as if the equipage had just sailed in from Zanzibar. I lay back in the deckchair and let it float into my head, closing my eyes.

'Tell me what happened,' he said.

So I told him, from the meeting with Prudence the night before her murder, to my beating up in the car park thirty-six hours ago. Only two things I left out: the draft pages and any reference at all to Kay. I was too confused about Kay to talk. I opened my eyes now and again to see how he was taking it, but every time he was just sitting forward in the other deckchair with a look of polite interest, his knees nearly touching mine. When we'd come below he'd put on a big mohair dressing-gown, thick and new looking, It was too big for him and made him look like a soft-shelled turtle.

'So I came to you,' I said.

He nodded. 'Yes, that was right. Everybody comes to Uncle Lazarus.'

'Prudence did,' I said. 'And Milord and Duncan and the rest of them.'

'Everybody.'

'Them especially. I want to ask you about them. That's the only way I'll get clear of all this.'

'Clear of what?'

It was like being an undergraduate again, at a tutorial. The questions were simple, but must be treated with care.

'Clear of murdering Prudence. I can only get there if I find out who really did it.'

'What else?'

'Clear of wondering who wrote the book. And that other murder. And the woman.'

I said it all in a breath. By the time I'd got to the last three words my voice had nearly run out, but he heard.

'The woman in the book?'

140

'The woman in the book. She made somebody else commit a murder, and after nearly thirty years it still matters. That was why Prudence was killed.'

'Why were you interested in the book?'

I could have made up some answer, but I didn't think he'd believe it.

'The acceptance of cruelty, the certainty of it . . . '

He leaned forward and ran a finger lightly along my jaw at the precise point where it hurt most. 'Certainty like that?'

'Like that. And a woman was watching while they did it.' It was the nearest I'd got to talking about Kay.

'What kind of woman?' I asked him. 'You knew them.'

'The woman who wrote the book, or the woman in the book?'

'It was a woman who wrote it then?'

He smiled, showing two rows of teeth, yellowish but complete.

'I don't know who wrote it.'

'But you knew them all. You knew Cardell.'

He nodded.

'And you know the book?'

'Oh yes.'

'They all talked to you. You must know.'

'Perhaps they did and I've forgotten.'

'You can't have forgotten.'

Instead of answering, he moved his hands a few inches, indicating I should look around me. I noticed that, as well as the pictures stacked against the walls, there were more hanging from bolts between the portholes: a group photograph of parents and children with the name of a Negev kibbutz underneath it and an inscription in what I took to be Hebrew, a cartoon of two 1960s students, male and female, toting their rucksacks among reindeer with 'Thanks Pal' scrawled underneath it.

'A lot of cruelty,' he said. 'A lot of people trying to escape.'

It sent him off again. Sometimes we were back to Franco, sometimes he was assuring me he'd get me to my friends in Stockholm by a route the CIA didn't know about. Once he

141

seemed to take me for a Jewish resistance worker who might, with luck, make it to Switzerland. The place seemed crowded with them, fifty years of shadowy figures who'd come to Uncle Lazarus for refuge while *Rêveuse* rocked her bric-a-brac cargo on the turbulence of the western world. I could only wait for them to go, occasionally dropping in a question about Prudence or Milord or Duncan to try to remind him of my problems. It was a mention of Angela Arless that snapped him out of it quite suddenly.

'Mimi. You've seen her?'

'I told you I had, at Duncan's. She said Nicolle wrote the book.'

He ignored that.

'Has Mimi got children now?'

'I shouldn't think so. I don't remember any reference to them.'

'She regrets it?'

'She didn't strike me as the maternal type.'

He sighed. 'And poor Prudence was so jealous. So jealous.'

I sat forward in my deckchair. It was the first voluntary piece of information about the Cardell circle that he'd given me.

'Jealous of what?'

'Of Mimi's child. Before she had the abortion.'

'Prudence had an abortion?' I thought of Kay.

He shook his head. 'No, not Prudence. Mimi, Angela. Prudence didn't need an abortion, that was why she was jealous. Prudence wanted children, but she couldn't have them.'

'How do you know?'

'She told me. Some illness. That was why she came to Paris. So when she knew Angela was expecting Duncan's child—'

'But Duncan . . .'

He smiled. 'Duncan was a very attractive man, to everybody.'

'Let's try to get this straight. It's important. You're telling me that Mimi, Angela Arless, was expecting Duncan's child but had an abortion. You're sure she did?'

142

I was thinking of Kay again, and the resemblance to Duncan.
'Yes. I was there.'
'You mean when she had the abortion?'
He nodded. 'I was there. Duncan didn't know. Nicolle paid. Nicolle offered to go with her, but she didn't want Nicolle.'

Another side of their *vie de bohème*. The glamorous Angela on a divan in some dingy concierge's flat, only Uncle Lazarus to comfort her and Duncan goodness knows where.

'And Prudence. She definitely told you she couldn't have children?'
'Yes.'

So how to account for Kay? I was beginning to wonder if I'd imagined her and her sudden appearances on the dark hillside, in the cucumber house, the unseen presence in the car park.

He asked: 'You're surprised?'
'I'm surprised. What happened after that?'
'Angela and Prudence had a fight in a café and Nicolle told Cardell he must send Prudence back home.'
'And did he?'
'She wouldn't go home, but he sent her away somewhere for the summer. Brittany, I think.'
'Was all this before or after the book was published?'
'The spring and summer before.'

The answer came without hesitation. Once his attention was anchored, the information was all there. The problem was, keeping him from drifting off again.

'How could Nicolle tell Cardell what to do?'
'She had the money. She paid for most of the books he published.'
'And she and Angela were great friends even then.'
'Oh yes.'
'More than friends? Lovers?'
'Nicolle dedicated her first book of poems to Angela.'
'And Milord, where did he come into all this?'
He shrugged. 'As a young man with time and money.'
'Duncan's lover?'

143

'Possibly.'

'You know who Milord is now?'

'Duncan tells me he's at the Home Office.'

'You've seen Duncan recently?'

'Not for years. He never comes to Paris now.'

'Have you been to England?'

'No. I haven't left Paris since 1945. It's a kind of sickness, to go to other places if you don't need to.'

'He telephones?'

'No telephone. I do not like speaking to people when I can't see their eyes.'

'He writes?'

'Sometimes.'

'Do the others keep in touch with you at all?'

'No. They don't need me now.'

'But Duncan does?'

'Sometimes.'

'Do you know where Nicolle lives?'

After all the people who claimed not to have written the book, Nicolle was the only one who'd been fingered to me as its author. I had my doubts, but I needed to see her and this latest information about her relations with Angela and Prudence made it more urgent. Something had happened to me on *Rêveuse*, whether from the breathing techniques of Uncle Lazarus or the company of all those decades of other battered ones. I was hunting again.

'Yes.'

'Will you give me her address?'

'I must ask her first.'

'How?'

'I'll go and see her. You must rest.'

He disappeared into a cubbyhole behind piles of books and I heard a kettle boiling. After some time he reappeared, carrying a glazed pottery bowl steaming herb smells.

'Drink.'

I took it awkwardly between my fingers, staring at him over the brim.

'Drink,' he said again.

It smelt of cinnamon and lemon grass and something else that I couldn't quite place.

'Camomile?'

'Camomile.'

It probably wasn't poisonous. I drank.

'Confusion to Franco.'

He led me to a divan in the bows of the boat, surprisingly clean and orderly, with a fresh sheet spread over it as if he'd been expecting me. He said it was always ready for whoever came. When I'd taken off my shoes and lain down under the sheet he covered me with a blanket, tucking it in carefully.

'You can sleep now.'

'You'll go to see Nicolle?'

'Yes.'

'Don't tell her what I've been asking you. Say . . . say I'm a lecturer from Oxford who admires her books and wants to meet her.'

He didn't object. He must have lied for other people in the past.

Before I went to sleep I saw him going up the steps to the deck-house in white shirt and baggy trousers, heard his steps cross the deck and then recede over the narrow gangplank. I wondered if Nicolle lived far away, if her hair was still red and how I could get a sample of her handwriting, and soon afterwards fell asleep.

When I woke up the light had changed and I had an idea it was late afternoon. I could hear somebody moving about quietly on deck and thought it was Uncle Lazarus. I called out to him, wanting to know if Nicolle would see me, but instead of coming down into the cabin the steps went away quickly, across the deck and over the gangplank, light steps but too quick for Uncle Lazarus. I got up and found the door at the top of the steps into the deck-house slightly ajar. I didn't think he'd left it like that when he went out. I ran in bare feet to the other end of the gangplank, looked up and down the embankment, but there were crowds out in the afternoon sun and I couldn't pick out anybody I recognised. When I went down to the cabin again I found I was shivering, although it

145

wasn't cold. I kept telling myself that it was just a kid or a tourist. Anybody could have walked on board out of curiosity and run off, embarrassed, when I called out from below decks. It probably had nothing to do with me. The trouble was, I didn't believe it.

After that the boat didn't seem a safe refuge any more. My teeth and ribs began aching again and I was full of restlessness and the need to be somewhere else, though I knew I had to wait for Uncle Lazarus. I decided to start looking round, in case there was anything in his piles of keepsakes about the Cardell group. It was a breach of his generous hospitality, but I'd have to settle that with my conscience later. I picked up a blade of lemon grass from his kitchen cubbyhole and sucked it to freshen my mouth, then began the search. There was no hope of being methodical about it because the strata of several decades were jumbled together: an old snow-shoe with mildewed leather straps weighting down piles of last year's magazines, art catalogues propping up a broken easel. I wandered at random, moving piles of books and replacing them, opening cases of clothes long out of fashion. None of it meant anything to me until I accidentally knocked over a pile of books and records and, in putting them to rights again, was struck by a glimpse of familiar handwriting. Prudence's handwriting. I'd seen it just once before, in the note to Gus Prothering, but the aggressive scrawl of it was unmistakable. It was on a single sheet of yellowed flimsy paper and, as far as I could tell, it had been tucked under a book of Bob Dylan guitar tunes for beginners. The address was in Brittany and it was dated 23 July 1958. The letter was short and to the point.

Dear Uncle Lazarus,
    We need more money for the doctor's bill so you must sell the one we left with you. Please try to get a better price for it than the last one and tell the bank to telegraph the money as we need it urgently.
    Best wishes,
    Prudence Belsire.

I stood there trying to work it out. Uncle Lazarus had told me he thought Prudence went to Brittany the summer before the book was published. Could the 'one' left with him to sell be the book itself? If so, why the reference to the last one and who was the other person who made up the 'we'? Angela Arless, post abortion, might have needed a doctor, but if she and Prudence were bitter enemies they were hardly likely to be spending the summer in Brittany together. While I was thinking about it I heard steps across the deck. I was still holding the letter when Uncle Lazarus came down the stairs.

Chapter Fifteen

He was clutching parcels to his chest and humming to himself, not a care in the world.

'Did you sleep?

'Somebody woke me. Somebody coming on board.'

He didn't seem bothered. 'Who was it?'

'I don't know. Whoever it was ran away when I called out.'

He shrugged. 'They'll come back.'

'You have nervous friends?'

'Some of them.'

He walked past me, taking a long look at my face on the way, and put his parcels down in the cooking cubbyhole.

I said: 'I found this letter to you from Prudence.'

He'd started pouring spices into a jar and didn't turn round.

'She was in Brittany. She wanted to sell something you were keeping for her. Do you remember?'

'There were many people I kept things for. Some of them didn't come back.'

'Prudence wanted the money quickly, more money than last time. Was it a book?'

He turned round to face me, wrinkling his forehead.

'Always books with you. No.'

'What was it then?'

'A stone. A sapphire.'

'And there'd been another one you sold for her before that?'

'Yes.'

'Where did Prudence get sapphires?' It didn't go with the plain vicar's daughter. On the other hand, it went very well with a blackmailer.

'I don't know.'

'We're talking about the summer before that book was published. And there'd been a murder, hadn't there? You knew about that. And suddenly Prudence has sapphires and goes off to Brittany. Who was with her?'

'I don't think anyone was with her.'

'She said "we" in the note.'

'Nobody from here. They were all in Paris that summer.'

'All of them? Duncan and Milord? You and Nicolle and Angela?'

'All of them. Away for a day or two perhaps, for a weekend, but no more than that.'

I looked at him and I'd never seen a face more open. No fear, no resentment, nothing more than a civil interest. It scared me.

'There'd been a murder by then, hadn't there? One of you had killed somebody.'

'There are always murders.'

'A man killing another man on the beach and the woman watching. You know who they were, don't you?'

'You and me. Me and you.'

'And Franco and Hitler and the President of the United States. But it's that murder I'm interested in.'

'The murder in the book.'

'The murder that popped up out of the book and killed Prudence.'

I tried to calm down, to match my face to his.

'I need to know, you see. People are following me. They did this to me.' I touched my face. 'They'll do worse if they find I'm still asking questions. The only way I can get out of this is by finding out what happened.'

'You'll be safe here.'

But I didn't feel safe there, not after those footsteps on deck.

'You won't tell me?'

'Listen.' He put his hand on my shoulder. 'Listen, if the police or the CIA or anybody else come looking for you, I tell them I've never seen you, I know nothing about you.'

'Thanks, but . . . '

'So when you come here and ask me who killed somebody, what do I tell you?'

'But I need to know. Somebody may try to kill me next.'

He took his hand away and shrugged.

'All right, my life might not mean a lot in the history of the world's massacres, but I'd quite like to keep it.'

'Then why did you read the book?'

'Is reading the book a death sentence?'

He didn't answer, just turned away and started crushing some things that cracked in his pestle and mortar.

'We'll eat soon. Something nourishing for you. I've been shopping specially.'

'Never mind eating. Did you see Nicolle?'

'Yes.'

'Will she see me?'

'You are to call on her tomorrow. Ten o'clock at 14 Rue du Vigneron in the sixteenth.'

That couldn't be much more than a mile away. He'd taken his time.

'You told her I'm an academic who admires her work?'

'As you asked.'

'I think I'll see her this evening.'

'She may not be at home this evening.'

'I'll try.'

After those few hours of exhausted calm on *Rêveuse*, my nerves were on edge again, urging flight. It was more than I could do to sit there all evening wondering what Uncle Lazarus and Duncan were plotting, or what Uncle Lazarus and Nicolle were plotting, or whose the steps were on the deck.

'Then I'll keep the food for you.'

I thanked him, I think, and crossed the gangplank to the embankment. After the water shadows in the boat's hold it surprised me to find full daylight outside with the sun still high over the river and crowds strolling along watching the boats. It was the hour of the pre-dinner saunter, with the less energetic already sitting over their apéritifs at the café tables and waiters lighting candles and folding napkins on the other side of plate glass windows. The sleep and Uncle Lazarus's potion had at least given me back some energy and I used it to weave at speed through the slow-moving crowds, making direct along the river to the Trocadero steps. I hurried because I wanted to get to Nicolle before Uncle Lazarus could warn her of my premature arrival and although I'd checked that he had no telephone, I could imagine him dodging along short cuts on his way to her. I tried to keep an eye open too for anybody in the crowd who might be watching me, but in Paris an aggressive stare is the social norm, and there might have been none or dozens. As for the three men from the car park, I couldn't even be sure I'd recognise them again by daylight.

Rue du Vigneron was a little street near the Museum of Mankind, a deep canyon of Belle Epoque flats with tangerine awnings over their windows and plump pigeons absorbing the evening sun on sills decorously fluffed with geraniums. Number Fourteen was, if anything, even more elegant than the rest of them, sheltering behind a gateway of curlicued copper. The top bell had Nicolle's name beside it, but when I rang it a concierge appeared and told me madame wasn't at home to anybody in the evenings. Madame did her writing in the evenings. I was an old friend, I insisted, come all the way from England to see her, but it got me nowhere. It would probably have been easier to interrupt Shakespeare. I said, humbly, that I'd come back in the morning and asked if the top flat was madame's. Yes, she said, thawed a little by my humility. Yes, madame had the top two floors.

In the sixteenth, that meant money. It also meant a roof garden. Stepping back from the closed door and craning my neck upwards, like a devotee visiting a literary shrine, I could see trees hanging over the balcony, even smell jasmine. I noticed too that the house next door was having repairs done and that scaffolding went all the way to the top floor. For security, the builders had tied a plank along the rungs of a ladder that gave access, but they hadn't made a very thorough job of it and it was quite easy to climb by wedging my toes on either side. I found myself doing it while I was still trying to decide whether it was a good idea or not. From the first floor, the next three stages were easy, just a matter of climbing up ladders until I reached the planking at the top. From there I had a better view than I wanted down to the pavement. I looked away quickly. The trees of Nicolle's roof garden were now a few yards to my left and about four feet above my head. By one committed movement, left foot on moulding above window, step up and left elbow hooked over the parapet, I could be there. I'd launched myself on it before I realised it and only desperation stopped me thudding backwards down four storeys to the street. I clawed at the parapet, felt something give in my shoulder as I hooked an arm over, pushed with my feet and found myself head downwards in a bed of white lilies that snapped and collapsed like trees in an avalanche. I rolled over and lay there gasping, looking at a pair of bony feet in lizard skin mules. Above them a voice was saying something in French, but I disregarded it.

'Good evening,' I said. 'I believe you must be the authoress of *The Martyrdom of Valentine*.'

The feet moved back a step.

'I detest the term authoress.'

So did I. I'd only done it to annoy because I was sure in advance that there was something wrong about Nicolle. The voice was husky, as if she smoked too many cigarettes, with traces in it of both Paris and Pittsburgh.

'Are you the one Uncle Lazarus told me about? You were supposed to come tomorrow. You could have walked in at the front door then.'

I made no attempt to rise from the lilies.

'I wanted to do something to show you how much I admire your work.'

'Get up.'

She made no attempt to help me as I brushed loam and petals off myself. I made a long business of it so that I could get a good look at her, the final one in my collection of Cardell's circle.

She'd probably never been pretty, Prudence had been right about that, but she'd put a lot of work into ageing well. Her hair was still red, assisted probably, and her face white. A

152

long nose and high forehead gave her the look of Cleopatra on coins, cultivated with fingers full of rings and heavy metal bracelets up both arms. It was cool on the roof but she wore a sleeveless culotte suit in black silk, the trouser part of it floppy so that it swung round her calves when she moved. This to sit up in her roof garden on her own and write. There was a table under a vine trellis and a stand with several fountain pens and a bottle of blue-black ink.

'You work here?'

'When I'm not interrupted.'

Still in the guise of a devout fan I moved over to the table and read what was on it, upside down. It seemed to be a review, in French, of somebody else's poetry. The point was that the handwriting, small precise italics, bore no relation at all to anything I'd seen so far, certainly not to the few pages of draft Duncan had taken from Prudence's cottage.

'Uncle Lazarus said you were an academic. You don't look like one to me.'

She had a point, I suppose. Bloody tee-shirt, leather jacket, two days' stubble bristling among the bruises. It seemed unjust to me, though, after all the assumed identities, that now I'd come full circle and was claiming to be what I actually was, I didn't look the part at all. Just as the true story, or the piece of it I'd decided to give her, sounded as unlikely as anything I'd made up.

'I am. High Anglican poetry of the nineteenth century. Only your book came up instead.'

'So you came straight over to Paris to see me?'

She sounded wary, but then she had reason to be.

'Straight away. I wanted to know more about it, and you. Like why you wrote it.'

She was quite tall but I could look down on her by a few inches. The obsessed stare I gave her might have worked better if one eye hadn't been puffed up. She didn't seem impressed.

'Are you planning to write an academic paper about this, or for a magazine?'

'Which would you prefer?'

153

'Because we're keeping the magazine interviews until the filming starts.'

'With Angela Arless?'

That surprised her.

'How did you know about that?'

'It's getting around.'

She looked neither pleased nor surprised about that, but I could see a lot of thinking going on behind those grey eyes. It told me one thing, at any rate: that my interview with Angela hadn't been passed on to Nicolle yet.

She made up her mind. 'If I talk to you, anything you get is embargoed until I say so, right?'

'Right.'

'We'd better go inside.'

She gathered up her pens and paper and led the way down white-railed steps into a living room that took up most of the upper storey. White leather chairs and white goatskin rugs on a gleaming black tiled floor. Just visible to the right through an alcove the tiny white kitchen of somebody who didn't do much eating in.

'I'd offer you coffee, only it's my housekeeper's night off.'

Style. She fitted a black Balkan Sobranie into a white ivory holder, without offering one to me.

'It's going to be tedious, everybody coming to talk about the book. It was a long time ago and I've written a lot of things since then.'

'Tedious but profitable,' I said.

She ignored that. 'Shall we get on with it?'

'The woman in the book,' I said. 'Is she you?'

'She's every woman.'

'Every woman who's wanted to destroy a man, you mean?'

'That's every woman at some time.'

One of her bracelets was a cobra, beaten copper and platinum, made in flat interlocking segments so that it moved every time she raised the cigarette to her lips. It would have worked better on a plumper arm.

'Did you write it for Angela?'

'I wrote it for nobody but me.'

154

'You were young.'

'Twenty-three.'

'What year was that?'

'The summer of 1958.'

'The summer before the book was published. The summer when Prudence and one other were away in Brittany. The summer Kay was born.

'Where?'

'Here in Paris. A little upstairs room opposite L'Ile de la Cité. I'd get up in the morning just before it got light and start writing while all the rest of the city was asleep. Ten, twelve hours a day sometimes.'

It was the liveliest I'd seen her since I arrived. Her eyes shone with recollected greed, like remembering a first love affair. I could almost have been convinced.

'Typewriter or longhand?'

'Longhand. I can't work creatively on a typewriter.'

'Did you keep the manuscript?'

'I keep all my manuscripts. I'll show you later.'

She stood up, but only to go to the kitchenette, and came back carrying a vast glass plate covered with seafood.

The absent housekeeper had gone to trouble: soused mussels and cockles, crab claws and big prawns in their shells prettily arranged on a bed of crushed ice with trails of seaweed. I like seafood. When I saw it my appetite came back for the first time for days. She put it down on the table beside her chair, returned to the kitchen and came back carrying brown bread and butter, a little silver hammer for the crab claws, plate and fork. One plate and one fork.

'You'll excuse me. I never eat lunch. There's champagne in the fridge.'

A half bottle. I made sure I took in two glasses and watched while she went through the seafood like a dissection class, gouging out the last remnants from the cockle shells, stripping the prawns of their body armour until they were no more than plump pink commas in her monologue. The organic relationship between a writer and paper and ink, that was what she was talking about. Also the need for self-discipline. Also of

155

the stricter demands of poetry as compared with prose. I sat there, sipping champagne, watching the prawns disappear, getting more and more annoyed.

When the plateful was reduced to detritus and melting ice, I asked: 'Why did you let it stay anonymous until now?'

She wiped her fingers on a napkin and threw it aside. 'The sixties hadn't happened then. You know they burnt it when we tried to publish it in England?'

'I knew the Customs impounded it. Were you that worried about notoriety?'

'No, but I was worried about the rest of my work. I was beginning to understand that I was a poet, I didn't want *Valentine* hung round my neck all my life.'

'But you're going to claim it now?'

'I've got my reputation now.'

An odd idea had come to me.

'It's a bit like claiming an illegitimate child thirty years on.'

'Children change, books don't.'

'Have you ever had a child?'

She shook her head. 'Never wanted one.'

'The others, weren't they curious about what you were doing that summer?'

'What others?'

'The Cardell set.'

'I was never one of a set.'

'They thought you were. Prudence and Duncan. Uncle Lazarus and the man you called Milord.'

'Who told you that?'

'Prudence.'

'Prudence was a jealous cow.' She drawled out the word cow, straight American. I'd managed to annoy her.

'You know Prudence is dead?'

'I haven't given a thought for years whether Prudence is dead or alive.'

'She was alive until a few days ago, then she was murdered.'

She lit another cigarette.

'I dare say she'd given plenty of cause.'

'I thought Angela might have told you.'

156

'Why should Angela be interested in Prudence?'

'She went to see her just before she died.'

'Did Angela tell you that?'

'Not exactly. I deduced it.'

'Then you deduced wrongly. Angela wouldn't go within spitting distance of Prudence.'

'They had a fight, didn't they, back in Paris? You got Cardell to send Prudence away for the summer.'

'I may have done. Angela was no more than a child having a bad time, and that bitch was making it worse.'

'Did you talk to Prudence about the book?'

'Why the hell should I talk to Prudence about it? She was only Cardell's secretary, for heaven's sake. Did you break in here to talk about Prudence or talk about my work?'

'Your work. I'm just trying to get it in context.'

'Prudence isn't context. Prudence isn't anything. Shall we go downstairs?'

She got up in a whisk of black silk and I followed her, down a staircase plastered left and right with photographs of Nicolle, some at literary functions, some solo portraits. It looked as if she wasn't the only one to take her poetry seriously. I'd liked to have looked for pictures of the younger Nicolle, but she wouldn't let me linger.

'This is the manuscript room.'

For Baudelaire it might have been just about adequate. For Nicolle, it looked like narcissism run mad. Quite a big room, as large as an average dining room, with shelves and cupboards round the sides and glass-topped showcases down the middle with oiled silk blinds over them. *Juvenilia*, said the label over the bookcase closest to me. It was crammed with the sort of thing even fond mothers clear out when the kids leave home: exercise books, scrap books, piles of yellowing paper tied up with raffia. Other bookcases had book titles and dates over them and box files marked *Working Notebooks*, *First Drafts*, *Corrected Proofs*. She switched on the striplights.

'It's documenting my development as a writer.'

'What a pity Shakespeare didn't think of it.'

157

She stood there while I looked round, even let me pull things out and look at them. It was all in that same italic hand I'd seen upstairs.

'What about *Valentine*?'

There was no sign of that on any of the shelves or files. She took a key out of a drawer, unlocked a cupboard under the showcases and took out a new box file.

'Here it is.'

There was a table and chair in the corner. I sat down while she watched and lifted out a great bundle of handwritten paper. I'd been so sure she couldn't produce the manuscript, but there it was. It looked as authentic as anything I'd seen and matched perfectly Nicolle's description of how she'd written it in long bursts in one summer. The paper was thin and cheap feeling, but the italics went marching confidently on, sometimes in blue-black ink, sometimes in black, clear and precise at the beginning of each day's work, a little ragged towards the end. Here and there a word or phrase was crossed out and another written over the top in different coloured ink. Occasionally she'd strike out whole paragraphs with an impatient Z stroke.

'You didn't correct much,' I said. 'Was this a first draft?'

'There was only ever one draft. Not like poetry.'

I read the first scene in the garden, in St Paul's, then the murder on the beach. As far as I could remember, word for word as printed. I could feel her watching me all the time. When I got to the point where Valentine's friend was lying sacrificed on the beach with the blood running from him I threw myself across the floor and landed kneeling at her lizard skin mules. Clutching desperately for her right hand, I drew the hand down to me and kissed it, finger by finger, taking my time. It smelt of nicotine and seafood. Her arm went tense.

'Get up,' she said.

I got to my feet slowly, looking into her eyes.

'You,' I said, 'are a literary imposter.'

She dragged her hand away and clawed it down my cheek. I could feel the skin peeling like wallpaper. I grabbed at her

158

wrist and caught it again, then, with my left hand, drew out her clenched middle finger from her palm. It was harder than crab claws.

'But a very determined one,' I said. 'Ten, twelve hours a day.'

I made her look at the hard, ink-stained pad of calloused skin on the inside of her middle finger, half as wide as the finger itself.

'You don't get that from redrafting lyrics. You get it from copying out a whole book by hand. Somebody else's book. There was a first draft, and I've seen it. That murder scene was written quite differently in the first draft.'

'It was as I wrote it.'

I think she'd really convinced herself by then that she was the author. Copying it out had turned into an act of adoption.

'There really was a murder, only it didn't happen the way it does in the book. It was a fight over the woman that went too far. That's the way it was originally written.'

'The only murder is the one in my book.'

'There was a real murder,' I said. 'The author knew about it, but you didn't.'

'A murder in the imagination.'

'Prudence wasn't murdered in the imagination either. She had her throat cut with a pruning knife.'

She was sitting down now on the chair by her pile of manuscript, running a nail under a front tooth, probably to prise out the fragments of my skin.

'The question is, where you and Angela fit into it. Was it Angela's idea that there's money in the book now, or did you think it was a nice little touch of spice for the reputation of a fading poetess?'

'Poetess' was meant to hurt, but then so did my cheek.

'But you could neither of you risk it if the real author was likely to turn up and claim it, which means either the author had to be in a position where he or she was never likely to claim it, or the author had to be safely dead. Which was it?'

She said nothing, just sat there looking at me like a praying mantis sizing up a mate.

'Did you tell Angela it might be a good idea to go along and delete Prudence?'

I sketched on the air her Z crossing-out sign.

'You're talking nonsense and you know it. Has somebody put you up to this?'

'No one.'

She considered me for a while, then stood up.

'I've got something to show you. Come on.'

I followed her across a hallway through a door on the opposite side. Her bedroom, as white as the inside of an apple. Double bed with duvet cover in white linen, two Doric pillars at the head of it, walls padded in fine white kidskin. The only touch of colour was the painting, more than lifesize, over her bed between the pillars. It was the woman from the book, in her garden, and I couldn't help giving a gasp when I looked at it because she was so much as I imagined her, so like Kay. She smiled when she heard it.

'Duncan's,' I said.

I'd seen the Circe painting of Angela. His style didn't seem to have changed much in thirty years.

'Yes. It's one of a series. He was obsessed with the book, like you are.'

'Where are the others?'

'I don't know. He wanted to give them all to me, but I'd only take this one. Now do you believe me about the book?'

'No.'

I'd thought that she'd brought me in there to show me the painting. I stood there, staring at it, not thinking about what she was doing. A mistake. When I looked at her she was still there as before, smile included, but with one important difference. She was holding a small pistol and pointing it at me.

I think from its flat shape it was probably a Walther, but I've never been technically minded about guns. Up to then they hadn't played a large part in my life and I stared from the gun to her face and back again, hoping there was some mistake.

160

'Hey,' I said. 'You can't go round rubbing out visiting academics.'

'You're not an academic.'

'That's not a capital offence.'

I looked round, wondering whether to make a dash for the door. It struck me that the white leather padding was probably effective sound-proofing.

'It would make a terrible mess in here. Your housekeeper wouldn't like it.'

I was sweating and she could smell it. She enjoyed it.

'I'm not going to hurt you. I'm just doing what I should have done when you first arrived: showing you off the premises.'

'You only had to ask.'

I backed towards the door and she followed, keeping exactly the same distance between us, holding the gun steady.

'I always keep a gun by my bed,' she said. 'Paris is a dangerous place for a woman living alone.'

'It's not so good for a man either.'

We arrived in the hall and I got my hand on the front door knob.

'I'll say goodnight then. Thank you for your hospitality.'

'Not that way,' she said. 'You go out the same way as you came in.'

I thought of the gap between parapet and scaffolding and the sense of relief I'd been feeling ebbed away again.

'It'll be worse going down.'

'You should have thought of that before you came up.'

She indicated with the gun that I should go upstairs to the living room. There was still some champagne in my glass. I stopped and drank it.

'You know the Buddhist fable about the man and the grapes? Make a good poem.'

'It would make a very hackneyed poem. Now move.'

Perhaps she was better than I'd thought. We went single file up the steps to the roof garden. It was just getting dusk and the scent of jasmine was swamping the place. She gestured with the gun towards the smashed lilies and the parapet wall.

'Try not to do any more damage when you go.'

161

I'd got it worked out by then. She expected me to fall. And if I did, especially the way I was looking, that would be one more desperado getting his just deserts in an attempt to pillage the sixteenth arrondissement. It was even neater than she knew, because there'd be no identification on my body. If I didn't fall, still no problem. I was hardly in a position to report her for pulling guns. Nicolle couldn't lose, No use arguing. I got astride the parapet.

'I hope you and Angela are going to invite me to the première.'

I was light-headed from the champagne, but that was what I'd intended. Sober I hadn't a chance. The last sight I had of her as I lowered myself down until my feet were resting on the ridge above the window showed her standing there looking politely interested, gun still at the ready. I drew my head in quickly. If she'd shot me then it would have been legitimately alarmed householder taking extreme measures with intruder. In the sixteenth, probably not all that extreme either.

It was as bad as I'd imagined getting back to the scaffolding. Cars went along the canyon underneath, making me look down when I didn't want to. I dared not look up in case she was leaning over the parapet. I inched along, crushed against the wall, past caring about my ribs. When I got my feet on the scaffolding planks I was shaking so much I had to sit down and do some of Uncle Lazarus's breathing exercises before I could tackle the ladders. As I slid down the plank over the last one, down to the pavement, all that was left in my mind was finding the nearest café for a small coffee and a large brandy. It had to wait.

'Somebody wants to see you,' said a voice in my ear just as my toe was touching ground. A gravel voice that had absorbed a lot of cigarette smoke, waiting in a lot of dark car parks. Even before I saw his face I knew who it would be and my whole body curled up and shrank. The other two were there as well, waiting in the shadow of the scaffolding. One walked beside me, the other two just behind, as we went down the street.

Chapter Sixteen

There was a car with French numberplates parked just round the corner. The thick-set man with the gravel voice drove, leaving me sandwiched in the back between the other two. We screeched round a couple of roundabouts, but no faster than most law-abiding Parisians, and it was no surprise to me when, a few minutes later, the headlights showed trees on either side of the road, Bois de Boulogne. Typical of the French to have their place for dumping unwanted things so conveniently close to the city centre. In London, at least, I'd have got a ride as far out as Epping Forest. Gravel voice parked the car in a lay-by, opened the back door and the other two herded me out. Very cautious about it they were too. My right-hand partner got out first and stood only a few inches from the door, while left-hand partner shoved me towards him. It didn't occur to me to wonder if they had guns. I'd seen what they could do without them.

'I kept quiet at first and went along passively. Gravel voice was in front, the others one on either side of me as they'd been in the car. They weren't quite holding on to me, but at every step the shoulder of one or other of them brushed against mine. We had to go single file after a while to pass through some bushes. No help there, with number two treading on my heels and number three right behind him, but I worked out that there had to be a split second of confusion when we formed up as the path got wider again. As far as that went, I was right. Number one waited in front, looking back at us. Number two stepped up on my left. Before number three could get into place I dived off to the right, running like mad in the direction of the orange glow that marked the centre of Paris. Useless. Number two jumped like a frog. Number three was a little slower, but not much. From then on they got a firm grip on my arms and kept it.

It occured to me later to wonder why I hadn't yelled, on the chance at least that there were other people around in the trees. It was as if the violence was just above my head somewhere, like an unstable rock roof, and raising my voice would have brought it crashing down. Even when I started talking it was in a whisper, just loud enough to carry to number one up ahead.

'All right. I know you told me to keep out of it, but I did, didn't I? I even left the country, for heaven's sake.'

No answer.

'I'm just paying social calls on a few friends in Paris. It's got nothing to do with the other business.'

'No answer.'

'Who are you supposed to be working for anyway?'

I hadn't expected an answer to that. I suppose even if I had shouted it wouldn't have made any difference. The habitués of the Bois after dark are mostly transvestite prostitutes and their clients, far too occupied with their own affairs to worry about a simple little business like a murder going on next door.

After another ten minutes or so of walking the moon was beginning to come up and I recognised, from the visit with Andrea, that we were in the part of the Bois set out as a running track for the more energetic Parisians. Every few hundred yards or so there are rustic parallel bars and climbing frames, for exercises in between the bursts of jogging. By day it had looked depressingly healthy. At night, with the three toughs in attendance, it looked far from healthy but even more depressing. The man in front came to a halt by a climbing frame in a clearing and signed to the others to stop. At that point I made another, more desperate attempt to break away, kicking shins, dragging one arm loose and getting a grip on the ear of the one on my left, but all it got me was a clump on the side of the head that left me sick and giddy. I was hardly resisting at all when they dragged me to the climbing frame and tied me to it by the wrists. Then they lit cigarettes

164

and waited, facing away from me and into the trees, for all the world as if I were nothing to do with them.

Five or ten minutes passed. I could hear cars in the mid distance on one of the roads through the woods. People coming from dinners with friends, people going to their own beds or other people's beds. My heart was thumping so hard I could feel it vibrating through the wooden bars against my back. I wondered what we were waiting for. When it came, it was no more than a pinpoint of light, the sort of torch careful types carry in their overcoat pockets in case they lose their own keyhole. The light dithered around in the darkness.

'We're over here,' the first man said.

Steps crunched on last winter's dried leaves and the pinpoint came towards us. The figure behind it was wearing dark trousers and jacket, so the first thing I saw was a white face, then long dark hair, not falling over her shoulders this time, but caught up in a bundle at the back of her head. It made her face look colder.

She stood surveying me, playing the needle of light over my face so that I had to screw up my eyes and turn my head aside. Her expression stayed in my mind, even when my eyes were closed: lips a little apart, like a mask, and a look in her eyes of fear and excitement.

'Where did you find him?'

I opened my eyes and found she was talking to the first man.

'Where we expected.'

She switched off the torch so that, under the moon, there were two white faces looking at me, plus two dark backs of the guards looking outwards to the trees. The first man had come to stand close to her, practically touching her, and I noticed she took a step to one side.

'You broke your promise,' she said. 'You've been finding out things about me without telling me.'

'No.'

The air was cold against my face and pinioned hands, but I could feel sweat breaking out all over, great drops of it running down my forehead.

165

'I don't like people knowing more about myself than I do. You wouldn't like it.'

The first sentence was a threat that made me sweat and shiver at the same time, the second the pathetic appeal of a self-justifying schoolgirl. It was the combination of the two of them that scared me, plus the way the man was looking at me, as if working out where to plant the first punch.

'I don't . . . or not much anyway. Nothing that makes sense.'

My voice trickled away into the silence. A match cracked and flared as one of the guards lit a cigarette.

'Don't let them start on me again.'

'The ring,' she said. 'What did he tell you about the ring?'

Already Lord Talisby in his library seemed a long time away.

'It had been in his family. He wanted to buy it, but I wouldn't sell.'

'Where is it?'

'Still in my pocket, I suppose.'

'Which pocket?'

I couldn't remember. She climbed up beside me, her feet on the bottom rung of the climbing frame, and searched me, first my jacket pockets with her long fingers prodding my hip bone, then the front pockets of my jeans. When she let her hand travel slowly across my stomach, my cock strained against the fabric. I knew she must have felt it and her face was close enough for me to see her lips widening a little and her breath coming faster. She found the ring in the second pocket and juggled it onto her middle finger, the other hand still holding on to the climbing frame. I remembered the last hand that wore it was Prudence's, dead. Or so she said.

In spite of having the ring she didn't get down but balanced there, watching my face from a few inches away. The finger with the ring on it crossed my cheek quite softly, tracing the scratch Nicolle had left.

'That's not one of yours. Jealous?'

She frowned. I wondered why, when she'd watched the three thugs doing much worse, this scratch should bother her. She looked up at my wrists and ran her fingers round the left one, above and below the rope.

'Does it hurt?'

I said nothing, not wanting to encourage her. Her face had the unfeeling curiosity of a child experimenting.

'They'd kill you if I told them to,' she said, very quietly, and yet I had a feeling she was experimenting with that idea too.

'Then you'd never know what I've found out about you, would you?'

It was all I had to barter, my store of scraps, but it was in my mind that if I could spin it out long enough she'd make them let me stay alive through the short night, till daylight brought the early joggers padding over the grass to the rescue.

'Sit down,' I said. 'Get comfortable. There's a long way to go.'

To my surprise, she did exactly that, her back against the climbing frame and her knees drawn up, face turned towards me, like a schoolgirl in a gym. The first man stayed exactly where he was, looking alternately down at her and up at me, but I sensed I'd got him off balance. A story-telling session wasn't what he'd expected. As for the other two, they stayed facing outwards, giving no sign of interest in what was going on behind them.

'Once upon a time, twenty-nine summers ago, a little girl was born in a little house near the great big Atlantic sea.'

'Me?'

'You. A very expensive little girl she was, too. Just to get a doctor to come and let her into the world, a man in Paris had to sell a very precious sapphire.'

'My father? Was he . . . ?'

'Be a good girl. Don't ask questions, just listen and you'll hear all in good time.'

I might be imagining it, but it seemed to me that the sound of cars crossing the Bois was dying down, as if the city were settling into the deepest part of the night. From somewhere not far off I heard a high-pitched giggle, soon cut off, of tranny with client. No good calling to them for help. Even if they came, they'd just think everybody to his

167

tastes. I stood on tiptoe to take some of the strain off my wrists and went on.

'A very expensive little girl, and a very unusual little girl, even before she was born. You see this little girl' – I drew the words out – 'this little girl had one, two, three mothers.'

There was a sound of protest from her that made the guards turn round and the first man took a threatening step towards me before he realised I hadn't moved.

'Fathers,' she said. 'Not mothers, it's my father.'

There was panic in her voice. The ice I was treading on was very thin.

'Listen. Just listen to the end of the story.'

Except that it still hadn't got an end. The man was looking as if his interest in fairy tales was near its limit.

'You'll have to keep him under control,' I said. 'If he knocks out any more teeth I shan't be able to talk anyway.'

She mumbled to him that it was all right and he took half a step back. I felt his eyes on my ribcage and thought it was probably knives rather than punches he had in mind.

'You might ask him to untie me,' I said. 'I could tell you a lot more easily if I were sitting beside you.'

'No,' said the man.

She didn't argue with him, just asked me again in that panicked voice what I meant about three mothers.

'Mother number one was very young and very beautiful. Long chestnut hair she had, and long white legs.' I thought of Angela Arless in Duncan's studio. 'Everybody loved her and she loved everybody and when she got drunk she'd dance on café tables and cause fights and everybody loved her even more. Then, that summer twenty-nine years ago, she went to a wise old man who was living on a boat, and she said to this wise old man: "Help me, I'm expecting a baby."'

Kay drew in her breath. She was looking up at me hungrily, so close to me now that her shoulder was pressing against my left calf.

'The baby was me? But Prudence . . . '

I let her wait, drawing it out for five heartbeats, wondering how many heartbeats till morning.

'But the wise old man thinks the baby wasn't you.'

'Who is this man? What does he know about me?'

'The wise old man's got a good reason for thinking the baby wasn't you. He says the beautiful girl with the long white legs whom everybody loved asked him to go with her when she walked off the boat and all through the streets until she came to the house of . . . ' I was deliberately dropping my voice, making her crane her neck to hear me. ' . . . to the house of the abortionist.'

She recoiled as if I'd kicked her, crouched against the bars in foetal posture.

'No. Why are you telling me this? Why are you telling me?'

'The question is, was the wise old man telling the truth? Are wise old men allowed not to tell the truth?'

I waited till that sunk in, then added in my ordinary voice: 'And do you know an odd thing? That girl with the long chestnut hair went to Prudence's house the day before Prudence was killed. Did you know that?'

She shook her head, so that a swathe of hair flopped down, but I had the idea the man had suddenly started concentrating. That wasn't what I wanted. I went back to my fairy-tale voice.

'Number one's the beautiful mother. Number two's the wicked mother. She's got red hair and a big beaky nose and a nasty little pistol. She writes lots of poetry and nobody likes her very much. She likes one person very much though – and that person's mother number one, the beautiful mother. The wicked mother would do anything for her, but she doesn't like men at all.'

'Are we going to be here all night?'

The question came suddenly from the guard who'd lit the cigarette, turning round to the first man. Kay jumped up and stood alongside me, facing them.

'You stay here as long as I say so. You know that.'

Because I was so close to her, touching her, and because I was scared myself, I could feel the fear running through her body. But the voice was strong and authoritative, a world away from the girl who'd been crouching and listening to me. For a

169

few seconds, until the man with the cigarette turned his face away, mumbling, it was the two of us against the three of them. And yet, not long ago, she'd said they'd kill me if she told them to.

She settled back down and that crisis was over, but it was still deep night and the big man was taking an interest.

'If this woman's a dyke, how come she's supposed to be her mother?'

'I suppose anyone can experiment. And if she isn't Kay's mother, there's one thing that needs explaining.'

'What?' Kay's voice, soft again.

'Why there's a big painting of a woman who looks exactly like you hanging over her bed.'

It was cheating. I didn't tell her about the illustrations for the book, but why should I be the only one playing fair?

'A woman in a garden,' I said. 'As like you as anyone can be. Only the date on the picture is twenty-nine years ago – the year you were born.'

Kay said nothing, but the tension from the guard's question still hadn't gone out of her.

'A very remarkable little girl, wasn't she?' I said. 'The wise old man went to her abortion, but she's still here. An artist painted her portrait as a grown woman several months before she was born. And somebody – one of her mothers probably – put her in a book before she even existed.'

She was shivering, head bent, hair disordered. I felt a sharp pain in my wrists and realised that what I wanted to do was put my arms round her to keep her warm. I soon stopped that.

'You can't be cold,' I said. 'You don't exist, so how can you be cold?'

The big man said, in his gravelly voice: 'What about the other mother?'

I wished I knew what direction I was facing. There was no sign that I could see of daylight, only the orange glow from Paris.

'All right,' I said. 'Mother number three. The real mother. Strong and loyal. Face like a bull pup, hard-working brown hands. Slaving away in her garden, working all hours to bring

170

up her beautiful little daughter with her big brown eyes and her long black hair, who doesn't look in the least like a bull pup, but then daughters don't always take after their mothers, do they?'

I was talking at the big man now, but that was a mistake. It was Kay I had to hold, and she was looking up at me with signs of impatience in her face.

'But if she's my real mother, why did you . . . ?'

'A real mother. The sort who'd give her heart's blood for her daughter. You remember that, her heart's blood? The way it ran over the floor? You must have had to kneel in it when you took that ring off her finger.'

'My father's ring,' she said.

She held it close to her cheek, fist clenched.

'We'll come to that later. But she didn't do badly by you, did she, poor Prudence? Seeing that she was never your mother at all.' I waited two heartbeats before adding: 'Or so the wise old man says.'

'Of course she's my mother. Why would she have brought me up?'

Yet Kay, so determined to find her father, semed more annoyed than distressed at having a mother taken from her.

'And yet, she told the old man she could never have children.'

'Who is this old man you keep talking about?'

The question came from gravel voice, in tones more impatient than I wanted to hear.

I said to Kay: 'Didn't it strike you sometimes that Prudence wasn't your mother? You don't look like her. You didn't even like her much, did you?'

'I didn't kill her.' It came from her in a wail. 'You can't make out I killed her.'

'I'm not saying that. I'm not accusing you of anything. I'm just pointing out that, out of three available mothers, one was infertile, one was lesbian and one was aborted.'

'But the ring. Why was she wearing his ring?'

Still wailing, but I had to admit that her mind seemed to be working. Either that, or it had got slotted onto the tramlines

171

of the Talisby family and couldn't be jolted off them. Still, if that was what the customer wanted, I was in no position to refuse.

'Interesting, isn't it? For a start, he prefers men. At least, he did in Paris that year you were born. So why does arrogant young Cambridge homo give poor ugly secretary the family ring?'

It was the big man who answered, not Kay.

'Perhaps he was hard up and sold it to her.'

'No, I don't think so. They all thought Milord was rich. Your turn, Kay.'

It was as dark as ever and the moon was going down. She said nothing and I couldn't see her face.

'Blackmail. Have you thought of that, Kay? Do you think Prudence would go in for a spot of gentle blackmail? Quite profitable, it would be, now he's in the government.'

The guard I was beginning to think of as the awkward one turned round and asked if they were all supposed to stay there till they turned into bloody statues. He added that it would be light in a couple of hours. Too long, too long. I willed her to answer, to argue.

'Have you thought of that, Kay?'

'I . . . I don't know. I don't care. I'm not interested in Prudence. I want to know who my father was, that's why I'm paying you.'

'But I am interested in Prudence. I'm interested in who killed her, and so should you be. Because back in England the police have got descriptions out on both of us.'

She disregarded it, didn't react at all. You'd have thought being hunted by the police was a fact of normal life for her.

'You do realise we're the two prime suspects, don't you? At least, two of the three prime suspects.'

'Who's the other one, then?' Gravel voice again. A bit above your usual class of hired thug, I was beginning to suspect.

'Oh him,' I tried to sound as casual as I could, shivering with cold as well as fear now, arms aching. 'Oh him. One of her possible fathers, that's who.'

172

'Who is he? Who is he?'

That had brought her to life anyway. She was back with one foot on the climbing frame and I could see her face again, gaping and greedy.

'Just a simple painter. Name of Duncan McMahon.'

'Where is he?'

'You weren't far away from him the night Prudence was murdered, if you'd known it. He was there just after I'd found her body.'

'Where is he?'

'In Brum. Running a hostel for distressed rent boys. He's homosexual too, as it happens. Your pedigree does sound a little problematic, doesn't it? Are you quite sure you exist?'

'She exists,' said gravel voice. 'She exists.'

I wondered whether it was worth starting a symposium on the logical criteria of existence, but I didn't think I'd get a quorum.

'But then I don't suppose he was above a bit of experimenting either, and there'd have been enough opportunity. Mother Angela still walks round his studio with no clothes on. Mother Nicolle – that's the wicked one – she's still got the picture he painted, and Mother Prudence thought he was the most beautiful man she'd ever seen.'

'What's he like now?' Her voice wasn't much more than a whisper in my ear.

'A bit worn, but still good looking. Quite like you.'

'And the book? Did he write the book?'

'That's the problem. I don't think he did. But he knows something about it. They all know something about it.'

'I want to see him,' she said. 'I want you to take me to him.'

'Two little problems there, Kay. One, if we go back to England, one or both of us will be arrested for killing Prudence. Two, your little friends threw me out of England and now they don't seem to think Paris is far enough. A little consistency would help.'

'He's not going back to England until he's told to,' gravel voice said.

Kay got down and moved away from me, shoulders hunched.

173

'Isn't she the one giving the orders, then?'

'It doesn't matter who's giving the orders. You were told to keep out of it, right out. You're still going around asking questions.'

But there were only two people in Paris who knew that: Uncle Lazarus and Nicolle.

'Literary research. It's part of my job.'

'You were told to keep out.'

He hadn't given orders to the other two, but his voice had changed in a way that made them turn round and move in towards me. When they started walking they were no more than lumps of darkness, but there was something about the way they moved that set my heart pounding and stripped away the pathetic sense of security I'd had while they were letting me talk. I heard my own voice blabbing that I hadn't meant to, that I'd done nothing, that I'd go away, right away, if only they'd tell me where. All the time she kept her back turned and her shoulders hunched, outside the semicircle of the three men closing in on me. The smallest of the three was asymmetrical. He had an arm inside his jacket. A knife, I thought, not a gun. Even in the Bois somebody might react to a gunshot. This way, in the morning, some health freak would find a knifed body tied to climbing frame. Mafia war, drug smuggler or some such. When description got back to England the police would compare it with man wanted for the Prudence murder inquiries and everyone would think he got what was coming to him.

Then I remembered there'd be no description; that, from the time I'd found Prudence's body, I'd been divested, stage by stage, by other people's actions or my own, of everything that made up my identity. The clothes I was sweating into weren't my clothes. My passport, even if they left it on my body, wasn't my passport. Since the book came to me I'd given myself so many identities, so many occupations, that no two consecutive people knew me as the same person. The question I'd thrown at Kay to make her speak, 'Are you quite sure you exist?', came sliding back at me and the fear I felt, even more than of the knife the smallest man might be holding under his coat, was of this scattering of existence that already felt like death. There was only one thing that could bring it together again, the thing that had scattered me in the first place, brought me there and turned away from me. I stopped babbling at the men and spoke to her back, hearing my voice quite calm.

'Look at me. You might at least look at me.'

I thought her shoulders moved.

'You've done it, haven't you, just like you did in the book. Taken my identity. Taken everything. At least tell me why.'

And yet, in the book I remembered, she'd never told him why and he hadn't asked. The three of them had stopped, a yard or so away. The smallest one still had a hand under his jacket. She'd said something and they were stopping to listen. It took a while for it to get to me.

'I'm not in the book.'

'Written the summer you were born. Your face in the picture before you even had a face.'

'No,' she said. 'No.'

She'd turned round at least. I could see her white face. More than anything, I wanted her to come towards me, to touch me.

'Do it yourself then, if you want to. Don't leave it to them.'

'No.'

But this time it was to the big man, not to me. She stepped forward, into the semicircle, stood there and screamed at him, 'No!'

After her scream it was very quiet. I could hear the traffic noise again, late cars going home or early cars coming in.

'I need him,' she said. 'The old man talks to him.'

What surprised me was that gravel voice listened to her. It would have been easy for just one of them to keep her quiet while the others attended to me, but there was no move to do that. She was still scared of him, I could see that, but she seemed certain he'd do as she asked.

'I want to see the old man.'

'Now?' gravel voice protested.

175

'Now.'

The smallest one had to climb up and untie me. I told him to be careful not to drop his knife.

They needed no directing to *Rêveuse*, which didn't surprise me. I'd been almost sure that the footsteps I'd heard retreating the day before had been Kay's, and if the toughs hadn't been trailing me round Paris, how had they known to wait for me under the scaffolding at Nicolle's? It was night still, but with the beginnings of lightness in the sky, when we parked the car under a plane tree on the embankment. I was in the back seat, of course, with a tough on each side, gravel voice in the driving seat with Kay beside him. I staged a protest before I got out.

'He's an old man. He'll probably die of shock if we all rush in on him. Anyway, he won't talk to her if you're all there.'

It was the best I could do. I knew I shouldn't be bringing Uncle Lazarus into this, but couldn't see an alternative that didn't involve a knife in the ribs. In the end they agreed that they'd wait in the deck-house while Kay and I went below. When we got out of the car and went down the steps to the quay my legs were shaking and my head swimming so that I could hardly stand up. The small man helped me quite kindly down the steps and up the gangplank. I got the three of them settled in the deck-house and looked at Kay properly for the first time since she'd stopped them killing me in the Bois. She had on her greedy look again, lips apart. I grabbed her and forced my lips against hers, my tongue into her open mouth and to my surprise and, I think, hers, she responded, clinging to me, pressing her whole body against me, with the three of them watching us. Then, just as suddenly, she moved away, wiping her lips with her sleeve like a workman after the first gulp of drink.

'The old man,' she said.

'The old man.'

I led the way down the steps.

Chapter Seventeen

We walked down into a sea of shadows and I heard her catch her breath when she saw the tidemarks of detritus his waves of refugees had left. The stacks of books and papers and pictures that dominated even in the daylight had taken over completely now, in the wavering yellow light of one oil lamp.

'Who is he?'

'He's known everybody in trouble for fifty years past. He knew your father and your mother – whoever they were.'

I couldn't find him at first. In his kitchen cubbyhole, the pestle lay neatly alongside the mortar with a few curled dried leaves inside it. I found another oil lamp there and lit it while she watched, fumbling because the circulation hadn't come back into my hands properly.

'Where is he?'

I tried not to let the fear in her voice get to me, carried the lamp carefully along the cabin between stacks of paper. He was there in the bows, on a little seat I hadn't noticed before. His eyes were wide open and he didn't blink when the light fell on them. When he spoke I nearly dropped the lamp.

'How is Nicolle?' he said.

'Oh, fine. She tried to kill me.'

He nodded as if that was only to be expected.

'She's taken up forgery. Or was that always a hobby?'

He didn't answer. Either he couldn't see Kay behind me, with the light dazzling him, or he was choosing not to notice her.

'I've brought somebody to see you.'

I grabbed her cold hand and made her stand beside me, holding the lamp so that he could see her face. It did something I hadn't thought possible: changed his expression. Until then, nothing I'd said or done had been able to shift that look of tired tolerance, as if whatever happened was just another one for the string of universal worry beads. It had been on his face when I arrived, when I told him about Prudence's death. But now, seeing Kay, his eyes closed and he made a little 'Tch, Tch' sound with his tongue, like somebody being told bad news.

'What is it?' she said. 'What's up?'

'What do you want?' he asked her. His voice was non-committal to the point of being cold.

'I want to know who my father is.'

'Beware of what you want.'

'Why?'

'Because what you want is what you get.'

He'd been rearranging the stack of pictures. When I was in the bows a few hours before they'd all been turned face towards the wall. Now there was one beside him turned outwards, a big canvas taller than he'd be if he stood up, but in the dim light I couldn't see what it was. As he sat there, and he and Kay stared at each other without speaking, it seemed to me that he was growing smaller and the shadowy picture bigger, but I still couldn't make it out.

She broke the silence. 'Why are you scared of me?'

Silly question, seeing she had three toughs on a doubtful leash upstairs. I thought that, somehow, their cooped-up violence had filtered down to him so that he was expecting trouble as we walked in, had scuttled to the far end of his boat to avoid it. He didn't answer, but stood up and took the lamp from my hand, holding it so close to her face that she must have felt the warmth from it. Then he sighed a long sigh.

'Yes.'

He crouched down in front of the picture, letting the light play on it, and when she saw what it was she screamed so loudly I was afraid it would bring the three of them down, or perhaps it only sounded loud because Uncle Lazarus was quiet. I couldn't blame her. The picture in Nicolle's bedroom had much the same effect on me, and it wasn't even my face. Also, in Nicolle's picture there was no blood.

In this one, when the light fell on it, blood was the first thing I saw, running into pools at the bottom of the picture, pushing out towards you so that your first reaction was to step back in case it got on your shoes, very much like Prudence's blood when I'd found her in the cottage. After that, I saw the knees, a man nude and kneeling with his legs spread out and, in between them, another man with darker skin, head flopped sideways and eyes closed. The streams of blood were running from his ribs on the left side. The kneeling man had his left arm across the other man's chest, right arm raised. I thought at first he was pleading for help or vengeance for his friend, then I saw the right hand had a stubby little knife in it. A woman with Kay's face was standing watching them, but though it had made Kay scream it came as no shock to me. What I was looking at, when I'd got used to the blood, was the face of the man holding the knife. A handsome face, large-nosed and bearded – a face that looked very much like a younger version of the Duncan I'd met.

I said to Uncle Lazarus: 'It's his picture. He painted himself?'

Uncle Lazarus nodded, not taking his eyes off Kay. After the scream she'd frozen, staring at the woman in the picture.

'It's the murder from the book.'

Another nod. But I knew it wasn't the murder scene from the book as published. It was much closer to the draft in the unknown hand that Duncan must have stolen from Prudence's desk, where the two men are goaded by the woman into fighting and one of them dies accidentally.

'Who's the man?'

I laid a fingertip on the ribs of the dying man. The feel of the oil paint was harsh and clotted.

'An Arab boy, in Morocco.'

'When did Duncan go there?'

'The spring of that same year. March.'

He didn't need to explain he meant the summer of the book.

'I don't understand.'

179

A desperate whisper from Kay. It surprised me that Uncle Lazarus, who'd been so charitable to everyone else, made no move to help her, then I looked at the face of the woman in the picture and understood. I cleared a space for her to sit, on a pile of books, and put my arm round her shoulders.

'In the book, the woman makes him kill his best friend. I thought from the start it was something that really happened. That's why Prudence was murdered.'

'But the woman . . . ?'

'I don't understand that yet, either. Who's the woman, Uncle Lazarus?'

He shook his head: 'There was no woman.'

I moved the oil lamp to show his face and the picture went back into shadows. He was staring straight ahead. Now that I'd got Kay under my arm, it was apparently safe for him to look away from her.

'Of course there was a woman. The only question is, what woman? I don't suppose Duncan went off on his own to Morocco. Did the whole gang go with him?

'No.'

'But some of them?'

'One.'

'Which one?'

No answer.

'Come one. Which one of them?'

I let go of Kay and crouched beside him, staring up at him.

'Does it matter any more? It's a long time ago. A lot has happened.'

'It's still happening. Prudence is dead and I'm probably suspected of murdering her. Nicolle tried to kill me and there are three thugs with knives waiting upstairs. It's still going on.'

I just stopped myself shaking him. He'd been good to me. I made myself wait for the answer, and when it came I thought his mind had gone wandering off.

'What happens,' he said, 'if somebody gives you a . . . what do you call it . . . a dud coin?'

'I suppose I pass it on to somebody else as soon as possible.'

180

'And it stays a dud coin until the day it gets passed to a man who really needs the money and can't pass it on to anybody.'

'What's the alternative?'

'You don't pass it on. You say "dud coin" and throw it away.'

'Supposing you can't afford to?'

He shrugged.

'Are you saying that's what Duncan did? That he kept quiet for somebody else?'

Silence. I could hear feet shifting in the deck-house upstairs. I suppose he could hear it too.

'But it didn't work, did it? It's still in circulation, or else Prudence wouldn't be dead and Nicolle wouldn't be telling lies and . . . '

I waved towards Kay. She was sitting there on the books, head bent.

'So who went with him to Morocco? Prudence?'

He shook his head.

'Angela?'

Another shake.

'Nicolle?'

'No, not Nicolle.'

'Who then?'

The light was changing, the first pale water reflections coming through the portholes and the oil lamp burning acid yellow. I had to lean forward to catch the few words when he spoke them at last.

'The one they called Milord.'

'Talisby?'

He nodded. 'Milord had the money. He wanted to go, but not on his own.'

'So Duncan and Milord went off to Morocco, did they. And what did Duncan tell you when he got back?'

His eyes went all round the boat, as if looking for somewhere to escape.

'It's no good,' I said. 'Those three upstairs won't let you out until she says so. And she wants to know, don't you?'

181

She looked up, her face almost ugly with strain and weariness. Her hair had fallen down from its knot and was hanging down her neck, heavy as oil paint.

'I want to know about the woman.'

'All in good time. What did Duncan tell you?'

He was on the edge of telling me.

'It's all going to come out now anyway. If you tell me, I might be able to help him.' And me, I thought. And us. 'If not, one of us is going to get arrested for killing Prudence, and that will be it.'

It took him a while to get started even, and he kept pausing, looking for words, his idiomatic English deteriorating under the strain. We got the picture though. April, and the plane trees just in leaf on the embankment above a younger and whiter *Rêveuse*. Cardell and Prudence and the rest of them gossiping over their wine in the pavement cafés, laughing about Duncan's abduction to Morocco by the rich Milord and about what Milord's oh so correct fiancée would say about it. Then, late one night, Duncan's return to *Rêveuse* alone, drunk and haggard. Uncle Lazarus had sat him down, much as he'd sat me down, brewed soothing potions, waited. By daylight, Duncan had told him the story.

'Just a young boy, seventeen, eighteen perhaps. Called him Ahmed. Never even knew his proper name. Jealousy, of course. All the boys in Morocco, but jealousy over this one.'

'So Ahmed preferred Milord's money and Duncan killed him. Is that it?'

A barge chugged past, rocking us.

'Yes, probably.'

'Probably? But I thought you said he told you— '

'That there'd been a fight, through jealousy, and the boy was dead. I didn't need to ask him more than that.'

'But what were you and he talking about?'

He stared at me, looking sorrowful that I didn't understand.

'About what he should do next. He thought he should go back to Morocco. Confess. They'd got out, you see, before it was discovered. And even when it was . . . there were a lot of Ahmeds in Morocco in those days.'

'You advised him not to.'

'I told him there were other ways.'

And Duncan had found one of them. I thought of the gaunt house in Birmingham, the paintings in the games room for kids throwing darts.

'But the woman?'

I was surprised when Kay spoke. I didn't know how much she'd been following. As he showed no sign of replying to her, I put the question again.

'The woman in the picture. Didn't one of the girls go with them?'

'No.'

'Then who's the woman in the picture?'

He looked away from us, straight down the boat at the light ripples shifting over stacks of papers, books, ancient haversacks and abandoned suitcases.

'She's never existed,' he said.

A little cry from Kay. Tough to be told you don't exist, twice over by different people between sunset and sunrise.

'Of course she exists. She's in the painting. She's in the book. She's . . . ' I gestured at Kay, not being quite able to say she's here. He wouldn't look at her.

'She's, what do you call it . . . an allegory.'

'An allegory of what?'

'Of evil. Of what made him do it.'

'But why didn't he paint Milord there? It must have been Milord watching, if anyone was watching.'

'I don't know.'

I took Kay by the arm and got her to stand up, walked her in front of him so that he had to look at her or screw his head away.

'She's flesh and blood. Somebody gave birth to her, that year. Prudence was there. She wrote to you to sell another sapphire for the doctor's bills. But you say Prudence couldn't have children.'

Now that I'd made him look at her again he seemed hypnotised, couldn't take his eyes away. She'd changed too. She'd been inert, boneless, when I dragged her in front of him.

183

Now there was tension in her, all of it concentrated on willing him to answer. I thought again of the three men upstairs and was scared for him and all of us.

'I don't know.'

'You must know,' I said. 'You must have wondered.'

'I don't wonder. I hear things people choose to tell me, that's all.'

'Nobody chose to tell you about the book? Nobody chose to tell you about her?'

'Nobody.'

He managed to close his eyes and started breathing slowly and deeply, trying to blot us out by going into a trance, I think.

'What happens now?' I asked. They were her toughs. She had the initiative.

'I want to see him – the man who painted the picture.'

'You can't. He's in England, and if we go back we'll be arrested. I want to see Lord Talisby again too, but the same applies.'

'The police needn't recognise us. I'll cut my hair off.' She actually wound a plump twist of it round her hand and was looking for a knife.

'You'll go without me, then. Your three little friends told me to keep out of it, remember?'

I touched a bruise under the stubble to remind her. She looked as if it had gone from her mind entirely.

'They'll follow you,' she said. 'You can go anywhere you like, and I can go back.'

That took my breath away, the idea that I should become permanently one of the world's wanderers with those three in tow. But the more I thought about it, the more it puzzled me. Were they taking her orders or was she taking theirs?

'Who's paying for this?' I asked.

She misunderstood the question. 'I'll give you money. Plenty of money.'

I'd started trying to explain to her that it wasn't the point when we heard a sudden clamour upstairs. First gravel voice, calling out to somebody on shore, then at least two lots of steps on the gangplank. Gravel voice again, saying in English that it was private property, then a torrent of French I couldn't keep up with, and my name disconcertingly in the middle of it.

'What's he saying?' I asked Uncle Lazarus.

'He's asking if you are on board.'

'I'd gathered that. Who is he? What's the rest of it?'

Before he could answer, the door from the deck-house opened and a pair of black shoes hit the steps down to the cabin, followed by a pair of official navy blue trousers and, in due course, the full uniform of an *agent de police*. The man inside it was fair, with a little clipped moustache. He stood at the bottom of the steps and asked for me by name.

I walked forward, my steps sounding hollow on the wooden floor. I was telling myself to keep calm, ask to see the extradition warrant, get a lawyer, but another part of my mind was urging me to push him aside and run, up the steps and past the three of them, go anywhere. Big confused city, Paris. Lots more identities out there. I stopped and said good morning to him in French, waiting to hear that a warrant had been issued for my arrest on a charge of murdering Miss Prudence Belsire. He looked me up and down, posturing sod.

'You should take better care of your little brother,' he said in painstaking English.

'My little what?'

I stood there and gaped at him. I started explaining I'd never had a little brother, only a sister married to a chartered accountant in Milton Keynes, but luckily didn't get far.

'He arrived on the late flight to Charles de Gaulle last night. He's been walking around looking for this boat ever since. You should have been there to meet him.'

'Where is he?'

He shouted up to somebody in the deck-house and, after a pause, there walked down the steps as composedly as into a spotlight the red-haired kid I'd last seen at Duncan's hostel.

'Hello little brother.' I said. 'What have you been getting up to then?'

He played up to it, even letting me ruffle his hair with

185

a brotherly hand, until the *agent de police* had delivered a
lecture about family responsibility and left, then pulled out
a letter from his leather shoulder-bag. My name was on the
envelope in Duncan's handwriting.

'He said I was to come and give this to you if the police
took him away. They came yesterday. Have you got any
breakfast?'

I left him to Uncle Lazarus and sat down on the padded
trunk to read. Kay came to sit beside me, and I let her see
it. It was dated the day after I left England.

Dear Colin,
    Soon after you'd gone the police came round again to
look at the car. They said they were only doing another
routine check but wouldn't tell me what for. Probably
only a matter of time before they come back again, then
I think they'll arrest me.
    This is to say, if they do you mustn't worry about it too
much. I don't think you started this – or even if you did
it would probably have happened at some time anyway.
Anyhow, if they do charge me with killing Prudence I'm
going to wait until I'm in the dock, then I'll let out a lot
of things I should have said a long time ago. What I'm
worried about, though, is I might not ever get into the
dock. A lot of odd things happen in police stations these
days, don't they, and who cares about one middle-aged
pervert more or less, especially if he goes around killing
people?
    Anyway, as I say, don't worry. The point is, though,
that I think you should keep clear for a while. I'll try not
to tell the police about you being there, but if they shut
me up and keep on at me, I might not be able to manage
it. So, if I were you, I'd stay in France or somewhere else
until it all dies down in a year or so. Uncle Lazarus will
help. I remember when he had a lot of deserters from
the Korean war he found them all jobs as waiters and
one of them's the Maître d'Hôtel now at a very famous
place in Nice, so it all worked out rather well in an odd

186

sort of way – though not the way they expected.

It's the same with Prudence. I want you to know, Colin, that I didn't kill Prudence and I don't think you did either, only I don't know who did. But a long time ago I was involved in something I should have been arrested for and wasn't, so if I'm arrested now for something I didn't do, that evens it up in an odd sort of way, so don't worry. You can ask Uncle Lazarus about this if you like. Tell him I told you, and send him my love.

That was it, except for a scrawled 'Good luck' and his signature. I let the letter thump down on my knee. Kay, a slower reader, took it from me. I turned to the boy, who was stirring morosely a dish of cold grain porridge.

'They came and arrested him?'

'Yes, I told you. Yesterday. Has he got any baked beans or something?'

Kay asked: 'It's the man who painted the pictures?'

'That's right.'

I took the letter from her and gave it to Uncle Lazarus.

'What do we do now?' she said.

'It sounds as if I'm booked for the hotel trade. Perhaps Uncle Lazarus will get you a job as a chambermaid if you ask him nicely.'

Further and further away from everything I thought I was before the book found me. Years now, not days or weeks, and no guarantee I'd ever get back. Duncan wanted me to go away. The three toughs, or whoever was paying them, wanted me to go away. Andrea – well, she'd had enough of me anyway. As for my work, I'd known when I started it that nobody wanted it but Lagen, and even then only so that he could be sarcastic about it. *Rêveuse* rocked gently up and down as the traffic on the river increased and I rocked with it, deciding that they were right, that all I could do now was disappear and let the rest of them sort out to their satisfaction who wrote the book, who killed Prudence, who produced Kay.

187

I said to her: 'Why don't you come with me? We could go somewhere warm – Australia, Uruguay.'

She stared at me. 'I told you, I want to see Duncan.'

I howled: 'But he's in prison.'

'Get him out of prison then. He says he didn't do it.'

'Oh fine. I suppose we go along to Wormwood Scrubs or wherever and say, "Excuse me, sir, my friend didn't do it. Can he come home with us, please."'

'But he's probably my father.'

'Yes, for what it's worth, Duncan probably is your father. But for heaven's sake, it was only a moment of aberration. He's got enough problems.'

Then Uncle Lazarus put in his oar. 'I think you should go back and do what you can for Duncan. You may regret it if you don't try.'

'I'll bloody well regret it if I do. I'll get arrested myself.'

'But they won't be looking for us,' Kay said. 'Not now they've arrested him.'

'It's all right for you. He's probably told them about me already.'

'I don't think so,' Uncle Lazarus said. 'Not yet anyway.'

There they were on either side of me, ignoring each other but both intent on pushing me to the same decision. If I'd had anything to oppose them with except the prospect of years or a lifetime of wandering, I might have been better at resisting them. But my rags of identity, if they were to be picked up at all, were on the other side of the channel, and that, far more than any concern for Duncan – though I was sorry for him – made the decision for me.

'If we do go back it will be on my terms. You do what I say.'

Her great dark eyes stared at me, my stomach churned and I knew it was a lost cause, but persisted.

'For a start, you send those three back to their kennels.' I jerked a thumb up towards the deck-house.

'No.'

'You're scared of them, aren't you? You let them out and now you can't control them.'

She bit her lip but didn't answer.

'I'm not going back to England with you unless you get rid of them.'

'They won't let us go without them.'

'Unpaid bills, is that it? Set them onto me and now you can't afford them?'

Still biting her lip, she nodded.

I wasn't sure I believed her. There was more to it than unpaid bills, but if I'd won my point there was no need to argue.

'In that case, we have to get out without bothering them. Have you got a couple of hundreds?'

She gave me two hundred-franc notes. I gave one of them to Uncle Lazarus, the other to the red-headed boy.

'Get up there and talk to them,' I told the boy. 'If they ask you what we're doing say we're arguing with the old man. Keep them occupied as long as you can, then Uncle will give you the other instalment.'

He looked at the note suspiciously.

'How much is that in money?'

'About ten quid.'

'Double it.'

The look on the boy's face would have skinned alligators. I nodded to Kay and she gave another note to each of them. As soon as he'd disappeared up the steps I opened a porthole on the river side of the boat and drew the trunk up beside it. Uncle Lazarus watched but made no move. Her presence exhausted him. He kept looking from her to the picture, then closing his eyes.

'I'll get out first,' I said, 'and hitch a lift for us.'

Parisians wouldn't lift a hand to help anybody in boring trouble but they dearly love a crisis with some originality to it. That was what I was relying on as I stripped off shirt and jacket, stood on the trunk and pushed head and shoulders through the porthole.

'Ahoy,' I called to a passing barge. 'Au secours,' and waved dementedly.

I had to call loudly enough to be heard over their engines and I hoped the trio in our deck-house wouldn't come to

189

look over. With luck the boy would be making them pay for their scraps of information. The object was to get a lift before they outbid me for his services. The first barge passed without stopping. From the second one a woman on the deck waved a hand as she hung out her washing, a baby in a play-pen beside her. Behind me I could hear Kay tapping on the wall, probably trying to ask me what I was doing, but she'd have to wait.

'Au secours, s'il vous plaît, for goodness sake give us a lift.'

I was so busy shouting and making lift-thumbing motions at the barges going up river that I didn't notice the rubber dinghy floating down it until it was bumping against the side.

'Hi,' said a large green fish. 'Need a lift?'

The fish was about six feet tall, wearing grey track shoes and spoke with an American accent, from Texas by the sound of it. He was looking at me from eye slits on a level with his gills. In the back of the dinghy some species of mollusc supervised the outboard motor and what looked like a crayfish was composing its spare limbs in the bottom. Above them a banner said, in French and English: 'Don't murder our rivers'.

'How far do you want to go?' said the fish.

'Anywhere, as long as it's fast.'

'Allée des Cygnes do you? We're doing a performance by the Statue of Liberty.'

I said Allée des Cygnes would do just fine, and could I bring a friend.

'As long as she's a little one.'

The fish took my arm and pulled and I felt my hurt ribs go crunch as I came through the porthole. I didn't see Kay following because the crayfish and I were disentangling ourselves, but when I looked round the fish had his green rubber arms round her and she'd landed safely. The dinghy by now had settled low in the water but that didn't seem to bother any of them. The outboard motor roared and off we went. Kay, slimmer than I, had only needed to take off her jacket and was in black trousers and silk blouse. The

190

fish put her down quite gently beside me in the bottom of
the boat.

    'What's wrong with you?'

    'Don't worry. Only another dozen or so broken ribs.'

    'It's a cruel old world,' said the fish.

Chapter Eighteen

They didn't ask any questions. A few barges hooted at us as we chugged down river, though we couldn't tell whether it was support or derision, and children looked down and waved from the bridges. There was no sign of pursuit from the *Rêveuse*, either on the river or along the embankment, so it looked as if we were getting our money's worth from the red-haired boy after all. The World Preservation Theatrical Collective handed us out cautiously onto the steps by the replica Statue of Liberty at the sharp end of the island called the Allée des Cygnes, and accepted our regrets that we couldn't stay to watch the show. It's hard to convince a man dressed as a fish that you feel conspicuous without a shirt. We collected a few curious glances as we walked side by side under the chestnut trees to where the island joins the Bir Hakeim Bridge, but that was probably her rather than me. Even by Parisian standards and after a sleepless night she was beautiful, and could no more help looking it than I could help looking battered.

In a shopping centre not far from the bridge we bought a shirt, jacket and disposable razors for me, using her money. She'd had the sense to hand her shoulder bag out first when we came through the porthole. Come to think of it, even the money I'd left in my jacket on the *Rêveuse* had been hers as well. All I'd got left was my false passport in the back pocket of my jeans, and even that was crumpled from coming through the porthole. She left me drinking coffee and cognac in a café while she went off on a shopping trip of her own. Halfway through the second medicinal brandy it struck me that I was an idiot, that she'd gone to find the three thugs and set them

192

on me again, but she was back before I'd finished it, looped round with carrier bags. She even looked as if she'd been enjoying it, and announced she was hungry.

'What do we do now?' I asked as she scanned the menu.

'Oh look, they do palm hearts.'

I waited till she'd made up her mind and I'd given the order to a waiter. Then I started telling her the plans I'd been making, wondering when she'd interrupt, wondering when the next punch would come.

'I thought we'd go back by boat. Less conspicuous. We can take a taxi to the Gare du Nord and a boat train to Calais. Have you got enough money?'

'Plenty.'

But her attention was on the pale cylinders of palm heart as she cut them into regular lengths and ate them.

'The question is, what are we going to do when we get back?'

'Get Duncan out of prison.'

She said it as if it would be as easy as ordering dessert.

I said, trying to speak slowly and reasonably, 'We can only do that by proving somebody else killed Prudence. Do you think anybody was blackmailing her?'

She shrugged and shook her head.

'She kept handwritten pages from the book in her desk – the pages about the murder. Then there's the ring, Lord Talisby's ring.'

I remembered her fingers moving across my stomach from pocket to pocket when she'd taken it from me. I wondered where it was now and guessed she'd stowed it in her bag, hanging from the back of the chair.

'We can't just demand another interview with Lord Talisby and ask him politely if he had Prudence murdered to stop her talking about what happened in Morocco.'

'But he didn't kill the Arab boy,' she said. 'The old man told you Duncan did that.'

She was staring at me, knife and fork poised. It surprised me that she'd been following things so closely, scared me

193

even, because it was a reminder of a resourcefulness in her that was hidden in this passive, abstracted mood.

'Then there's Angela,' I said. 'Suppose she got jealous and followed them out to Morocco without Uncle Lazarus knowing about it. A bit of scandal's all right for an actress, but not sadistic murder.'

'Does Angela look like the woman in the picture?'

From her voice, that mattered to her as much as anything.

'No. She must have been beautiful, but not like that.'

She went on eating her salad, bright green chicory fronds. I wasn't sure whether I was talking to her or myself.

'Nicolle too. She wants the book and she wants to please Angela. It's not far from Paris to Shropshire if you're rich. Nicolle won't talk, but Angela might.'

Angela, as far as I knew, didn't carry a Walther.

'The thing is,' I said and leant across the table towards her, 'the thing is, can we get to Angela or anybody else without your three thugs catching up with us?'

That got through to her at least. She dropped her fork and stared at me, then looked at the door as if she expected to see them walking through it.

'The big one's quite bright, isn't he?' I said. 'They might have tracked us as far as the Allée des Cygnes by now. They might be waiting for us at the station.'

'What shall we do?'

'I think we book in at a hotel for a few hours, change, rest, then we'll go for one of the overnight boats. Perhaps they'll have given up waiting by then.'

She wouldn't stay for coffee. We found a modest place not far away where they didn't even blink when we registered as Mr and Mrs Henry Wood of Kensington. I was allowed first go at the bathroom while she unpacked her bags, and I showered and soaped where I could in-between the places that hurt most, broke razors on three days of stubble. The face that emerged scared me: sharp and pale, with mad eyes. I'd have arrested it on sight. When I came out of the bathroom she was wandering around, stripped to the skin, holding a big new pair of scissors. I nearly bolted inside again.

'I want you to cut my hair.'

Why she had to strip to have it done, only she knew. She gave me the scissors and I stood there holding them, stupidly.

'Why?'

'So they don't recognise me.'

'Who? The minders?'

'Or the police.'

There was a mean little dressing table with a mirror. She sat down on the stool in front of it, crossing her long legs.

'Come on. It's not difficult.'

But when I touched her neck awkwardly, every muscle of it was tense. She sat sideways on to the mirror, her back to me. I picked up a swag of hair and it lay in my hand, quiet and heavy. I wondered why I thought of the trails of blood.

'Come on,' she said again.

I cut across it at shoulder length, finding the trick of holding the scissors at an angle, and jumped back when it fell inert to the carpet like a dead animal.

'Not like that. Short, really short. Close to my head.'

Without looking at me, she touched her neck just below the ear.

'Are you sure . . . ?'

'Get on with it.'

Feeling sick, I made one cut, then another and another, fast and desperate to get it over, until the faded carpet was littered with great dark swags that glistened chestnut brown when the sun caught them. Several times I pricked her neck with the scissors, but she didn't move a millimetre, and when I looked at her reflection in the mirror her eyes were closed. I put the scissors down.

'That's it.'

She stayed there, eyes closed still.

'You could stab me in the neck and kill me. Quite easily. They're sharp. I made sure they were sharp.'

'Why should I want to kill you?'

I looked down, and great tears were forming under her closed eyelids. I didn't know whether, after I'd asked why I should want to kill her, I'd added 'I love you,' or only said it in my head. To make sure, I said it again.

'I love you.'

She flopped head and arms down on the dressing table, hard enough to make the mirror tremble, and her thin back heaved up and down with great gasping sobs.

I knelt in front of her with my arms round her, my face against her stomach, uselessly telling her that it would be all right, all right. After a while she tried to say something and, once she'd got the words out, couldn't stop.

'I'm scared. I'm scared. I'm scared.'

I picked her up, one arm round her back, the other under her knees, and carried her over to the bed. She went on crying, but more softly, while I stroked her cheeks and forehead, whispering meaningless, comforting things. Once I let my hand stray down to her small breasts but she went as tense as a spring so I stopped. She didn't object though when I lay down on the bed beside her, even opened her eyes and tried to smile.

'Do I look different with my hair cut?'

She did. Younger and less guarded.

'Just as beautiful.'

She shook her head. That wasn't what she wanted.

'Do I still look like that woman in the book and the picture?'

'Not so much.'

Not quite so much.

Soon after that she fell asleep and, watching her, I slept too. I hadn't slept since the few hours on *Rêveuse*, so perhaps it wasn't surprising that I blanked out, completely and dreamlessly. When I woke up I could see from the slant and colour of the sun that it was well into the afternoon and the traffic underneath the window sounded like rush hour. The bed space beside me was empty and I jumped up in a panic, but her bags and the make-up things she'd bought were still scattered round the room. I was relaxing, thinking she must be in the bathroom, when the outer door opened and she walked in from the corridor, dressed in the denim jeans and jacket

196

she'd bought that morning, short hair brushed and gleaming, lips glossed.

'Where have you been?'

'I went to ask the woman at reception if she'd got any safety pins.' She showed me how the waistband of the trousers gaped, too wide for her.

'And had she?'

'No. I'll just have to start eating.'

She might have been a different woman from the one who'd been crying on the bed a couple of hours ago. I said nothing, just watched as she collected up her old clothes and her make-up and stowed them into one of the bags. The scissors were still on the dressing table.

She said: 'We can leave those.'

But when she wasn't looking I picked them up and put them in the pocket of my new jacket.

At the reception she gave me her wallet to settle up while she went outside and waved for a taxi. It struck me suddenly as I was counting out notes that the woman behind the desk had a little glass dish with handy odds and ends in it like paper clips and rubber bands – and safety pins. I asked, making sure Kay was still on the other side of the swing doors, if the bill included madame's telephone call. Oh no, said the woman, pleased with her own honesty, madame paid for that just after she'd made it. Would monsieur like a receipt for his bill? When I joined Kay on the pavement she was triumphant at having caught a taxi and asked me why I looked so worried. Trying to work out what to do when we got back to England, I said.

I saw nobody I recognised at the station. Kay slept peacefully for most of the journey to Calais, lips apart, hand going to her neck occasionally to feel for the drifts of hair that weren't there any more. I thought of her voice when she'd said I could kill her with the scissors, of how she'd gone tense when I touched her breasts, and I felt like crying. I slept fitfully between stops at numberless stations and dreamt once that I could see somebody writing in the only hand I hadn't identified, the unknown hand that had drafted the murder scene, but when I tried to look closer Kay's hair swept across the page, trailing blood, blotting everything out. At Calais, where we had to wait on the quay for half an hour, she was hungry and I found cheese rolls and strong coffee in paper cups. She ate my roll as well when I couldn't finish it, saying she needed to fill out her new jeans. I said nothing to her about safety pins.

On the voyage we drank cognac in the saloon and discussed again what we should do when we got back to England. I said I was getting the glimmerings of an idea but wouldn't tell her till I'd worked it out. When the Tannoy told us we were twenty minutes from Dover I decided I needed fresh air to drive out the cognac fumes and persuaded her to go up on deck with me.

It was dark by then, with lights on in the buildings round Dover harbour and a breeze coming off the cliffs. She shivered and I put my arm round her shoulders.

'Ah, love, let us be true to one another!'

'What do you mean?'

'Just quoting. My job once.' I didn't give her the next bit about the world without certitude or peace or help for pain. Just as well, because I'd have been interrupted by the ship's public address system hounding drivers towards their cars. There was a general scramble off the deck and towards the doors and I watched it over her bent head, trying to remember what it felt like to know where you were going and be in a hurry to get there. Then I saw Nicolle.

I could hardly have missed her because, typically, she was going against the current. As the rest of them crowded off the deck she strolled onto it with such an air of possession that they made way for her. She was a driver too – I could see the keys with the Porsche tag she was dangling quite clearly in the light from the lamp over the door – but she wasn't letting any processed male voice tell her what to do. She strolled past us without a glance and leant over the rail watching the harbour. I tightened my arm round Kay's shoulders and led her inside.

'Did you see that woman?'

'The one with the dyed red hair in the black trouser suit?'

'Nicolle.'

She twisted round, trying to look at her through the glass of the door.

'Careful. I don't think she noticed us.'

'But what's she doing here? Is she following us?'

It sounded genuine. I wished I knew if that phone call from the hotel had been local or long distance.

'It can't be a coincidence. It must be something to do with the book.'

Whether or not Nicolle was on the boat because Kay had phoned her, the course of action was the same: stick with Nicolle.

The question was, how did we, without transport, stick with Nicolle in her Porsche. By the time we found out whether she was following us or we were following her, it would be too late.

'Have you got your driving licence with you?'

She had. Mine had been lost several identities ago.

'And enough money to hire a car?'

That too. Where did it come from, this money of hers? She objected, though, that it took ages to hire a car and, by that time, all the other drivers would be out and away.

'I'll take care of that. Just get one as quickly as you can and meet me on the other side of the gates.'

I could trust her to do that, at any rate. If there was a plan for my future, or lack of it, it would involve more than leaving me stranded at Dover harbour.

'She'll be miles away by then.'

'Don't worry. Just leave that to me.'

I told her to go below and make sure she was first in the queue for car hire. It was a change to give orders, a surprise when they were obeyed. Only, as she went down the stairs, she turned.

'You're not trying to get rid of me, are you?'

I bent down and kissed her like anybody else with his girl. 'As if I could.'

Once I'd seen her on her way, the delicate work started. I had to see Nicolle to her car without being seen. Luckily there was a luggage space just inside the deck doors, and every time they opened I was bent over, fiddling with the straps of somebody else's haversack. The fourth time I did it, a pair of slim, trousered legs sauntered through, sheer stockinged feet and shiny wedge heels. An angry Australian turned up to claim the haversack a few seconds later, but it didn't matter by then because the red hair moving down the stairs among the thinning crowds was as clear as a beacon. I told the Australian to keep his cool and followed it to the car deck, arriving just in time to see her sliding elegantly behind the wheel of a white Porsche. That was all I needed. When they let the pedestrians off I was near the front of the queue, only a dozen or so behind Kay, who seemed to be following my instructions exactly. I made sure that she and a few others went ahead of me through the green channel at Customs then, trying to look conscientious but awkward with it, approached a uniformed official.

'Look, I'm sorry to bother you and it's probably nothing really, only I know how careful you have to be and . . . '

He was patient and helped me get my story out. I'd been approached at the bar on board by this woman, very friendly, quite sophisticated, middle-aged. We'd chatted and, towards the end, she'd said would I do her a favour? She had this case, quite small, but awkward to carry because she had slight arthritis in both wrists. Would I take it off for her? Well, I'd have liked to help, but you have to be careful, don't you. The odd thing was, I'd seen her later getting into the driving seat of a car. Yes, a white Porsche. French registration, but I thought she had a slight American accent.

By this time we were in an office of the Customs Hall and I was mentally screaming at him to get a move on. He telephoned somebody in the end, but not before he'd taken my name and address. Thomas Sterne, I think, from some college in Cambridge. I accepted his formal thanks for my public-spirited attitude and left. As I walked out of Customs and towards the gates I was gratified to see that the queue of cars coming off the boat was moving very slowly. Possibly it contained a high quotient of female drivers in white Porsches.

200

At the other side of the gates I leaned against a fence post and waited. Released cars hurtled out, hooting and raising dust, but no sign of Nicolle. Twenty minutes later, after midnight, a silver Polo came out and drew up beside me, Kay in the driving seat.

'I couldn't get anything faster.'

'Did they seem interested?'

'Not very.'

It had occurred to me while I waited that if the police still wanted to question Kay, the car hire people might have been told to watch out for her name on a driving licence. No good sharing that worry with her now.

'Is she out yet?'

'No. It might take her quite a while.'

When I told her about my tip to the Customs officer she stared at me for some time without saying anything. The short hair made her eyes look even bigger.

'Are you used to this kind of thing?'

'No more than you are.'

I wanted to take over in the driving seat, but she wouldn't let me. It was nearly one and the stream of cars had slowed to a trickle before the white Porsche came through the gates.

Chapter Nineteen

After being taken apart by the Customs, I expected her to shoot off into the night at a speed that would leave us standing, but she didn't seem to be in a hurry. She filled up at an all-night garage while we lurked round the corner, managing the operation as decisively as she'd handled the gun. I don't suppose she even got a drop of petrol on her new shoes. From the docks to the main road there was enough traffic to keep a couple of vehicles between us, and Kay managed it without any hints from me, as if she'd been shadowing cars all her adult life. I tried to ignore, for the while, the nagging feeling that it was easy enough if you were in partnership with the person being shadowed, but the thought of the phone call wouldn't go away. We followed her to Folkestone.

'I should keep to the outside of the roundabout. She'll probably take the London road.'

Kay ignored my advice, which was just as well. The white Porsche took the last exit, signposted for Hastings and the West, and settled to a sedate fifty-five on the open road. We followed, with no cars between us now, but as far as I could see Nicolle was showing no signs of worry. Just after Hythe she turned into a lay-by and we had to keep going. Tucking in behind her would have been a declaration of war. I cursed and told Kay to get into a side road and turn round, ready to follow when she passed.

'No. She's probably just looking at the map. She's bound to notice us if we pop out of a road behind her.'

Sure enough, the Porsche passed us a few miles on and we settled into formation again as we crossed Romney Marsh. It was a starry night but the flat pastures drew darkness into themselves like blotting paper. When I wound down the window I could hear waves pulling and sucking at the beach like animals at a great teat.

'Shall I drive for a bit?'

'I'm all right.'

She was intent on the road and the car in front. My hand was twitching to move itself to her thigh, not to do anything, just to lie there, but I sensed it wouldn't be welcome. Her chopped hair ended in little jagged points round her ears. As we passed Winchelsea there was already a crack of light in the east and by the time we'd found our way through Hastings it was more day than night. The breeze coming off the land already felt warm and the sky was cloudless, with that keyed-up feeling about everything that comes at the start of a hot day.

On the outskirts of Eastbourne Nicolle nearly wrong-footed us, first stopping in a lay-by again, then – when we'd driven on as far as the town – failing to reappear. We stopped in front of a line of guest-houses and argued for a bit. Kay thought she might have been feeling drowsy and have stopped to sleep or breathe some sea air. I couldn't imagine her giving in to such simple human weaknesses and said she'd been playing with us, knowing we were there all the time. In the end we drove back and found the lay-by empty.

'See, I told you.'

The very emptiness of the road made me scared. I looked along it the way we'd come, more than half expecting the three toughs on our tail. Nothing. Kay seemed unworried.

'If she was looking at the map she might have been going to turn off somewhere.'

Disregarding me, she turned up a narrow road on the left and, within yards, came to a hotel sign and the white Porsche parked on a sweep of gravel outside a place encrusted with Edwardian turrets and plaques from various good food guides.

'What on earth's she doing here?'

The answer turned out to be very simple: Nicolle was having breakfast. I didn't discover that until half an hour or

203

so later, after we'd sat in the car discussing things and Kay, her face nearly transparent with tiredness, had leant back in the driving seat and closed her eyes. For a while I sat and watched her, wondering what thoughts made her eyes move so restlessly from side to side under the blue-veined lids, looking at the long sweep of eyelashes that, with everything else going on the day before, she'd carefully stroked with mascara. Even so my mind was on Nicolle and in the end I got out, closing the passenger door as gently as I could, and walked up the steps. The swing doors were unlocked, but there was nobody at the reception desk or occupying the islands of chintz chairs in the hall. Sunlight slanted uninterrupted onto polished parquet floors and the only sign of life was a clattering from what must be the kitchen area. The reason for the noise became obvious when I peered round a rampacious house plant and saw Nicolle sitting on her own at a table, quite composed, with a cup and coffee pot in front of her.

It said something for her force of character because there was a notice at reception saying breakfast was served from seven thirty to nine, and it was then barely half past six. As I watched, a harassed-looking night porter in uniform trousers and a crumpled shirt came in with a tray. He apologised in a soft South of Ireland voice that there were no croissants until the lad got there, but would she try some nice fresh wholemeal toast and yes, there was honey, he was sure he could find her some honey. More clattering from the kitchen. The honey was brought but madame still wasn't satisfied. Papers? Yes, the girl would be bringing the newspapers any moment. Was there any particular newspaper? At that point a bicycle skidded on the gravel and a bundle of papers came through the doors and slid across the parquet at me. The night porter was so absorbed with keeping Nicolle happy that he hardly gave me a second glance as he bent to pick them up. When he took her the *Telegraph*, she hadn't even unfolded it before another need occurred to her. Telephone, yes certainly. There was one in the booth by reception. He'd put a line through to her from the switchboard.

There was a porter's chair with its high back towards the reception desk. I dived into it and curled up just before her wedge heels came clopping over the parquet. Either the phone booth door didn't fit properly or she hadn't botherd to close it, because I could hear quite clearly. She dialled five digits, not enough for an international call or even to London. It took some time for the other end to answer, and her voice sounded impatient when she gave her name.

'You're expecting me at ten o'clock? Yes.... You did what I asked you? No, it's no good just thinking. I want to know.... All right, so you'll check. And the other thing? ... Yes. Sunday night only.... Good. When is he arriving? Good .... No, I was delayed, I've been travelling all night.... Yes. I have the directions. I shall be there at ten.'

Which left me not much wiser, except that whatever was happening next couldn't be far away. She came out of the booth and went back to the breakfast room, pausing to ask for more coffee, only could he please brew it freshly this time and not just heat up last night's. The porter said yes, yes he'd do that, in a voice that suggested he'd do his best for the golden apples of the Hesperides as well, if that was what she fancied to follow. It made me shiver. If Nicolle could achieve Parisian coffee in an English seaside hotel, there was no limit to her powers.

I shifted in my chair and watched as she ate toast and honey and scanned the paper. She seemed to be quite at her ease. It was so quiet I could hear the paper rustling and the little snaps of her teeth into the crispy toast. I was just wondering what would happen if I went and joined her when something broke the rhythm. The toast hit the plate and the paper crackled more urgently. I risked another look round the foliage and saw she was staring at something at the bottom of the front page. The porter came out, smiling nervously, with a steaming coffee pot.

'The other papers. Have you got any of the other papers?'

Long-suffering, he came to where he'd left them on the reception counter and sorted out a *Guardian*, an *Independent*, a *Sun*.

'Be with you in a moment, sir,' he said in passing.

His eyes weren't on me. While Nicolle's attention was on the papers, I slipped out and woke up Kay as I scrambled into the seat beside her.

'She's arranging to meet somebody not far from here at ten o'clock, but she's seen something in the papers that worries her. We'll go and get some.'

The town was coming to life by now, with milkmen and joggers in the streets. We found a newsagent, bought the whole range of papers and parked on the promenade to read them. The story she'd read in the *Telegraph* didn't take much finding, although it was no more than a short paragraph headed '*Cottage murder remand*':

A man appeared in Ludlow Magistrates Court yesterday charged with the murder of Prudence Belsire on June 17. He was Duncan McMahon, a painter, of New Park Street, Birmingham. Miss Belsire, 54, was found stabbed in her cottage near Clun, Shropshire. The accused was remanded in custody until 1 July. Reporting restrictions were not lifted.

The reports in the other papers were much the same. Nicolle could have saved her money.

'What do we do now?' Kay was staring at me, wide-eyed.

'It doesn't change anything. We knew it was going to happen.'

But it did. Seeing it in cold print was a reminder that it wasn't just our worry, that there was a whole apparatus of police and law and state teasing away at the ragged edges of twenty-nine years' deception. I thought of the *Telegraph*, with that same paragraph, lying on Lord Talisby's breakfast table, although he wouldn't have had to wait to read about it in the papers; wondered whether they'd let Duncan himself read it in prison.

'I don't see what it has to do with them,' Kay said, echoing my thoughts.

I was angry with myself. 'It's got everything to do with them. She was murdered, wasn't she? It's not our private property.'

'He's my father.'

'We think. He's also a murderer.'

'The Arab boy? That was a long time ago.'

'In another country, and besides . . . Oh, never mind.'

'She made him do it.'

'But who is she? If it was a she.'

'But the picture, the one— '

'The one that looks like you? I've been thinking about that. Suppose Uncle Lazarus was right and there was no woman – just him and Talisby. But, when it came to it, he couldn't accuse Talisby and he painted the woman instead.'

'But where did she come from? Why did she look like me?'

She was raking her fingers through her short hair, trying to reassure herself, I think, that she looked different now.

'Suppose he painted himself twice over in the same picture once as a man and once as a woman? Himself and his self?'

'Bad self . . . a woman?'

'That's how it might have seemed to him.'

'But . . . ' Her fingers were going past her hair, raking the empty air where it had been till yesterday, looking for a comfort that wasn't there.

'But he couldn't create me, just by painting me.'

It was more of a question than a statement. I tried to calm her by talking about what we'd do next.

'I'd say Nicolle's comfortable in that hotel for the next hour. Wherever she's got to be at ten can't be far away, so we'll park on the main road near the hotel turning from about half past eight on, and follow when she comes out.'

'What will we do when we get there?'

'Depends on where it is and who she's meeting.'

The papers said the day was Saturday, the first date I'd been conscious of since the book. In the phone call she'd talked about something on Sunday. It wasn't only the heat that made me feel things were coming to a head. We drove to the main road, with Kay making no resistance when I took over the wheel and, for nearly an hour, we waited with the windows open to the sea breeze and a stream of cars went past with suitcases on roof racks and kids staring out of back windows. It was half past nine before the Porsche shouldered its way into the stream, Nicolle driving. She'd changed at the hotel and was wearing a blouse or dress in turquoise silk, with big billowing sleeves. The roof was down and her red hair was blowing in the breeze. I let another three family carloads through before we followed.

The road rose up and over the edge of the South Downs, already shimmering in the heat. Beachy Head was just off to our left, but we kept straight on until the road dipped again, where the chalk hills of the Seven Sisters end in the Cuckmere Valley. Here the white Porsche turned out of the main traffic queue and up a smaller road to the right, signposted Alfriston. I nearly missed it, turned suddenly without signalling and got a hoot from the car behind, loaded to the gunnels with disposable nappies. To each his own problems. We fo' her up the side road, then into a smaller road on the with trees hanging over it. If she hadn't noticed before that she was being followed she must have guessed it by then, but she didn't react. I was becoming certain that she'd known since Dover, or even before it, and was deliberately leading us into a trap, a lonely chalk quarry, say, with our three friends waiting. We'd already passed several driveways and I decided that I'd turn round in the next one and drive back to the main road like a bat out of hell.

Kay said: 'There are a lot of cars behind us.'

There were, too. A few minutes ago we'd had the narrow road to ourselves. Now we were number two of a convoy of half a dozen, all crawling along behind Nicolle. What the sudden attraction was on this country road I couldn't imagine and I started sweating, feeling closed in. At least the car immediately behind us looked reassuring, an elderly Morris being driven by a woman with glasses and straight cropped grey hair. I was craning my neck and swivelling the mirror, trying to get a look at the others, when Nicolle slowed to a crawl and turned right into a driveway between high brick walls. A sign on the gate said something Institute, but we were past before I could read it as we tracked the Porsche down a drive with lawns and beech trees on either side. The Morris fell in behind us, and the queue of other cars as well, following the parking signs to a wide sweep of gravel at the side of a red brick château. A minibus was disgorging people and suitcases onto the steps.

'What is it? What's happening?' Kay sounded really panicked.

As for me, when I watched the people getting out of the bus, all apologetic laughter and after you's and sloping shoulders, I was hit by a feeling of familiarity.

'It's a convention,' I told her. 'It's a bloody literary convention.'

Nicolle, of course, had taken the last convenient parking place near the steps. I watched her strolling up them, Gucci weekend bag in hand as the rest of us blocked each other off and got bad-tempered. She was wearing tight black trousers under the blouse, cut short to show off her ankles, and getting some lustful glances from the dandruff brigade struggling out of the minibus. Once we'd parked I practically had to drag Kay out of the passenger seat.

'What are we doing here?'

'Watching her.'

Kay stayed close beside me as we went up the steps. The sign by the door identified the place as the Morgan B. Pencluft Institute for Literary Understanding. I knew it by reputation: a respectable enough transatlantic body with more money than discrimination. People like my studies supervisor, Lagen, kept themselves in claret by contributing the occasional learned article to its spasmodic publications. We walked into the shadowed hallway, smelling of conscientious pot pourri, where a plump man with sparse hair and fat woman in a kaftan presided over a reception table. The banner over their heads welcomed us to the Morgan B. Pencluft Symposium on Eroticism in Literature. There was no sign of Nicolle. She'd presumably been whisked off to whatever luxuries the

209

institute kept for its visiting literary celebrities. The woman in the kaftan made some trouble about letting us in because she couldn't find our registration forms, but my plaints about the post office, plus a little judicious name-dropping, carried the day. I signed in under my own name, feeling a shock of non-recognition when I saw it on the page. Of all my pack of identities, none felt as odd to me as the one I was claiming now and, even though some of the delegates around me were giving me anxious smiles of half recognition, having shared the same tables in the same libraries, I expected any moment to be denounced as an imposter. I introduced Kay as a colleague, printed her name down firmly on the list as Kay Smith, not wanting to ring any bells with Belsire. When I handed the pen over to her I tried to signal with my eyes that she should sign in under the false name. She did it, but so awkwardly that I'm sure the woman would have noticed if somebody hadn't been distracting her with questions about meal times.

We'd been handed leaflets with the timetable on them as we signed in, and I studied mine while waiting to be allocated our rooms. The first name that hit my eye was Nicolle's, down to speak at two o'clock that afternoon on 'The Symbiotic Fallacy: A post-feminist perspective on sexual poetic imagery'. I felt Kay's elbow in my ribs and jumped. A red-faced bore was heading her way.

'I don't think we've met before. What's your field?'

I could hardly blame him for trying. There aren't many new female faces on the conference circuit.

I answered for her. 'She's researching castration fantasies in schoolboy comics of the 1930s. She'll let you have one of her questionnaires when she's unpacked.'

He turned a brighter shade of red and I dragged her away, through some French windows and down onto a lawn with cherry tree and bird bath. She was furious.

'Why did you tell him that? My father's in prison and we're playing silly jokes with your friends. I want to go away.'

'I don't think you do.'

I opened the programme and showed her something: not Nicolle's lecture but the main attraction of Sunday afternoon.

'The Political Dimension. The junior Home Office Minister, Lord Talisby, will be examining the effects of government policy on the literary sexual ethos.'

'Can you think of a better chance to get at him? You want to ask him about the ring, don't you? About what happened in Morocco? We wouldn't get within miles of him any other way.'

She stared from his name on the paper to me, and back again.

'Nicolle knows about it. Perhaps she even arranged it. I heard her talking on the phone about something on Sunday. Whatever's going to happen next is going to happen here.'

She still didn't say anything. The French doors opened and two men strolled down the steps. They were deep in academic gossip and didn't notice us at first. One of them was the shape of a Beerbohm caricature, the other tall but stooping, grey-haired and craggy-faced. His voice when he saw me rumbled like a landslide.

'Colin, what the devil are you doing here?'

I turned to Kay. 'Miss Smith, let me introduce you to my supervisor,' I said.

Behind him, Gus Prothering eyed Kay and waggled his egg-shaped eyebrows up and down.

'Acquired any interesting editions recently?'

He stepped onto the lawn, treading delicately with his little feet.

Chapter Twenty

'Just one,' I said, 'but then I lost it.'

He made a regretful puckering motion with his lips. Lagen meanwhile was looking at me over his glasses as if I were a misplaced footnote.

'Who invited you here?'

'Oh, I get around.'

'It's not your field.'

I told him I'd found some surprising by-ways in nineteenth-century Anglican poetry, annoying him more from force of habit than because my mind was on it. What concerned me was whether the police, looking for the mystery man who visited Prudence, had traced me as far as Oxford. Surely if they'd questioned Lagen or Prothering about me, it would have been the first thing they'd mention.

'I wouldn't have thought you'd got time to spare for by-ways.' He was being openly offensive now, not only in the words but in the way he was looking at us, implying Kay was one of the by-ways.

Admittedly we were an unlikely academic couple. I needed a shave again, and the last time I'd looked in a mirror the bruises had ripened to purple and yellow. Kay, in her denims and cropped hair, had a look of aggro and glared at him, not trying to hide an instinctive dislike.

'I heard you were lecturing here,' I said, having spotted his name on the programme, 'so naturally we decided to come, didn't we darling?'

Prothering giggled and Lagen looked daggers, willing to pick up a cheque lecturing at some second division establishment, not so eager to have it advertised in Oxford circles.

That, at least, was one explanation for his obvious disgust at the sight of me. Another was more worrying – that he had some inkling at least of what was going on. In support of that was the presence of Gus Prothering. He, after all, had directed me to Prudence and, if his bibliophile's ivory tower admitted anything as common as newspapers, he'd know she was dead. We stood there on the lawn, Lagen glaring at me, Kay glaring at Lagen and Prothering's eyes skipping from one to another, registering, as far as I could see, nothing but mild malice.

At this point the balding little man who seemed to be organising the symposium appeared at the top of the steps looking even more harassed than before.

'Professor Lagen, I wonder if we could have a word, please?'

Lagen grunted but went inside and the rest of us followed. The heat in the hallway had risen by several degrees and a power struggle was in progress. On one side, a thin, middle-aged man with rimless glasses was pointing to the timetable, explaining in courteous East Coast American that it could not be altered without great difficulty. His second, the woman in the kaftan, was looking pink-faced and satisfied like a connoisseur of rows. On the other side, with no second but not needing one, was Nicolle. She was simply standing there, arms folded, repeating her ultimatum at regular intervals.

'Either I lecture tomorrow afternoon or I don't lecture at all.'

The balding man, with Lagen in tow, came bustling up like a UN peace-keeping force.

'Director, I was wondering . . . '

It was some time before he got a chance to put his peace plan: that Lagen, who'd been due to speak on Sunday just before Talisby's session, should swap with Nicolle and perform that afternoon. I could have told him it was no use trying to shuffle Lagen and was expecting a further outbreak of hostilities, but I'd underestimated Nicolle yet again. As soon as the plan was suggested she walked over to Lagen, laid her thin white hand on his shirt sleeve and said huskily, upping her French accent several notches:

213

'Oh Professor Lagen, could I ask you to do that?'

He um-erred and was lost. She poured out her gratitude, how she hated travelling, what a dreadful crossing it had been (here Kay glanced at me because it had been mill-pond smooth), how she, as a mere poet, was nervous about speaking in public, unlike such a very well known academic who was doing it all the time. Result, complete capitulation of well known academic, relegated to Saturday afternoon slot, and gracious ascent of the poet to relax and study her notes upstairs. I'm not sure Lagen didn't actually kiss her hand as she went. That is, I saw him do it and I still don't believe it. Just one thing, if one were being hypercritical, marred the gracious ascent, and that only briefly. It was the point when she paused at a turn in the staircase, caught my eye and gave me a look all to myself that was neither gracious nor poetic, a look that said she'd noticed me don't kid yourself, and steps will be taken. Then she disappeared and the little crowd that had gathered to enjoy the scene drifted away to lunch.

I said to Kay: 'I wonder why it's so important to her to speak just before Talisby?'

But Kay wouldn't talk about it. She claimed to be tired, which was fair enough after being awake for most of the past two nights, and decided to follow Nicolle's example and go upstairs. I saw her to the door of her room and came down again, feeling far from tired myself. The need for sleep, as well as the need for food, seemed to have got left behind in another existence. Thinking that I should try to eat, I wandered experimentally into a dining room packed with sweaty-faced people bellowing inquiries to each other about who'd got what jobs as they jostled for sandwiches. I withdrew after fielding questions from two acquaintances on when I was going to publish and breaking one of my temporary fillings on a piece of celery. My mind wasn't there. It wasn't even, as it should have been, trying to sort out what Nicolle was doing there, what would happen when Talisby came, whether Lagen and Prothering were coincidences. No, it was full of the need to be with Kay, imagining her upstairs, naked between cool sheets, wanting to slip in beside her or, if that wasn't allowed, sit on the floor

214

and watch her as she slept. I wanted to be back in the hotel room in Paris, with her on the bed beside me and her hair, cut by my hand, congealing on the carpet. It got so bad that I even wanted to be back in the car park with the three men working on me, as long as she was there.

I went out of the French windows and into the garden to get away from the heat and voices, crossing the lawn where we'd met Lagen and down some more steps to the back of the house. In spite of the academic mediocrity of the Morgan B. Pencluft Institute, it did itself well by way of land. A winding path led down a series of terraces, its turns arranged to give alternate views of downland and sea, crossing and recrossing a little stream that was invisible for most of its course under drifts of meadowsweet. Every terrace was different. First you went over a rustic bridge into tangled English, the air full of the smell of pinks and honeysuckle, bumble bees head first into roses, furry backsides quivering. The next was Japanese, where the stream broadened out into a pond with carp and stepping stones, then formal Italianate, with stone nymphs and closely clipped hedges. I stood there for a while looking at the sea in the distance then went back to the English garden and sat on a stone bench under a weeping ash tree, where the stream poured itself over a six-inch waterfall.

At first I was thinking about nothing but the sound of the water then, without forcing the pace, letting things fit together in my mind, rearranging what I knew, guessing at what I didn't know. Some of it was clear to me by then but, clearer than anything I could put together, was the sense that the process I'd started was moving with an unstoppable momentum to answer the two questions that had, in my mind, become one: where did the book come from and where did Kay? I hardly spared a thought for Duncan in prison, or even the probability that, as the suspect of Prudence's murder, I was first reserve if the police should tire of him. I had an inexplicable confidence that once my question was cleared up, the problem of the murder would be settled as well. I'd even lost the guilt of the idea that if I hadn't started asking about the book, Prudence would still be alive. They'd all piled up an avalanche waiting to go and if I were the first pebble I couldn't be blamed for what followed me.

I dropped leaves in the stream, watching them hesitate on the lip of the miniature waterfall and go over. I was leaning over watching one that determinedly refused to go, wondering whether to help it along, when Nicolle found me. I didn't look up when her feet came clacking over the rustic bridge, knowing very well who it would be, and waited till I could feel her standing behind me.

'Hello,' I said, still watching the leaf. 'I was expecting you.'

She walked round and stood in front of me, pausing to send the leaf on its way with the toe of her shoe.

'Why are you following me?'

'I wasn't, not on the boat. That was coincidence. The rest was curiosity.'

'I'm going to tell them to throw you out.'

'You can't. I'm a bona fide academic, registered and paid my fee.'

I had too, on Kay's money.

'You admit you followed me here?'

'I was curious to see what you'd do next. I think I've guessed now.'

'So what am I going to do?' She was standing over me, one foot on the end of the bench.

I smiled at her. 'You're going public. You're going to use this occasion to admit in passing, in your admirably academic lecture, that you committed an erotic novel twenty-nine years ago. You'll manage it very delicately, very allusively, but there it will be on the record.'

'I wrote it.'

'And once you've got it on the record, before suitably academic witnesses, off you go – interviews, chat shows, film, nice part for Angela . . . '

She didn't say anything, but I could see her go tense.

' . . . though why you think Angela's anything like the woman in the book I can't imagine. That alone would prove you didn't write it.'

216

That, and the fact that she hadn't said a word about Kay. Even with the cropped hair, she should have recognised her.

'You've even got a picture of the woman in your bedroom. Are you telling me you can look at that every morning and imagine her played by a middle-aged soap opera seductress like Angela?'

I thought she was going for my face again and put a hand up to shield it. She laughed.

'I'm not going to hurt you. Are you disappointed?'

I let my hand drop back and said nothing, but I'd proved that Angela was the weak spot.

'And if I do claim my book tomorrow,' she said, 'are you going to stand up and say it isn't mine?'

I didn't answer.

'Won't you feel a little stupid, a little at a loss, when they ask you how you're so sure of it?'

I threw another leaf in the stream, pretending to be absorbed in its progress.'

'And won't it be a little awkward for you to explain about Prudence and Duncan and the rest?'

I said, looking up at her: 'Convenient for you, isn't it? Of the others who might have written it, one's dead and the other's in prison. Couldn't have been better if you'd planned it.'

'Am I supposed to have killed Prudence?' She sounded genuinely amused, far less tense than when I was talking about Angela.

'And then, such a very neat way of dealing with one of the other candidates. Piquant that, having Talisby actually sitting up on the platform listening to you when you tell them you wrote it. I wonder how he'll react.'

'Milord couldn't write. That's why he went into politics.'

'Nice situation for a sadist, making him sit there and look interested while he wonders if you'll tell them about what he nearly did thirty years ago.'

'I shan't.'

217

'Of course not. Far better to keep him worried. No censorship problems if you've got a Home Office minister owing you a favour.'

She said calmly, as if discussing the weather: 'And would your Home Office minister owe me a favour if I tell him he's got the wrong man in prison for murder?'

'Duncan?'

'Duncan's a gentle man. He wouldn't kill anybody, not even a bitch like Prudence.'

'Talisby might need more proof than that.'

'Suppose I told him about a violent young man obsessed with a book, a young man so obsessed he even breaks into my apartment and threatens me.'

'Suppose I told him something else. Suppose I told him about an actress who'd always hated Prudence, who went out of her way to call on Prudence the day before she was killed.'

I don't suppose Nicolle had ever needed her self-control more. I felt it like a rise in air pressure as she first lurched towards me then drew back, forcing herself to sit down on the other end of the stone bench. She even managed to cross her legs elegantly, drawing her black silk trousers up at the knee and tucking one ankle behind the other, but she couldn't take the fear out of her eyes when she looked at me.

'Who told you?'

I lied. 'Angela.' But the next bit was true. 'She had no choice. I'd found a map in her car with Prudence's cottage marked, and she'd dropped a theatre programme in the living room.'

'Angela was always so untidy. She won't change.' There was pride in it, as well as love, as if Angela's untidiness were to be cherished.

'Does her untidiness extend to leaving bodies lying about?'

'Don't be ridiculous.'

'If you were to tell Lord Talisby about me, then of course the police would have to question me, and I'd have to tell them about Angela.'

'There's nothing to tell about Angela. She went to see Prudence because I asked her to.'

'Why?'

'Because I'd decided I was going to acknowledge my book this weekend. Prudence was always avaricious. I though when she knew there was going to be money in it, she'd probably claim to have written it herself.'

'So you sent Angela to warn her off?'

'No. I sent Angela to make her an offer.'

'What sort of offer?'

A bee, drunk and heavy with plunder, brushed against her shoulder, buzzed off, leaving a little smudge of pollen on the turquoise silk. She didn't move.

'Prudence would make problems out of pure malice. I expected her to do something when I announced I'd written the book.'

'Like proving that you hadn't?'

'Like deliberately confusing my claims to authorship. We'd decided to head off this possibility by offering her a business agreement.'

'Flat rate or percentage?'

'Percentage.'

'So Prudence was to get some of the profits as long as she didn't go casting doubt about. But it didn't work. Were you surprised?'

'Yes. Prudence liked money.'

This with the scorn of a woman who'd always had plenty of it.

'Did she give any reason?'

'She hinted to Angela she'd had a better offer.'

'Did she say who from?'

'She appeared to connect it with a visit she was expecting later that day. The visit from you, perhaps?'

How did she know I'd visited Prudence? I'd never told her.

'I didn't have any money to offer, at least, not the sort that would compare with yours.'

A flash of satisfaction in her eyes told me I'd fallen straight into the trap. Until then she'd only been guessing.

'That wasn't what Prudence seemed to think.'

'She must have been expecting somebody else.'

219

Duncan. But Duncan didn't have money to throw around either.

'Perhaps.'

'Somebody who was blackmailing her about the book. Somebody who didn't want it known that he or she wrote it.'

She smiled at me, like a glint of light on a scalpel. 'Why are you so reluctant to believe that I wrote it?'

'Because you didn't. Because you don't know anything about that book. You didn't even recognise the woman when you saw her.'

'What woman?'

'You told me the murder never happened. It did. It was in Morocco. Duncan and Talisby were there. Uncle Lazarus told me.'

'He gets confused, poor old man.'

'I've seen Duncan's picture of it.'

'Of course. Duncan illustrated my book.'

'But the date on it was months before the book was written.'

'How do you know when the book was written?'

'That summer in Brittany.'

'I never spent a summer in Brittany. I wrote it in Paris.'

A bell rang from the house. She stood up. 'I must go. It would be impolite of me to miss Professor Lagen's lecture.' She paused at the rustic bridge and turned back. 'I do hope you're not going to make trouble tomorrow. Dealings with the police are always so tedious.'

I stood up. 'I'm sure Angela would agree with that.'

She was looking down at me from where she was standing and I could feel her weighing me up, wondering if I meant what I said. I tried to make my eyes as hard as hers, returning her stare. At last she turned and click-clacked away over the bridge without another word.

I naturally had no intention of going to hear Lagen on 'The Semantics of Sexual Attraction in the Nineteenth-century Novel'. I stayed in the garden for a while until the sun shifted so that my ash tree was no longer shading me, then strolled up the path, looking at the first floor windows and wondering which one was Kay's and whether I should wake her. I decided against it because my head was full of questions I knew I should be asking her, if it weren't that I was scared of her answers. The path, turning away from the house, gave me one of its views of the sea and a need to walk on the beach and watch waves came to me so strongly that it seemed a solution in itself. I followed a path leading out of a side gate and down to the valley, where it joined the broad concrete path to the sea.

The sun on my head felt as hot as Morocco. When I got to the beach the tide was well out, with only a few picnic parties on the shingle. I stripped to my underpants and swam and, although my ribs twinged and the salt bit into me, felt better for it. I lay down where the shingle and sheep pasture met to let the sun dry me, blocking out the family parties on the beach, putting there instead the tableau of Duncan with the dying boy and the woman watching. I must have slept deeply because when I woke there was a breeze blowing and the sun had started to move down towards the west, so that the woman's shadow slanted across me from the direction of the sea. The sound of the waves was closer and I sensed, without looking up, that everybody else had gone.

'You've been here before,' I said. 'When the boy was killed, with Talisby and Duncan. Who were you then?'

The shadow didn't shift.

'Who are you now? Who were you telephoning from the hotel in Paris?'

It wavered a little.

'Was it Nicolle? Don't be afraid to tell me. You know you can't do any wrong to me, whatever you do.'

I could hear her breathing, short, harsh breaths across the sound of the waves.

'Only if it is Nicolle, you shouldn't trust her for your own sake, Kay. Better to tell me. You can still go on spying on me.'

Still no response.

'Or is it Lord Talisby who's paying you? Did you make it up between you, the story about the ring on Prudence's finger? Did he send you?'

221

'Nobody sent me.' Her voice, when it came at last, was as flat and emotionless as ever. 'I've got something for you.'

When she said that, it was in my mind that she'd come to kill me. I sat up slowly so as not to scare her, expecting a gun or a knife, looking not at her hands but her eyes. They were wide and nervous, fixed on mine.

'This.'

Then I looked at her hands. She was holding something wrapped in a plastic bag; sat down on her heels to give it to me.

'I thought you'd want it.'

I unwrapped it and, for the first time since it had been taken from me in the car park, saw the book, unquestionably the same book in its primrose cover that had come to me in the Bodley. When I opened the front cover there inside, where I'd left them, were the three draft pages in the unknown hand, telling the story of the murder in the book as I now believed it happened, not as the writer had tidied and ritualised it.

'Why . . . ?'

'I knew you wanted them. I stole them.'

'Stole them from . . . ?'

'I can't say who from.'

I thought it must have been the three toughs, perhaps when she was with them in Paris.

'I don't understand. You watch them while they're half killing me, then you do this for me.'

'What do you mean?'

I touched the bruises on my ribs and face. 'This. You were there in the car park watching them. I know. I could feel you there.' I was on my feet by then.

She looked scared; took a step away from me. 'What car park? I don't know what you mean.'

'The car park where you were supposed to meet me. Don't worry, I'm not angry about it. I just want to under-stand.'

'I wasn't there.'

I groaned, put my arms round her and let my head rest on her shoulder. At first she didn't move, then I felt her denim

222

arms brushing my bare ribs, her hands against my back, and held her to me more tightly.

'I don't want to hurt you,' she said.

'It doesn't matter.'

We parted when somebody came down the path walking a dog. The book was lying on top of my clothes and I gave it to her to hold while I dressed. As she handed it back to me she said: 'Now what are you going to do with it?'

It was in her mind, I think, as a kind of talisman that would clear up all the questions about her birth, if only I could be persuaded to get it to work.

'Wait and see tomorrow.'

I'd have opened every cell in my brain to her if it hadn't been for the thought of that phone call.

'Why? What's going to happen?'

'I don't know yet.'

We walked up the path with the sun behind us, not hand in hand, but arms touching now and then. Back at the house, they'd got themselves into discussion groups on literature and censorship and were cooking up nasty questions to throw at Talisby next day. There was no sign of Nicolle. At Kay's door I took her in my arms and kissed her goodnight, looking longingly at the narrow white bed inside. She didn't invite me in so I went to my room and sat all night at the open window with the book in front of me. The night was almost as hot as the day had been, with no moon but dry lightning flickering over the sea. When it got light I read the two descriptions of the murder again, the one in the draft and the one in the printed book. By the time the first steps were shuffling down to breakfast, I'd decided what I was going to do.

Chapter Twenty-One

Neither Nicolle nor Kay appeared at breakfast. I collected coffee and a sachet of sugar and took them up to Kay's room. She opened the door as soon as I knocked, in jacket and bare legs, hair disordered.

'I've been thinking . . . '

'With sugar?'

I stirred it for her, waited while she sat down on the bed and took a sip or two.

'I've been thinking,' she said. 'Why don't we just go up to him this afternoon and ask him about it?'

'Whether he killed Prudence? Whether he wrote the book?'

'Prudence and Duncan. I don't think he wrote the book.'

'Why not?'

'It was a woman, wasn't it?'

I felt disturbed and excited. Until then I wasn't even sure that she'd read it. I asked her why she thought it was a woman, not admitting that I still believed that too.

'Because of the woman in the book. At first, I couldn't understand why she was doing it. Then I started to see why, and it was something I'd sort of half thought only . . . '

I was holding my breath, but let out just enough of it to say, 'Go on.'

'She was saying to him, to all the rest of them: "Make things real. Stop playing games about everything."'

'I thought she was playing games with him.'

She shook her head. 'No, all the other things were the games, his work, his politics, that girl he was going to marry. She was saying to him there must be something that matters, something you'd die for.'

'You mean, you know it's real when it hurts? But mightn't that be part of the game too?'

She wriggled her shoulders resentfully. I'd lost her with my academic habit of argument.

'I don't know. I'm not a professor, am I? I just think it was a woman.'

Having messed up one tack, I started on another. 'So your idea is we go up to Talisby this afternoon and put it to him that Duncan's innocent and he's guilty, that it?'

'I've been thinking about the Arab boy, the one in the picture.'

'Well?'

'The old man said Lord Talisby was in Morocco too. Supposing he killed the boy and Duncan took the blame.'

'Why should he?'

'Lord Talisby was rich and had a family. Perhaps he paid him.'

It wouldn't have needed money, I thought. The guilt and self-sacrifice were already there in Duncan's character. But he'd have regretted it, surely, three decades later when Talisby sold them all out with his new law.

'Suppose Prudence could prove it,' she said. 'Suppose that was why he had her killed.'

'And that was what you were planning to do this afternoon, was it? Stand up and accuse him? You think he'll just collapse and admit it?'

She'd gone to stand at the mirror, combing her hair and trying to get it to lie flat against her cheeks, apparently taking no notice of me.

'Kay, leave it to me please. I know what I'm doing. Just stand back and let me get on with it.'

But I could get no promise out of her, and precious little else. I left her trying to get her hair to see reason and, for want of anything better to do, sat in on a lecture on 'The Phallic Fallacy in Fanny Hill' by a Cambridge lesbian. By mid-morning, with the heat bludgeoning and the atmosphere bad-tempered, I noticed that even more people were leaving than seemed accountable by the subject matter and gathered

225

that the focus of attention had shifted to something going on outside. I followed the drift out to the front steps in time to witness the triumphant entry of Angela.

She'd made it up the steps from the car park by the time I got there, and was being warmly embraced in succession by Nicolle, the director and as many of the assorted academics as could get within range. Most of those present were of an age to remember her at maximum sexual voltage, and her cream halter top with slit skirt seemed calculated to jog a few memories below the belt. Even Lagen and Prothering were watching, though pretending elaborately to be talking about something else. I heard one of my neighbours asking what she was doing here, and somebody explained that she was going to be in a film by Nicolle. The publicity department obviously wasn't missing a trick. Angela emerged from a scrum of welcome and noticed me. She hardly hesitated for a second.

'Darling, you owe me a new bra. You snagged it when you were taking it off.'

Considering how our meeting had ended and that our host of that day was, as she must know, in prison awaiting trial for murder, I gave her full marks for coolness.

'One of the risks of the profession, darling,' I said loudly over the intervening heads.

Nicolle shot me a look and a dozen mouths fell open. The expression on Lagen's face was worth a year's research grant. I was watching the director and Nicolle pretending I hadn't happened when I was aware of Kay standing beside me.

'Who's that?'

I told her.

'Oh, the one who had me aborted.'

In the nature of these things it came, quite loudly, in a pause in the conversation. Angela turned round and stared at her, surprise and direct sunlight fleetingly making her look all of her fifty years. The director said something and she turned away, all smiles again. Drinks on the lawn were offered and accepted. I followed uninvited and, turning to look for Kay, felt a firm grip on my shoulder.

226

'Who's that girl you're with?'

'Duncan's daughter – I think.'

Her hand kept me turned away. I couldn't see her face.

'Where can we talk?'

'There's a sort of Japanese garden, down the second lot of steps.'

I waited by a pagoda summerhouse and she came within ten minutes, holding two tall glasses.

'Mint juleps.'

'Which one's got the poison?'

She let me choose. It tasted like superior mouthwash.

'What did she mean about the abortion?'

'She was born that year you were all in Paris.'

'You said Duncan's daughter.'

'Don't you think she's like him?'

'Yes.' Her voice, for once, was quiet and serious and yet she'd had only a glimpse of Kay.

I said, 'I suppose in those days he was bi-sexual.'

'Oh yes, a lot of women were interested in Duncan.'

'Including Mimi?'

'Including poor Mimi.' She swept her hand side to side across a juniper bush, stroking it as if it were a cat, absent-mindedly.

'Was it Duncan's baby you had aborted?'

'How would I know, darling?' The hardness and flippancy were back. 'I suppose it was Uncle Lazarus who told you. Funny.'

'Why funny?'

'I trusted him.'

'He didn't want to. I'd convinced him he had to tell me all he could, to prevent something worse happening.'

'Worse than what?'

Prudence's death didn't seem to lie heavily on her.

'Worse than Duncan being in prison on a murder charge.'

'Oh that.'

'I thought you cared about him.'

'Duncan's got this drive towards martyrdom. He's probably happier in prison than he's been for years.'

227

'He wasn't always like that, though, was he? Something happened that year that made him take to homosexuality like a crusade.'

'What year?'

'The year the book was written.'

'The year Nicolle wrote the book.' She looked up and smiled as she said it, inviting me to argue. I side-stepped.

'Did you ever wonder what it was? Did you notice a difference in him?'

'Darling, I was twenty. I was too busy living my own life to go round analysing everyone else's.'

'You'd have taken an interest, though, if you heard one of your friends was pregnant?'

'With Duncan's daughter, you mean? That didn't have to be one of us though, did it? It could have been any little Left Bank scrubber.'

'What about Prudence?'

'Prudence?' She stopped stroking the bush and stared at me. 'Prudence have Duncan's daughter?'

'What's so odd about that?'

I didn't tell her what Uncle Lazarus had said about Prudence being unable to have children. I wanted her reaction.

'I can't imagine Prudence having anybody's daughter. Little calculating machines, that's what Prudence would have.'

'She hid herself away somewhere all that summer, didn't she?'

'As if I'd know. I didn't give a fart what Prudence was doing.' She pronounced it with precision, like Eliza Doolittle saying 'bloody'.

'And yet you went all the way to Clun to see her, the day before she was killed.'

She clunked her empty glass down on a ledge of the pagoda so hard that it cracked from base to rim.

'Who told you about that?'

'Nicolle.'

'Nicolle wouldn't.' There was hurt and fear in her eyes.

'Only because I'd guessed anyway. Nicolle's an intelligent woman. She knew she'd only make it worse by lying.'

'Guessed? How?'

I told her about the map in her car and the theatre programme on Prudence's floor.

'I didn't leave it there. Why would I carry a programme, for goodness sake? I'm in the thing.'

I didn't pursue it. The map was enough.

'Why did you go?'

'Didn't Nicolle tell you?'

'She said you were going to offer Prudence a percentage of the book and film profits, on her behalf, providing she didn't challenge Nicolle's claim to the book. But Prudence didn't bite.'

She shrugged. 'Well then, you know it all. It's not illegal.'

'It's not illegal, but it could be inconvenient. The police might like to know about it.'

'Why? It's got nothing to do with her being killed.'

'They can't be sure of that. And, quite apart from the police, it might spoil your little publicity launch if people started raising doubts.'

'What do you want out of this?' Her voice implied that it was money.

'Three things. I want to know who killed Prudence. I want to know who wrote the book. I want to know about Kay.'

'Kay?'

'The one you saw.'

'God help you. I can't.'

'You can tell me what happened when you saw Prudence.'

'You know already.'

'Not the details.'

'How will they help?'

'I don't know. Just tell me.'

She sat down on the little stone bench in front of the pagoda, crossed her long legs, and got on with it.

She had an actress's memory for appearances, like how Prudence looked when she came round the side of the house, hands covered with soil, sneering like a pug offered the wrong brand of dog food.

'It was like being back in Paris again, the way she'd look when I was getting all the attention, hating it, but drinking it all in as if she couldn't get enough of it. I said straight out that Nicolle had sent me to talk business, and at least that got me inside. More like a potting shed than a living room, it was.'

Prudence had listened while Angela put their proposition. A cool five per cent of Nicolle's profits was on offer for doing nothing but keeping quiet. Angela had Nicolle's instructions to go up to as high as ten per cent, and did in two stages.

'I remember wishing my agent could bargain like she did. Anyway, she was just playing with me, as I might have expected from Prudence, because when she got me up to the ten per cent she just grinned and said no deal.'

'Did she say why not?'

'She said we weren't the only ones in the market. She said she'd had a phone calll from somebody else who was coming to see her the next day, and whoever it was might be making her a more interesting offer.'

'But . . . but she can't have meant me.'

'Were you making her an interesting offer?'

'Twenty per cent of a book on French publishers I wasn't going to write anyway.'

She stared. 'But that was nothing like what she'd have got from us.'

'So it can't have been me she was talking about. Did she say anything at all about who this person was supposed to be?'

'She hinted – I've been trying to remember the exact words ever since because Nicolle wanted to know, but I can't – she hinted it was somebody who knew who wrote the book.'

'But what did she say?'

'It was a kind of warning to Nicolle that things were waking up, or breaking up, I can't remember which. She said I should ask Nicolle if she was quite sure she'd got all the documentary evidence.'

I thought of the few pages of manuscript in my room.

'A friendly warning?'

'No, of course not. Teasing. No, more malicious than teasing – making fun, as if she knew something we didn't.'

'What did you do?'

'What could I do? I just thanked her politely, to disappoint her, and left.'

I sat and thought about it, not even noticing that I was staring at her leg. The leg noticed, though, and responded, re-crossing itself, letting the sandal dangle by a thin strap from her toes, instep arched like a wave breaking.

'I must go,' she said. 'Nicolle will be waiting.'

It was nearly twelve o'clock. We walked back together to the house, earning me jealous glances from every male who saw us, but all I could think of was what Prudence had said about documentary evidence. That, and why it should matter about a theatre programme. When I heard camera shutters clicking I didn't at first take in what was happening. Nicolle did, though. She was between us in seconds, cutting me out, directing the photographers.

'No, you don't need him. He's nothing to do with it.'

My first impression of a posse of photographers resolved itself into three, once I'd found out what was going on. There were two from the tabloids that didn't mind collecting a few pictures of Angela on a quiet Sunday plus one from the *Guardian* – Nicolle having done some research into who'd go for 'American poet admits I was mystery author'. They drifted down to a lower garden for photographs, the director fussing in their wake, half thrilled at all the publicity, half horrified that it might rebound.

'What's going on?' one of the academics asked me.

It was a reminder that, although the news editors presumably knew what Nicolle intended to spring that afternoon, the conference didn't. I told him I gathered Angela had just signed up for a new film and Nicolle was scripting it.

'You seem to know her well.'

More snide envy in the voice than if I'd landed a professorship. I told him we were childhood friends, left him trying to work it out and strolled casually with the rest of

231

the stream to watch the photographs: Angela barefoot on bench by pagoda, Angela leaning over rustic bridge, dress becoming more low cut by the minute. Nicolle meanwhile, remote and unsmiling, was co-operating with the *Guardian* man who had arty ideas about leaf shadows. The director, who seemed to think I was somehow responsible, asked me if I thought the papers would mention the Institute. Sure to, I said. He looked from Angela, perching on the rail of the rustic bridge, to Nicolle's sharp profile, half invisible behind the foliage, and did not seem comforted.

'I hope they're going to make it clear this is an academic occasion.'

At this point the woman in the kaftan appeared at his elbow and whispered something. He looked distinctly miserable, gave me an absent-minded apology which I didn't need and followed her, at a pace too fast for the heat, back up the lawn. Since I'd heard what the woman in the kaftan had whispered I followed but, as they went round to the front of the house, made sure that I stayed out of sight round the side. An aggressively thorned climbing rose screened me as I watched him going into the celebrity welcoming routine for the second time that day.

They were taking their time getting out of the Montego. The chauffeur opened the door, Lord Talisby emerged clutching a thin black briefcase, then turned back to help out Lady Talisby, cool in cornflower blue silk. Her presence was unexpected and bothered me. She'd seen me twice to his once and was already proven to have a memory for faces. I'd have to keep out of the way of both of them until I'd had a chance to spring my trap. Meanwhile, hidden by my rose, I watched with some security as the director advanced down the steps to meet them, walked backwards up the steps in front of them uttering apologies for the heat, telling them how honoured the Institute was by the ministerial presence. Since most the the academics and writers present had spent much of the weekend working out nasty remarks to throw at Talisby, I thought it was overdoing things, and the polite arrogance of Talisby's smile showed he thought so too. He said something about coming as a Daniel to the lions' den, but with a drawl that suggested he'd seen the lions before and thought them a fairly mangey bunch. I could see the director throwing nervous glances down the garden, hoping that Angela and the photographers wouldn't reappear until he'd got his latest guests safely alongside dry sherry in the library. He nearly managed it too. He and Lady Talisby were halfway up the steps with Lord Talisby just behind them, when the pack reappeared. They swept past me without a second glance, round to the front of the house.

I gathered the idea was to get some pictures of Angela sitting on a stone lion at the bottom of the steps, but that was dropped as soon as they saw a much better photo opportunity.

'It's that bugger Talisby. What's he doing here?' The cry went up from one of the photographers and all was lost. Talisby looked furious and on the point of bolting inside, but Nicolle, moving even faster than the photographers, cut off his escape. She was up the steps in two bounds, shaking his hand, shaking Lady Talisby's hand, with the director flapping his arms and trying vainly to usher them inside to safety. In a ringing voice, as if opening a public meeting, Nicolle said to Lord Talisby:

'How very nice to see you again, after all this time.'

Then she dragged Angela into the group by main force, the shutters clicked, and there was tomorrow's front page photograph.

I've seen those photos since; three versions all much the same because, in the split second afterwards, the Talisbys made their escape inside and there was no chance for more shots. They're frozen there, the five of them in the sunlight between the creepers and the climbing roses: the director on the right, mouth open; Lady Talisby flashing that tense, frenetic smile with which politicians' wives the world over will probably greet Armageddon; Lord Talisby, stern and serious but unable to avoid Nicolle's hand; Angela, unregarded for once on his left, smiling by instinct straight into camera. All there. There's just one other photo with them all on it together (not counting the director, of course) and that was taken twenty-nine years ago. The door opened for the five of them, closed again and the photographers were left outside, still asking each other what Talisby was doing there. The woman with the kaftan was sent out to scold them: a private visit, an academic occasion, if you are going to use it be sure to spell the Institute's name right. They packed up their camera cases and left.

If Angela, Nicolle and the Talisbys sat down together at the lunch table, it must have been one of the most fraught hours the director ever suffered. I've no way of knowing because naturally all hoi polloi got were salads and one glass of hock in the buttery. I went in and collected two glasses, one for Kay. I couldn't find her there, nor in her room and, for a bad moment as I stood outside the door, wondered if she'd gone, but her clothes and make-up were still scattered around. I spent too long with them, staring at the colours of her lipsticks, smelling her moisturiser, telling myself I was waiting for her. By the time I'd realised she wasn't coming it was fifteen minutes before the start of Nicolle's lecture, allowing me no more than a fleeting search of the nearer parts of the garden. When the lecture began I still hadn't found her.

It was a full house. Even if they didn't know what Nicolle was going to say, word had got round that it would be more interesting than adverttised. For an added bonus, there was Talisby sitting on the platform. Academic courtesy dictated that he must listen to Nicolle's talk before delivering his own and he seemed, from the expression on his face, to have settled for a policy of distant interest. I could see no sign of Lady Talisby and assumed she was in the garden smelling the flowers.

I found one of the few spare seats at the back, trying simultaneously to keep my head down and look round for Kay. As far as I could see she wasn't there, but aat least Talisby gave no sign of having noticed me. Nicolle did, though. After the introduction from the director, including a quote from one of her poems in Boston French, she came to the podium and surveyed her audience with a coolness that didn't go with her claim to be a simple poet, scared of public speaking. She let her eyes rest on me for what seemed a long time, so long that I imagined Talisby and the rest must be looking at me as well, wrongly I think because when she moved on nobody seemed to be paying particular attention to me. She'd had long enough, at any rate, to deliver me a personal message and that message was sharp and clear: shut up.

She made us wait. The first part of her talk was as advertised; that is to say, I'm no expert on post-feminist poetic imagery but it seemed dull enough to fit and I could feel everybody around me relaxing, sated with heat and the hock ration, into the familiar state of academic semi-coma. With Angela absent, they were beginning to wonder what the fuss had been about. Even Talisby seemed to be relaxing a little, giving the occasional half smile that had no reference to what Nicolle was saying. Then, very gradually, the rhythm of the talk changed. She dropped in one about making love on a boat, more openly erotic than what had gone before, doing it, of course, to demonstrate a reverse sub-text simile in the last stanza. Of course. The audience woke up and showed a sudden interest in reverse sub-text similes. She paused between the French and English translations, looked round and smiled. I could read her thoughts: it was time to give it to them.

I could feel the dry lightning, a current coming from her, connecting with Talisby and with me, with all the rest sensing something was happening but not knowing what it was. She picked up my book, the twin of it, and read from it matter-of-fact and without emphasis, a few lines describing a conversation between the woman and Valentine. I recognised it as the scene where she's first put into his mind that he should kill his friend, but unless you'd read the book you wouldn't have known that. I watched Talisby while she was reading. He was leaning forward, with an expression of a man puzzled but disposed to be tolerant. I forget what literary point the passage was supposed to be illustrating. As she closed the book and administered a proprietary pat to its primrose cover she apologised for again quoting from her own work. There was a little gasp from somewhere, I'm nearly sure from Gus Prothering, that gave her as much cue as she needed.

'*The Martyrdom of Valentine*. A curious child of my youth that may, in these more enlightened times, be acknowledged safely at last.' A sharp sideways glance at Talisby. 'Always supposing that the noble Lord permits.'

Naturally, most people assumed she was taking a dig at the Government's known enthusiasm for accepted artistic guidelines, alias censorship. There was a little surge of laughter at Talisby's expense. I noticed that next to me a man I didn't recognise was taking notes in shorthand and realised she must have briefed the writing press as well as the photographers. Talisby's smile was noticeably tight by now. He took the strain off it by tipping back his chair, staring at the ceiling as if none of this had anything to do with him. She paused and looked at him, making sure he wasn't going to answer, before gliding back to deep academic waters.

She didn't mention the book again, but then she didn't need to. After another minute or two's exposure to the theory of similes the journalist got up and left with the air of a job well done. The pattering of applause at the end was no more than polite and when the director rose and asked for questions there was hardly a sign, apart from Lord Talisby's continuing pretence that he was on another planet, that anything out of the ordinary had happened. The first two questioners, obviously planted by the director, aired respectful opinions and were duly patronised by Nicolle. The director was on his feet again, getting ready to introduce Lord Talisby and my mouth went dry and my heart started thumping as I thought I'd missed my chance.

'If nobody's got any more questions . . . '

'Yes. I have.'

I was on my feet, but the voice was not mine but Prothering's, from his seat near the front.

'I have to confess that my interest is more bibliophilic than literary, but did I understand Miss Banderberg to say that she is the author of *The Martyrdom of Valentine?*'

'Yes, I am.'

She was smiling at him quite warmly. Prothering was um-ing for a supplementary question, but I got in first.

'Oh no she's not.'

These are not, I admit, the terms in which debates are usually conducted in literary circles. They weren't even quite the words I'd intended to say when I'd rehearsed in my mind. Still, they served. The director looked as if somebody had punched him in the stomach, Nicolle froze at the lectern and Lord Talisby decided abruptly that there were some earthly matters worth his notice after all. There was a buzz all round me not, I think, of disapproval but of pleasure that things were getting vulgarly interesting again. The director found some breath and began saying he didn't think this was the place to go into . . . I stayed on my feet and kept talking.

'Miss Banderberg no more wrote that book than I did. She's claiming it now because she thinks there's money in it. I have documentary evidence that she is not the author.'

After that I didn't wait to see if the Morgan B. Pencluft Institute employed bouncers. I took one last look at the platform party and walked out past lines of shocked, pleased faces that said another one spun off the track, another competitor gone in the race for academic survival. I'd no doubt at all that they were right.

Chapter Twenty-Two

I'd have liked to stay and hear whether Talisby said anything about it, but now I'd taken the irrevocable step there was something more urgent than that. I had to find Kay and, having found her, make her keep clear. If I could, I'd persuade her to go away somewhere and wait for me, impress on her that she must trust me and not interfere. I calculated that I had an hour perhaps to find her before Talisby's talk ended and they were all on the loose again. Outside the lecture hall the place was quiet, the air heavy with heat. I went upstairs and checked my room first, but there was no sign that anybody had been in it since I left. I went and knocked on her door, paused for a half minute, called her name and went in.

It was only a small room, but its emptiness made it seem vast as a barn to me. When I'd been there before the lecture started I'd seen the litter of her things, denim jacket, make-up, the bag she'd bought in Paris. Now there was nothing. The bedclothes were pulled back, the smell of her perfume, a green ferny smell, was still in the air, but apart from that, not a sign of her. I think I stood there for quite a long while, incapable of thinking or moving. I've a dim memory of looking into the narrow wardrobe, under the bed, calling her name as if trying to entice a kitten. When I saw something catching the light on the floor by the wash-basin pedestal I pounced on it with relief to find anything at all, but it was no more than a lipstick. I pulled the cap off and registered that it was the apricot colour she'd been wearing that morning, one side of it already worn down. Current favourite, then. She'd have wanted to take it with her. Easy enough to find if she'd looked, so she hadn't looked, hadn't had time to look, gone in a hurry.

I put it in my pocket and went down to the car park. The hire car was still there where she'd left it. She had the keys. I remembered her picking them up off the table when we'd registered. She could have driven herself away but she hadn't. I checked the other cars. Nicolle's still there. Angela's still there. The Talisby Montego was gone, but that didn't signify. Chauffeurs have to eat. It came to me that she might be on the road hitching and I ran down the drive to the gates, gravel scrunching like breaking eggs, smell of cut grass heavy in my lungs. I'd like to give a rational account of what I did in the next few hours to find her, but I wasn't rational. I didn't even know whether I hoped she'd gone of her own free will or been taken away by force. I only had a certainty that she couldn't be far away and if I didn't stop, I'd come to her.

I ran all the way down the side road to the main road, stood for a while half hypnotised by the streams of holiday cars going past, staring into them in case she should be there. I met some hitchhikers, asked them if they'd seen a tall woman with short dark hair. Nobody like her. After some time I tore myself away from the traffic and went back up the side road, stopping at every lay-by, every clump of trees, in case there was any sign of her. On the way back cars passed from the opposite direction, bearing the early leavers away from the symposium. Some recognised me and I got curious looks as I glared in through their windows. No Kay with them, unless she was lying down on the floor. Back at the Institute there were still quite a few cars left, Nicolle's and Angela's among them.

By then I'd convinced myself that Kay hadn't gone by road at all, that she'd taken the path through the garden, out through the valley to the sea. I had such a clear mental picture of her standing alone on the beach, waiting for me, that when I got there and found it crowded with kids and swimmers and family parties packing up to go home I felt physically sick with disappointment. I suppose I'd been on the move for two or three hours by then, mostly running, under the hottest sun we'd had all year and exhaustion had caught up with me.

At least that exhaustion brought with it a clarity of mind that had been completely lacking since I stood in her empty room. The idea that I'd find her by running far enough or looking hard enough disappeared. Whether Kay had gone of her own free will or been taken away, it was with the intention that I shouldn't find her. It was part of the same tangle that had been there all along, and unravelling it was the only way to get to her. So although one part of me still wanted to run on, run anywhere, I sat down on the shingle, watched the sea and did some of Uncle Lazarus's breathing exercises until the sickness had gone and I was thinking again. By the time I stood up, the sun had slipped another few notches seaward and the beach was almost empty. My legs had gone stiff and I had the washed-out feeling you get after running a high temperature. It was all I could do to drag myself along the path back up the valley to the garden gate and I told myself that I must eat something or drink something, that there was still everything to do.

The gate from the valley to the garden of the Institute is overhung with trees, birches and dark untidy rhododendron bushes that screen everything inside. As I put my hand on the latch I thought I heard a rustling from the other side, something moving cautiously, but too big for a cat or dog. I opened the gate very quietly and stepped inside, hearing the rustling again from somewhere on my left. There was a path I'd noticed only vaguely before, no more than a trodden line in the grass, leading at right angles from the path up the garden, disappearing into another thicket of rhododendrons. I took a few steps along it and found myself looking into the eyes of the gravel-voiced tough.

It was one of the oddest encounters I ever had. I knew he was looking at me, from his place behind a bush covered with creamy flowers, no more than ten yards from where I was standing. When I say I was looking into his eyes I had no doubt that he'd seen me, just as well as I saw him, yet neither of us did anything at all about it. I guessed that he'd been left there to keep watch on whoever came in or out by the back gate and that, beyond watching, he had no instructions to do anything about me for the moment. I stood long enough to let him be sure it was me, then turned and walked back up the path to the house. I told myself that if Kay had seen him or either of his colleagues it would account for her packing up in a hurry and going away without telling me. I hoped, but didn't believe now I'd seen him, that it was as straightforward as that.

Inside, the fat woman in the kaftan pounced on me.

'You didn't tell me you were staying for the Sunday night. That's twelve pounds each extra.'

I didn't know whether she'd heard about my performance at Nicolle's lecture or just disliked me on instinct.

'My friend keeps our money. I don't suppose you've seen her.'

'I wouldn't have noticed. There are too many comings and goings.'

'What about the VIPs? Are they coming or going?'

'Lord and Lady Talisby will be staying the night, so that he can get up to London first thing tomorrow.'

She liked using the words Lord and Lady, even to a scruff like me.

'What about Angela Arless and Miss Banderberg?'

'I believe they're staying too.' She said it with less enthusiasm, and sniffed at my sweat-stained shirt and creased trousers. 'I assume you'll be changing for dinner.'

I told her I wouldn't be dining. As I turned to go upstairs she said as an afterthought, 'I believe there's a message for you on the notice board.'

I grabbed it almost before she'd finished speaking, a square white envelope with my name on the front. I didn't recognise the writing, but then it came to me that I'd never seen Kay's writing. When I tore it open, though, the message inside had nothing to do with her and I stared at it stupidly until I saw the signature. There it was, ornate and self-satisfied, Augustus Prothering. If he'd been there, I could have shaken him for raising false hopes with his bibliophilic inanities.

241

My dear Colin,

I hope you will excuse an unsolicited approach but your interest in the book under discussion this afternoon leads me to wonder if you may perhaps have acquired a copy of it since we last met. In view of Miss Banderberg's revelations, some curiosity value will attach to the first – and so far, only – edition and I am venturing to write to you to suggest that, if you should consider disposing of your copy, you might allow me to make an offer which may well prove more satisfactory to you than that tendered by a dealer. I shall be staying here until tomorrow, and should be happy to meet you after dinner to discuss this matter.

I crumpled it, put it in my pocket and went upstairs, aware of the fat woman's eyes on me from the corner of the hall.

I didn't expect to find any trace of Kay in my room and there wasn't, except for the lipstick I'd brought with me in my pocket. I kicked my shoes off and lay down on the bed, winding the lipstick up and down, trying the colour of it on my hand, seeing it on her lips. It had come as a shock to me that I didn't know what her handwriting looked like, that I'd even mistaken Prothering's for hers. When so much in what had happened to us hinged on writing, it seemed a frightening gap, standing for all the other things about her I didn't know. Once my mind had started on that tack it moved slowly but with a certainty that I hadn't known since Prudence was murdered. Physically, though, I was inert, tiredness and hunger caught up with me at last, beyond sleeping or eating. I couldn't have moved from the bed unless the door had opened and Kay had walked in, and I knew that wasn't going to happen. The colour of the sunlight in the room changed from clear white to dusky yellow, became a shaft of apricot-gold and lit up the dust motes, making shadows on the walls of the creepers outside. Through the half-open window I was conscious of sounds of dinner being served and cleared away, of murmuring voices, occasional gusts of laughter from the lawn behind the house.

242

Through all this the unknown hand kept writing and, while it wrote, became so clear to me that I couldn't think what had stopped me recognising it before. I could have laughed, did laugh perhaps, at the simplicity of it.

Before it got quite dark, I found I could move again, though cautiously, with legs as stiff as sticks and a head that, for all its clarity, seemed only lightly attached to my spinal column, free floating like a balloon. I opened the window more and leaned out, getting wafts of warm scent from the garden and the sharper tang of the sea. The sun was down out of sight, but the sky still flared orange-red. I supposed it would be a matter of waiting, and had turned back into the room when I noticed something that had been waiting for me all the time.

I hadn't noticed it when I came in because it was such a very small change, so subtle that I might have missed it altogether, except the person who'd made the change knew me better than that. Sooner or later, from force of habit, I'd go to pick up the book as I did then when I turned away from the window. And I'd notice, as I noticed, that it wasn't exactly as I'd left it, that it had been turned sideways on to my pile of conference papers, instead of parallel to them. When I noticed that, of course I picked it up and saw what I took to be a sprig of grass tucked behind the front cover. It wasn't grass, though. It had started as something delicate and feathery, only the heat had withered it. When it crumbled in my fingers the smell that came out, unmistakable, musky and medicinal, was camomile. It had been put between the first page and the blank back of the copyright page. At least, when I'd last seen the book it had been blank. Now there were three words on it. 'Midnight. Last garden.' Tucked in alongside them, deliberately for comparison, my few pages of manuscript describing the murder in the unknown hand. I hadn't needed the comparison. I knew as soon as I saw those three words that they'd been written by the same person.

Waiting the next two hours was, I think, the hardest thing I'd ever done. It wasn't worry or even fear. I'd come through those to a kind of sandbank where they were all round me but, for the moment, without influence. It was simply the mental and physical effort of making the time pass, as if every second had to be pushed out of the way to make room for the next. I was conscious of every sound, of the last voices from the lawn retreating inside, of steps up and down stairs, doors closing, cisterns flushing, of the light going until only the white surfaces of papers showed up in the room. At twenty to twelve, taking no particular trouble to be quiet about it, I picked up my book and the manuscript pages and went downstairs.

There were still sounds of people awake upstairs, but I got down to the hall unchallenged and met nobody. The French windows onto the lawn had been bolted from the inside but not locked. They made a grating sound when I opened them, but nobody called out. Perhaps the kaftan woman was in bed with the director. I walked across the lawn, finding the top of the steps down to the gardens by memory rather than sight. The sky was matt black, with stars but not even a sliver of moon. I had a good memory map at least of the top two gardens, traditional English first where the path became meanderings of crazy paving and the smell of roses was heavier by night than day, the waterfall louder. I passed the black square of the summerhouse, negotiated the rustic bridge where Angela had posed for the photographers, into the Japanese garden where she'd sat on the bench outside the pagoda. Trampling the raked and patterned gravel, trying not to tread on prostrate junipers, I could have been heard from half a mile away. Once though, when I stopped to untangle my feet from some convoluted shrub, I heard a noise that wasn't of my making. It came from the English garden behind me and sounded like somebody coming cautiously down the path, rustling the climbing plants on either side. As I listened, the noise stopped. I went on again. I'd expected to be followed.

I'd known without having to think about it what the unknown hand meant by the last garden. The gardens sloped down in sequence from the house, following the stream. The last of them must be near the gate, along the narrow path where the tough had stood and watched me. I followed the straight flagged path of the Italian formal, beginning to adapt to the

244

minimal light that came from the stars, enough to distinguish shapes of urns and nymphs. More steps, where I waited a few seconds and heard scufflings on gravel from behind me, then on through Elizabethan, moss and musk smell, then something softer than grass under my feet and the scent of bruised camomile as sudden as an explosion. After that, only a little area of grass and shrubs before I came to the smaller path and had the bush with its white flowers to steer by. I passed it, tracing the path by the feel of it underfoot, went a few steps further and stopped.

The stream flowed into a pond there, with white water-lilies on it and great lumps of white stone round it. I didn't know then that it was an abandoned chalk quarry with the old workings terraced into hanging gardens. All I knew was a feeling of familiarity that stopped me in my tracks. I knew, though I couldn't see it, that there was a bamboo thicket on the other side of the pool, could even hear it rustling though there wasn't the slightest breeze. I've seen it by daylight since and I know now it isn't the garden in the book but at midnight I knew that it was. My heart started thumping and I realised I was clutching the book to me like a poultice. It was some time before I was conscious of the light.

It was a faint one, coming from somewhere on my left. I moved cautiously towards it and found I was standing in front of a façade carved into the chalk, like the rock tombs at Petra. No more by daylight than another ornate summerhouse: at night, with the light glowing from a window, as bleak as a skull. I walked up to it and found a metal door ajar, a crack of light showing through, pushed it open and walked inside. Greeny white of mould on chalk, like the inside of a skull that had been left a long time. My shadow bent across it from the light of a stubby candle on the floor, falling on something that was lying in the corner. That was white too, but not the skull white of the chalk walls. I shouted something, threw myself across the slippery floor towards the body of Kay. As I got to her, the door slammed shut behind me.

She was naked, her clothes in a heap beside her, curled up on her side like a child asleep. One arm was curved

245

over her head, the other stretched out, palm upwards, a puncture mark showing clearly just below the inside of the elbow where the skin was as pale as a plaice. Her breathing was shallow, uncertain, mouth a little open. When I got her in my arms her skin was as cold and damp as the chalk floor where she'd been lying. A syringe and some ampoules were scattered beside her bag.

I shouted, 'Kay's in here. She's taken an overdose.'

The windows were no more than slits in the chalk, but my voice must have carried through them. It echoed round the place, more of a cave than a room, as if inside my own head.

'We've got to get help for her. We can talk about the other thing later.'

No answer, but I was sure whoever had slammed the door hadn't gone away.

'Can you hear me? She's unconscious. She could be dying.'

Her narrow ribcage was hardly moving against my arms, her breathing a marginal activity, face quite calm. I laid her down, spreading out her clothes to make a mattress, covering her with my shirt for want of anything better. The iron door had a latch on the inside and was hinged to open outwards. I pushed at it, throwing all my weight against it, and heard a bar grating outside. For a moment I thought it was being opened and nearly cried with relief but when I pushed against it again it was as firm as ever.

'It's stuck. You'll have to run up to the house and get somebody.'

I'd believed up to then I was dealing with one of the toughs. Only when there was no answer or sound of movement from outside I knew I'd got it wrong. I threw myself at the door time after time, swearing, pleading, shouting. I found later that my chest and shoulders were lacerated and scaled with splinters of rust, but at the time felt nothing. When I stopped shouting, it seemed to me that Kay's breathing was even less regular than before. I went to her, took her in my arms again, rocking her until it went back to its uncertain rhythm, murmuring that it was all right, it would be all right. When I'd settled her I

went to one of the window slits and looked out. I couldn't
see anything after the candlelight but I knew now who was
watching and listening, no more than a yard or two away. I
didn't even have to raise my voice.

'She didn't do it herself, did she? You did it to her, or
made her do it.'

No answer.

'A deal. Let her out. Get help for her. We can think
of some story to cover it, no problem with that.'

The faintest of movement outside, no more than the shifting
of weight from one foot to another.

'I'll forget about the rest of it, about everything. It just
won't exist any more. Nobody cares about Prudence. Trying
to blackmail you again after all that time. She thought now
people were getting interested it was a chance to squeeze
some more out of you. If Nicolle hadn't stirred it up again
... then I ... '

I stopped, knowing it was true. My chance interest, coincid-
ing with Nicolle's, must have convinced Prudence there was
still juice in the orange.

'My fault, not yours really. Or if it was, you've got away
with it. Why spoil it now? None of it existed.'

Silence.

'I never existed. I'll go away, right away this time, anywhere you like. You can kill me if you like. Just get help for
her now.'

In the corner Kay moved an arm, made a little snuffling
noise.

'I haven't talked to anybody else about it. Nobody else
knows anything.'

A negotiating mistake, but then this was surrender, not
negotiation.

'It doesn't matter about the book either. Look, you can
have it.'

It was sprawled on the floor where I'd dropped it, pages
creased, cover already sucking in moisture from the chalk. I
smoothed it out, put the pages of manuscript inside so that
they were just visible and held it at arm's length through the

247

window slit. I remembered seeing a falconer once, holding out beef shin to a bird of prey, but there was no swoop and rush of wings this time. Simply, one moment I was holding the book, the next it had been taken from me. My shoulder was blocking the slit so I couldn't see, but I knew my hand and the hand that wrote the manuscript had been inches apart. I waited a minute or two.

'There, you've got it. Now please let her out. You don't have to stay. Just open the door and go.'

Kay made the snuffling noise again, but this time it sounded more like a groan. Her body felt colder when I put my arms round it. I pushed an eyelid back gently. The pupil was a pinpoint, with no sense or focus in it. I held her, trying to get some of my body warmth into her, wrapped the shirt more closely round her and carried her to the window with me.

'You needn't worry about her saying anything. She's kept quiet for you up to now, hasn't she? She didn't tell me. I didn't understand till today. She saw you kill Prudence. You managed her though, didn't you? Threats and kindness. The police might think she did it, but stick with you and you'd protect her. You'd help her find her father. Not difficult to keep her quiet. You didn't have to do this.'

I'd been scared by the harsh breaths. She was quieter now, and that scared me more.

'She worked well for you. She did a good job of spying on me in Paris. It wasn't her fault what happened.'

From outside the slight rustle of somebody changing position, and the panic cluck of a moorhen from the pool.

'That time in the greenhouse, when she gave me the ring, she wasn't meaning to go against you. She was just desperate. And she made up for it, didn't she? She told you she was meeting me in the car park. I even thought she was there watching them, but it was you all the time.'

Silence. I moved Kay closer to the light. There was a just perceptible movement of ribs and diaphragm, but perhaps that was no more than the candle flickering.

'She'll die,' I said, but might as well have been saying it to the wall.

'Duncan? I don't care about Duncan either. He wanted to be a martyr. He'll enjoy prison in his way. Kay never met him. If Duncan talks, nobody will believe him. Besides, he only knows about Morocco, not about Prudence. He can't be sure about Prudence.'

I crouched down beside the wall under the window slit, Kay across my knees.

'She's dying. They'll find us here tomorrow and blame me. That's the idea, isn't it?'

The movement outside was more decisive this time, a full step towards us. You'd have to crane forward to see us from the outside, where we were crouching.

'If that happens, I'll talk, you know that? I'll tell them everything I know.'

But they wouldn't believe me, not with Kay dead. Too many lies, too many identities. I don't know if that came into my head of its own accord or from outside. I felt soaked through with weariness, wanting nothing more now than to curl up with Kay in a corner and sleep until my warmth and her coldness merged into one. The rest of the world had gone away except for the presence outside and even that was moving into my own mind, inside the chalky skull, so that I didn't know where its thinking ended and mine began, whether its impulse or mine made my eyes go to the syringe on the floor and the unused ampoules beside it. And when that happened, the voice from outside the window said something at last.

'It was what you wanted, wasn't it? You wouldn't have felt like that about my book if you hadn't wanted it. You should be grateful to me.'

'No.'

'You play with the idea of wanting it, but when it happens you try to run away. It was the same with the two of them in Morocco.'

'You made him kill the boy.'

'You can't make people do anything unless they want to.'

My eyes went to the syringe again, glinting in the candle-light. When I put my hand on Kay's ribs and stomach I could feel no trace of breathing. The only movement was a vein

249

in my arm, throbbing and swelling. Suicide pact. Killed her, killed himself. Both of them killed poor Prudence. Duncan out of prison. Tidy. Tidy and restful. My free arm, the one not holding her, was stretching out across the floor when she made a little groaning noise and curled her body into me. I stood up, still holding her, and yelled out through the window slit:

'No! No, it isn't what I want. It isn't what she wants.'

And a voice, not the voice I'd been listening to but a civilised, affected voice, redolent of old books and dry sherry, came from further off, floating from the other side of the pond.

'My dear boy, whatever you want or don't want, there's no need to make so much noise about it.'

It was the book, I suppose, that saved us – or rather Gus Prothering's greed for it. He explained it to me, not at all shame-faced, around daylight the following morning with the rest of the house in turmoil around us and the police still taking statements in the director's study. Kay was in hospital at Eastbourne by then and I was desperate to get to her, only they wouldn't let me. Prothering came to where I was sitting in the hall, within reach of the phone. He was as neat and shiny as a pebble, quite unaffected by all that had happened, holding something out to me.

'Yours, I believe, dear boy. Scarcely pristine.'

The primrose cover was creased, smeared with chalky mud. She must have dropped it when she ran off and he picked it up. I wouldn't have noticed at the time. Although he was holding it for me to take, his elbow was bent, keeping it close to his body. I didn't reach out for it.

'There were some pages in manuscript.'

He shook his head. 'Not there. She must have taken them with her. One assumes they'll go to her next of kin.'

'One assumes.'

When he saw I wasn't going to take the book his arm began to move back and across his body, drawing it slowly away from me as he talked.

'Presumably they'll be produced at the inquest. They could be compared with other samples of her writing.'

'I don't suppose any of it will come out at the inquest. A middle-aged woman crashes her car into somebody's gatepost on a dark night. That's it.'

'But she wasn't just any middle-aged woman.'

'All the more reason.'

He nodded slowly, pursing his lips. The book was safely tucked between his left arm and his ribs by then.

'I gather it was your car she was driving.'

'Hired.'

'One might wonder how she came to have the keys.'

'One might.'

I thought of Kay, lying in a narrow white bed; wondered if it was too soon to phone the hospital again.

Seeing he'd get no further on that road, he tried another. 'And there's no doubt she wrote it?'

'None that I can see.'

'One wonders at her motives.'

'Scientific curiosity.'

He narrowed his eyes at me. 'Meaning?'

'She experimented with people. Including herself. Kay and I were the latest.'

He stood looking down at me where I was sprawled in the chair, rocking his weight gently from heel to toe.

'When you first came to see me you pretended you didn't know who wrote it.'

'I didn't. That much was true.'

'So how, if one may ask, did you find out?'

I was going to say by the usual academic methods, but took pity on him.

'When I managed to get samples of all their handwriting and none of them matched, I knew there was somebody I'd been missing. It had to be somebody who was there at the time, but hardly noticed. When I went back over what they'd told me, there was only one who fitted.'

'I see.'

He was positively cuddling the book by then. I wanted him to go so that I could telephone.

'Keep it,' I said.

251

A great smile came over his face.

'You'll sell it?'

He'd been watching me the evening before to see how I responded to his note. When I went down through the gardens he'd followed me, assuming I was going somewhere quiet to open negotiations with him.

'Why didn't you come when I shouted first?'

He blushed pale pink. 'I . . . um . . . assumed it was a case of, em, amorous disputes so to speak. I thought I'd wait and speak to you on the way back.'

And yet if it hadn't been for him, we'd have been going down in police records as a suicide pact.

'Not sell it,' I said. 'Give it.'

I owed it to him. Anyway, he must have noticed the Bodley stamp.

The thing about a high class hush-up job is, everybody is comfortable. I've been writing this at an exclusive convalescence establishment in the Highlands, not far from Pitlochry. I write in the mornings while Kay plays poker with her therapist, a cheerful red-bearded gnome from Liverpool who is, quite rightly, more interested in ospreys than in people. In the afternoons Kay and I go for walks on sheep tracks through the heather. She's getting much stronger now, and her hair is growing. We get newspapers here. Three things reported in them have interested us. The first, the inquest on Lady Talisby, got a half column in most of the serious ones, but then the details had been pretty widely reported the day after the accident and the inquest added little to them. Lady Talisby, having accompanied her husband to a literary conference in Sussex, was found dead in the driving seat of a car just after two o'clock in the morning, having crashed into a stone gatepost alongside a narrow country road in the Cuckmere Valley. From the force of the impact, a police expert estimated that she was doing between seventy and eighty at the time of the crash. No other vehicle was involved. The blood alcohol content of the deceased was consistent with the evidence that she'd drunk a glass of sherry before dinner and a moderate quantity of wine during the meal. It was slightly below the legal limit. Lord Talisby gave evidence to the inquest that his wife had seemed in normal mental and physical health on the evening in question. (I could imagine his black tie and statesmanlike tones.) The verdict was accidental death. One paper reprinted the photograph of the Talisbys on the steps with Nicolle and Angela and reminded readers that it had been taken a few hours before her death.

Kay and I talked it over on one of our walks among the heather, after she'd spent the morning taking five pounds fifty off the therapist. She said, quite sensibly, that she could hardly be expected to grieve for a mother who'd clearly resented her from embryo onwards, and no wonder she'd grown up disturbed, with all that hatred washing around in the amniotic fluid. She was entirely matter-of-fact about it. We discussed why the fiancée, as she was then, didn't get an abortion, and decided that hearing about Angela's experience might have had something to do with it. Kay has a theory that it was the anger and resentment of being made pregnant by Duncan in Morocco that made Lady Talisby write the book. I disagree. She'd already experimented with Duncan and Talisby by then, making them kill the boy. I said there's a strain of cruelty and curiosity endemic in most of us that happened to come out in her.

'Do you think it's in my blood too?' Kay asked me.

'No more than most of us,' I said.

She has a trick now of winding the Talisby ring round and round on her finger as she talks. She says before we leave she'll throw it in the pool under the waterfall, but not yet. I should have guessed, I suppose, when I first saw it that Milord would have sealed his engagement by giving the family ring to the fiancée. I could hardly have guessed, though, how Prudence had taken it off her, along with the sapphires and nearly everything else she possessed, in that summer of 1958 as part of the fee for being nurse and foster mother, as well as an insurance policy for the future.

'No wonder my mother hated me,' Kay said.

Another thing that worries Kay and makes her twist the ring round her finger is what she calls her lies to me. She had no choice, I tell her. Once she'd gone back to the cottage and found Prudence dead and Lady Talisby there – not knowing then who she was – it's hard to see, from her point of view, what else she could have done. Easy enough to say go to the police, but the unknown woman must have been terribly convincing when she stood there and explained so very cogently, all for Kay's good, that the police would think Kay had done it. It had been, Kay said, almost as if she'd known about the rows between herself and Prudence. Kay thinks, though she's not sure, that she may have talked in her shock about trying to find her father, and Prudence keeping him from her. The woman may even have offered to help find him.

For the time that mattered, she almost managed to make Kay believe in her own guilt: long enough to get her passively to London and stored away in Earl's Court while Lady Talisby planned what to do next. I had to point out to Kay that it had been brave of her in the circumstances, when she'd recovered a little, to make a break for freedom and follow up that clue of the ring. Pity that it brought her, inevitably, back into Lady Talisby's hands in the garden of their stately home, while I was confronting Lord Talisby inside. From then on, those hands had held her on a string, a long one when she was sent to spy on me in Paris, desperately short by the time Lady Talisby met her in that other garden at the conference centre and demanded a report. Kay's not a good liar. Not her fault, any of it. My fault, if anyone's, for not understanding sooner. Kay shakes her head. I haven't convinced her yet.

The second thing in the papers, soon after the inquest, was the news that Lord Talisby was giving up his post as a Home Office minister. He was photographed leaving Number Ten, looking years older than when I'd last seen him. Grief at the loss of his wife was the reason most of the commentators gave. Some of them speculated that this would mean the end of the Government's plan to silence homosexuals, since he was widely thought to be the instigator of it. We'd been given a promise before we agreed to go away to the Highlands, but this wasn't the fulfilment of it. We watched the papers and waited.

It came a week after Lord Talisby's resignation and was marked by just one paragraph in the *Guardian*, *Telegraph* and *Independent*. Duncan McMahon, a painter from Edgbaston, Birmingham, was released after being held in custody for three weeks, charged with the murder of Prudence Belsire. He was freed after the prosecution offered no evidence against him. Investigations into the death of Miss Belsire were continuing.

'But that's a lie,' Kay said, 'the bit about investigations continuing. Why do they print lies?'

I told her she'd have to get used to it and the conversation turned to whether Kay should meet Duncan when we leave here. At the moment she thinks she will, without obligation. Now she knows she's got a father, she's nervous about meeting him. I'd like to see him again because there's something I'm curious about. Duncan's release was the condition we made for keeping quiet: can it be that Lord Talisby's resignation was Duncan's? If so, we've most of us got what we wanted.

'Beware of what you want,' Uncle Lazarus had said, 'because what you want is what you get.'

Kay and I will be leaving here soon. Our conversations as we walk are turning more and more to what we do next. Oxford and Lagen and the Anglican poets are out of the question. They belong in another life and I've no wish at all to get back to it. Sometimes we think we'll run a herb farm, sometimes a bookshop. On days like today, with fat bees flopping through the heather, we ask each other whether we shouldn't stay in the Highlands and open a café for walkers. Then Kay says it will be cold in the winter and presses close to me as if she's cold already, and we end up in a naked clinch on a warm patch of peat. Soon I must write and explain to Andrea.